Also by Val Harris

Whisky 'n' Ginger (2007)
The Siren (2008)
Sea Creatures (2009)
The Song the Waves Sing (2013)

Masai Proverb

Coal laughs at ashes, not knowing that the same fate will befall it.

To Tautzi the best Vic in the world!

val harris

HUNTING GROUND

love + hugs.

Val x

CAVA BOOKS

(An imprint of Gingercat Books)

A GINGERCAT/CAVA BOOKS
Publication

First paperback edition published in
Great Britain 2017
www.gingercatbooks.co.uk

This is a work of fiction. Names, characters, places, locations and incidents are purely fictional and bear no relationship to any real life individuals, living or dead, or to any actual places, business establishments, locations, events or incidents.
Any resemblance is entirely coincidental.

Design and Typeset for this edition: Nick Ovenden www.nickovenden.com

Printed and bound in Great Britain by:
Biddles Books Limited www.biddles.co.uk

ISBN: (13) 978-0-9555997-1-2

A CIP record of this book is available from
The British Library

Prologue

MASAI MARA

June

*S*he drifted in and out of consciousness, bumping around in the open back of the vehicle exposed to the sharp wind. As she came to realise the hood covering her head, her mouth sealed with tape, the bindings on her hands and feet, confusion and fear sent her body into uncontrollable shaking. Bile rose up in her throat as she struggled to scream and get free. Dear God, what had happened? Who had done this to her? Where were they taking her?

The truck began to slow down and came to a halt. A door opened. Male voices spoke in Swahili. She turned her head to listen and heard a brushing sound as though something had been dragged aside, then the truck lurched forward for a short way before stopping again. This time the engine was switched off. The driver's door opened. She heard bolts being drawn and a metallic clang at the back of the truck where something, perhaps the tailgate, had been dropped down. Then the truck began to bounce as someone climbed into the back of it. Oh God, oh God! She smelled sour breath as they leaned over her and she whimpered and shrank back terrified, her heart racing. He said

1

something to the other man in Swahili then she was grabbed under the arms. She wanted to kick out and scream but she couldn't. His fingers dug in and pinched her skin as he hauled her to the front of the truck where she slumped against the side of it, her legs dangling over the edge. Someone cut the ropes at her feet but left her hands still bound behind her back. She was pulled out of the truck and she stood, trembling, terrified, wondering what were they going to do with her?

'Kwende,' a man said with a gruff African voice, 'let's go', and she was pushed forward, making her way with unsteady steps. 'Bend down, we go inside,' and she shuffled along, with her head and back bent, into a suffocating interior pungent with wood-smoke. Once inside the hood was pulled off but she kept her eyes closed, afraid of what she would see. One man said something to the other who grunted – then a hand slapped her face. Her cheek stung and her eyes flew open blinking from the chink of light that shone through a window slit. The dark shapes of her captors were silhouetted in front of her, masked to hide their identities. The sticky tape was still across her mouth and she longed to take a deep breath. A stifled sob escaped and, just as she felt she might faint, the tape was ripped away.

She licked at her stinging lips. 'Who are you?' she whispered, 'what do you want with me?' Tears filled her eyes.

Neither of them answered. One of the men sliced at the ropes binding her hands and then re-tied them in front of her. A bottle of water was put into her hands. She drank a little of it. Then the man pushed her backwards on the bed. Panic and fear returned. 'No, please, don't,' she begged.

He shook his head and frowned, impatient. 'Sleep. You sleep. No noise.' He took hold of her feet and twisted her onto the bed. An overwhelming fatigue coursed through her body *and she knew they had drugged her again.*

She moved through a dulled sense of awareness. Voices came and went and someone tried to make her drink, pouring water into her mouth and making her gag. She tried to focus on the figure, but her vision would not clear and she drifted back into a restless, nightmare-ridden sleep. Once she managed to speak a few words when someone tried to spoon a thin maize gruel into her mouth.

'Want my husband,' she slurred, the gruel running down her chin. 'No,' she said and turned her head away.

'You eat,' and the hard spoon was thrust into her mouth again, grazing her gums.

'No.' She tried to push it away with her bound hands. 'Who are you?' She closed her lips and struggled to focus on the figure in front of her, but her vision was still blurred. 'Why am I here? What are you going to do to me?'

They pinned her hands down and forced the spoon into her mouth.

'Stop talking,' they said.

Part One

AMBUSH

1

NYARA CAMP

March

Through the tent mesh at sunrise James Sackville watched a magnificent male lion go padding through the camp, its mighty roar resonating through his chest. He could smell the lion – its primitive scent of blood and testosterone. He saw its pale amber eyes as it swaggered by and he held his breath when the lion paused, sniffing the air, as though it sensed his presence. Then it padded on, melting into the bush and shadows.'

'You kept me awake,' James said to the departing creature.

'You kept me awake,' said his wife, Alexia, from the bed. 'You were restless last night.'

James turned to her with a twinkle in his blue eyes. 'I meant the lion.'

'I know,' she laughed. 'I bet the clients are already talking about that roar.'

'Isn't that what they come here for, to experience the thrill of being in the heart of the bush with wild and dangerous animals?' he frowned.

'Well that's the theory,' said Alexia stretching, 'but faced with the reality at such close quarters they may be feeling a little unsettled.' She threw back the bed covers and got up to have a quick shower, then she pulled on a pair of beige cotton shorts and a cream sweatshirt. She ran a hairbrush through her long streaked blonde hair and wound it into a loose plait.

There was a call of 'hello' outside and Alexia pulled back the sliding door. Silas had brought them hot welcome tea. He stood waiting for instructions, a tall and graceful Masai with his red and blue plaid cloak swept across his shoulders. 'Thank you,' she said, sipping at her tea.

'What's the news today?' James asked Silas. He caught sight of the beautiful plumage of a lilac breasted roller perched in a tree and a ring necked dove filled the air with its familiar bush call. It sounded as though the bird was calling: 'my father, my father, my father…'

'Lion and leopard here last night,' Silas replied, 'and Masigonde is out tracking.'

James stifled a yawn. Sleep did not come easy with so much to do and so many ideas buzzing around in his head. It was two years since Nyara camp had first begun to take shape and eighteen months since it had opened for business. The camp was owned by a venture known as the Monsoon Consortium, a group of wealthy individuals who had invested their money in a series of luxury camps across East Africa. James and Alexia had been recruited to manage the Kenyan camp from its inauguration. Nyara was situated in the middle of the Masai Mara, an area abundant with wildlife and their habitats. There were established lion prides, elephant herds, rhino, leopard, cheetah, hippo, buffalo, giraffe, antelope and some superb birdlife. It was not far from where the Talek and the Mara River converged, with two busy crossing points for wildebeest and zebra.

Since Nyara's first flurry of customers there had been no respite. Every day they were up at dawn, checking their emails for new bookings, organising the staff, placing orders, meeting and greeting the new guests, saying goodbye to the old. It was a busy life, but it was the life they loved and the place they both wanted to be more than anywhere else on earth. It was a joy to live with the sounds of the African bush all around them day and night; the leopards cough, the roar of lion, the whoop of hyena; falling asleep to the rhythmic lowing of the wildebeest or waking to the thunder of their hooves as thousands of them crossed the Mara River on their annual migration to the grassy plains on the other side.

James was six years old when he experienced his first crossing, sitting in a truck with his father, in a spot overlooking the river. On the opposite side a writhing mass of wildebeest and zebra, grunting in cacophonic unison, had gathered along the banks of the fast flowing Mara River. The animals were pushing in from the rear and putting pressure on the frontlines. His father told him that more than two million animals began the return from the western Serengeti to the Masai Mara, between July and October.

'Watch,' he said. 'It's coming.' A group of wildebeest had ventured down to the edge and more began to follow, slithering down the steep bank until the pressure of bodies was too much to hold back. Then they began to leap into the foaming swirl, mooing and grunting, plunging and tumbling on top of each other. He had watched in amazement as hundreds upon hundreds of the creatures followed, twisting and crashing into the water. Then began their battle against time and the dangers that awaited them in the rushing, churning river. The current took the weakest, sweeping them downstream, to drown or be snapped up on the way in the jaws of the wily crocodiles that lay in waiting. He saw the lucky ones scramble out of the water on the other side and gallop off towards the lush grasslands of the Mara. Minutes ticked by and still the crossing did not diminish. Then, all of a sudden, it ended as quickly as it had begun. A row of wildebeest dug in their heels and that was it. The crescendo of noise quietened down to a gentle grunting, the churning waters settled and the herds went back to their waiting game. It was one of the most wonderful sights he had ever seen and, James believed, it was that day that formed his love affair with the Mara.

Outside their camp was waking up. The first trucks had arrived with the workers – the cooks, the cleaners, the maintenance - to start the daily chores. They came from a second camp where the heart of Nyara's infrastructure was housed: car mechanics, an organic vegetable garden, a camp bakery, beehives and a chicken coop. What couldn't be home-grown was flown down from Nairobi or trucked in from Narok.

James and Silas made their way to the office tent. In a moment he would be communicating with the Masai trackers who were still out and sending back information. All day the guides and trackers kept in touch with each other, from camp to truck and truck to camp, reporting on the movement and whereabouts of the animals.

'Go ahead Masigonde,' he responded to a radio call.

'Rock Pride were near the camp last night – now heading towards Lookout Hill - six cubs from last year, three older boys, one girl and four mothers. Big male, I think you know, went through camp. Over.'

'Yes we heard him and I saw him. Any signs of rain?' They were on the edge of the expected long rains that fell from March to May.

'Not yet, the sky is clear as far as we can see.'

James turned to Alexia. 'I hope we don't have a drought again.'

'Don't worry, it's too early to predict how things will go.'

Their guests were beginning to emerge from their tents for breakfast and James and Alexia wandered amongst them checking for any specific requests or problems. The morning coffee, water and snacks were loaded onto trucks, the guests greeted by their drivers and guides, and off they all drove into the clear morning light of the Mara wilderness.

What more, James thought, could we wish for?

2

CHUI CAMP

March

Tessa Somerton was packing to leave Chui Camp for a well-earned break. The long rains were due but, so far, there had been no sign of them in the endless blue sky and the camp was due to break its dry season pitch and move to higher ground, away from the river bank. The plains were beginning to look parched, the waterholes were turning into dust bowls and the dry, straw-gold grasses were being over-eaten by the hungry wildlife. It was hard to imagine that, when the rains came, the whole area could be flooded and the bush roads made impassable.

She loaded her bags into one of the guide vehicles and her headman, Jackson, took her to the airstrip to catch the plane returning to Wilson Airport, Nairobi.

'Any sign of rain anywhere?' she asked the pilot, Anders, as they rumbled down the runway with clouds of red earth dust billowing around them.

'Not a teaspoon this way, but some has fallen up north.' The bush plane lifted, bumping against the crosswinds. 'The El Nino effect is promising a lot of flooding; just something else for us all to worry about as if the prolonged drought and the violence last year wasn't bad enough for business.'

Tessa agreed. And to top it all her own safari camp business was crumbling in its shabbiness that her husband, Ralph, seemed to think was acceptable. It was impossible to get him see otherwise; to see that if they didn't pull themselves into the real world and respond to the needs and desires of any prospective clients then they may as well not go back at all because there wouldn't be any clients to entertain. She knew the tour operators shared her exasperation with her stubborn husband who refused to act on their advice. The camp needed bringing into the twenty-first century, and the services they offered into line with other camps that were offering 'luxury' as far as a bush camp could. He had argued, 'where's the reality in that?' and Tessa had replied that the financial evidence, or lack of it, spoke for itself; but nothing she or the tour operators said seemed to be able to convince him otherwise.

Now Ralph was up in Nairobi where he was supposed to be touting for business and negotiating with the tour operators, but Tessa guessed a lot of his so called networking involved hanging around the Norfolk from lunchtime to midnight, drinking at the bar, meeting up with old friends and making friends with strangers. Meanwhile, she was left behind to run the camp for the clients that they did manage to attract.

'Everything okay with Chui?' Anders asked, making polite conversation, but Tessa knew he would have heard the rumours. He and Ralph had been friends for many years, long before she had become his wife and she knew where his loyalty lay.

She shrugged. 'As well as can be expected. Have you been in Nairobi? Have you seen anything of Ralph?' She looked through the window, down to where the earth was racing away, as though she might find him there.

'Not much, I'm afraid. I've been up in Samburu these past few weeks.'

Tessa guessed he wanted to avoid getting into the middle of a domestic quarrel. He turned his attention to the controls and Tessa leaned back her head and closed her eyes. She was looking forward to a rest. The days had been long and hard without Ralph and now, with all of it behind her, she was longing for the respite Nairobi would bring. Perhaps the lines, the pinched look and dark circles around her eyes would disappear after a few long sleeps and less responsibilities. The mirror that morning had shocked her. It revealed that her short blonde hair was dull and dry and her eyes had lost their sparkle. She had rifled through her belongings looking for a belt to hold up her loose shorts. Worry and sleep depravity seemed to have taken its toll of her and, even though she had not long hit her forties, she sometimes felt much older. God knows it hadn't meant to end up like this – the work, the strained relationship with her husband.

At Wilson Airport, where they landed, she took a taxi west to Karen, a sprawling area between Nairobi and the Ngong Hills. Here many old families of Kenya had made their homes, as her husband's had done, some as far back as the last century.

In their empty house she called her husband's mobile. 'I'm in Nairobi. Where are you?'

'I've been doing business,' was his curt reply.

'You're supposed to be going to Chui to break camp and move.'

'I'm flying out with Anders first thing.' She could hear the irritation in his voice.

'Are you coming back to Karen before you leave?'

'Yes.' He cut the call before she could reply.

Damn him, Tessa thought. First she needed a soak in a hot bath, the first for weeks, then a night out in the city. She turned on the tap, poured in some bath salts and started calling her Nairobi friends.

3

NAIROBI

March

Langata Road was already jammed with cars and trucks as Ralph drove home out of the city towards the west. The traffic crawled and, after getting nowhere for half an hour, his impatience got the better of him. He swung his truck off the main road onto a rough road that would take him through the outskirts of Kibera, towards a track that ran along the southern edge of the Ngong Forest.

Kibera, a huge slum on the edge of Nairobi, was not the safest of places to drive around, let alone through. It was a sprawling ramshackle settlement of huge proportions lying in a sweeping valley full of rusting corrugated iron roofs, muddy tracks and alleys and huge piles of discarded rubbish. Lawless, crime ridden and full of disease it was difficult for Ralph to imagine that some people saw it as a good place to live, but the innovation of the place was impressive and the good people who lived there were inspiring, despite the fact that most of them had no access to electricity, proper latrines or clean water. Kibera had been built from materials that the rest of the city residents of Nairobi had cast off and everything that was thrown away was seen to have a value in Kibera. The city slum teetered and tottered on top of itself, homes, shops, restaurants, schools, churches and cell phone shops – everyone seemed to own one. Cleaving its way through the heart of Kibera was the railway connecting Nairobi to places such as Kisumu and as far away as Mombasa and Uganda. Homesteads, shops and even schools stood right next to the tracks and the inhabitants lived in extreme danger.

Beyond Kibera, the road tracked through the Ngong forest, a beautiful place in the heart of it for wildlife, but not busy with motorists because of its reputation for being a carjackers haunt and frequented by the more desperate inhabitants of the slum. But it was still daylight and Ralph was not afraid of taking a chance. When he rejoined the main road he would at least be somewhere ahead of the jam.

Kibera Drive was pitted with potholes and he weaved his way around them, past the shanty areas where the smoke of cooking fires sent smoke up into the air like tribal signals. People slogged up and down the road bearing all kinds of goods in their arms and up on their heads. Goats and cows wandered the road at will and Ralph cursed and swerved this way and that to avoid them. People gave his car no more than a cursory glance; he had always been careful never to drive an expensive new vehicle that would draw undue attention. But, no matter who you were and what you drove, people would always hold out their hands for money as you passed or someone would try to wave you down to buy newspapers or water bottles for a sale.

As he left the township and got further into the forest area the traffic dwindled. He was thinking about Tessa, the cracks in their relationship and their dwindling business. It was all such a headache that he could do without and the more he thought about it the less he was paying attention to the road ahead. The setting sun played with his vision and he almost drove straight into a car turned on its side in the middle of the road. He jammed on his brakes and 'ambush' warning bells began to clang in his head. There was just about room to pass, but he would have to slow down and that would make him vulnerable. As he got nearer to the car he could see a man lying on the road; surely it was too orchestrated to be anything other than an ambush. Another man staggered out from behind the car with what seemed to be blood on his clothes and face, and just for a second his skepticism wavered. Then, out of the corner of his eye, he saw two men leap from the bushes to his right with rocks in their hands. They hurled them at his car and they bounced off the bodywork, just missing his side window. It would have been enough to panic a lesser man, but Ralph was a strong and able man of the bush and used to reacting in bad situations. He slammed the gears into reverse, put his foot on the accelerator and shot backwards as fast as possible with the men chasing him. Then, as they gained speed on him he changed gear, floored the accelerator and headed towards them; they hurled themselves left and right out of his way. Ralph kept going as he swung around the car parked in the middle of the road, bouncing over holes and rocks. He skidded and bumped off the side of a tree but he kept his foot jammed onto the accelerator, and somehow he kept going. One of the men scrambled to his feet and hurled another rock but it was a futile gesture. It bounced off the rear of the car and dropped away. Ralph looked in his rearview mirror and saw the face of a young man watching him go, someone high on chang'aa, the brew of poverty, and it was a face he knew.

His foot remained on the accelerator, heart pounding and adrenalin pumping him into superhuman action, despite the bad terrain which had the car sliding from left to right bouncing over rocks and rutted ground. Then, at last, he emerged from the forest and the car careered out onto the main Ngong road just missing a truck coming up behind him, its driver leaning on the horn.

People he knew had been hijacked and beaten for the sake of a mobile phone or a wallet. Sometimes they took the cars, leaving their victims stranded, and drove until the gas ran out; sometimes they beat the victim, but it was the thought of being hacked at with a machete that horrified Ralph the most. Last year, during the election violence, he'd seen people cut each other to pieces with machetes –it was the worst thing he had ever witnessed.

Safe at last, inside the walled and gated compound of his house, Ralph sat for a moment, taking deep breaths, until his heart had slowed to a more regular beat. He was a big man, tall and broad-shouldered and he had encountered enraged hippos, rhinos and elephant and, once, a near miss with a buffalo but nothing had made him feel quite as vulnerable as those few minutes in the forest.

'Don't you ever take a short cut through the forest,' Ralph thundered as he strode into the cottage, threw his keys on a table and sank into a chair, 'no matter how bad the traffic is!'

'Whatever happened?' Tessa asked as she hurried into the living room, towel drying her wet hair. She went to the bar and made him a gin and tonic.

'Bloody Kibera bandits or whatever the hell you call them. Parked their car in the middle of the forest road and tried to stop me. I got the better of them of course; they're damned lucky I didn't run them all down. Could have sworn one of them was that good for nothing brother of our maid!'

'Esme's brother?' Tessa handed him the drink.

Ralph took a large slug of it. 'Looked like him,' he said, 'from what I remember when he last came here.'

'That was a while ago. I know he hasn't been having an easy time, but carjacking? I hope you're wrong. Anyway it sounds like you had a lucky escape. I heard about someone else who got caught the other day. Gave them everything and they still beat him. He's lucky to have his life.'

'Safer in the damned bush,' Ralph grunted and held out his empty glass for a refill. 'So what are we doing tonight?' He caught hold of her hand. He'd missed her, despite the fact that they never seemed to do anything but disagree when they were together.

'I'm going out with the girls tonight,' she said, slipping out of his grasp. 'I need to unwind.'

'I was hoping we could spend the evening together. Why do you think I came back?' He could have stayed in the city, had some fun and saved himself the journey.

'You can get an early night and it's better you are here tonight rather than fighting the traffic to get to Wilson tomorrow morning. Esme's left something for you in the fridge and there's plenty of cold beer.'

It seemed like she'd got it all planned. 'What time will you be back?'

Tessa shrugged. 'I've no idea. I'm going out with Sophie,

so I presume late.'

'Sophie,' he guffawed, 'she likes to party.'

'Well good, I need a party tonight after being on my own in the bush.'

'Oh don't start that again,' he snapped, 'you know I've been in Nairobi trying to save the bloody camp.' Why did she have to bang on about it?

'I hope you've done a good enough job,' she snapped back.

'Jesus you don't have any idea, do you? For thirteen years I've been running Chui and it has never had the problems it seems to have now.' It was an ongoing argument they had about the camp whenever they were together.

'And the camp hasn't changed or updated itself in all that time. The clients are different now - they are just ordinary people, rather than adventurers, who just want to see animals in the wild but they want to do it without risk and in an element of style and luxury. Unless you accept what we need to do and we bring Chui into line with those requirements, of course we are going to have problems.'

He'd heard it all before. 'Yeah, yeah, yeah, so you keep telling me: baths with a bush view, hot showers on demand, somewhere to charge their ever increasing array of digital gadgets. It's ridiculous,' he shook his head, exasperated with hearing the same old thing.

'It might be to you Ralph, but if you want Chui to survive then you are going to have to accept that visitors and their needs have changed, as has the world. God knows even the old bush adventurers and game hunters liked their luxuries in an even more outrageous way.'

'Funny how our problems started when that new bloody

camp, Nyara, went up. Clients that might have been ours are being poached by that tented monstrosity,' he mused.

'You can't keep on blaming Nyara, but you might think about the fact that perhaps it's because they are offering their clients what they want, that people are clamouring to go there.'

'Oh what the hell do you know anyway,' he fumed walking off and slamming the door behind him. Nobody would listen to him, not even his wife. His business was falling apart, a family business that had been around for several generations one way or another. No wonder he felt resentful.

4

NAIROBI

March

Ignoring Ralph's bad mood and efforts to make her feel guilty about going out, Tessa called a driver to take her to the Mercury Lounge.

The Ngong road from Karen towards the city centre was heaving with the usual melee of lorries, buses, people, cattle and cars weaving their way around the potholes. Along the unmade roadside stalls displayed their wares of furniture, pottery, clothes, batik cloth, woodwork, crafts, metal work, tyres, gravestones, and all kinds of food. People billowed around the stalls like smoke from the wood-fires. She would take herself out there tomorrow morning, to find things to take back to the camp for the new season. Perhaps she and Sophie could share a spot of retail shopping in Kilimani and have lunch at the Muthaiga Country Club. That would be a real treat. It was good to think about things she could do without having to worry about the camp and its responsibilities.

Tessa resented the pressure Ralph put on her, confining her by his disappearances and leaving her to run the camp on her own. It wasn't that she was incapable or afraid of taking charge; she knew how to manage the staff, how to handle a gun and what to do if confronted by a wild animal. It was just such hard work. Up at dawn every morning Tessa supervised the breakfasts, the cleaning, and made sure the trucks were prepared for the clients. Things seemed to be running better than ever, although there were always problems – someone fell sick, a truck needed maintenance, an essential food item didn't arrive on time but, with perseverance and determination, Tessa kept the camp running and ensured the staff knew their responsibilities to make sure that the camp cogwheel didn't stop turning. *The clients are never to know there is a problem,* she drilled into them.

Her methods of obtaining obedience were not by barking out orders and making threats - something that often happened when Ralph was around. He had high expectations and a short fuse, and he had once threatened to beat one of the boys who had forgotten a part of his duties. When she had challenged him about it he had turned on her.

'Don't you dare question the way I handle my staff,' he'd roared. 'You should be supporting me.'

'I will not support your threats of a beating,' she'd retorted. 'What's the matter with you? You never used to treat them in that way, not by bullying them.'

'You just don't get it, do you?' he'd snarled. 'I've been in this business for long enough to know how to deal with these people. If you don't show them who's in charge, then they'll walk all over you.'

'If that's what you think, then you've been in it too long!' Tessa snapped back.

'You seem to know so much about it you can run the bloody camp on your own,' and he'd slammed his book down on the table and stormed off. That afternoon he had gone to Nairobi. It was what he did whenever they had a disagreement.

How different he was now from the man she had first known and fallen in love with. Her sister Lizzie had been the first to date him and had confided to Tessa later that, although he was good company, there was no dazzling chemistry between them.

'You should have a go,' she'd said. 'I think you'll like him.'

'Have a go? You make him sound like a fairground attraction.'

'Oh you know what I mean. He's a bit too bush for me, but you like that sort of man, don't you?'

'Do I?' she'd replied, wondering, but Lizzie seemed to think she knew what her sister needed.

'You'll get left on the shelf if you don't put yourself out there,' Lizzie had warned.

Tessa wasn't worried about that, but she knew it was Lizzie's worst nightmare. Her sister regarded ensnaring the right man into marriage as an absolute duty to the human race. Lizzie was their mother's daughter, a woman who had inherited from her mother a belief that the place of women was as a dutiful wife. She had attempted to drill into her daughters that same sense of position. Lizzie had revelled in the attention it had brought her; the parties; the clothes and the stream of suitable men, but it wasn't the life for Tessa. She detested that kind of attention. She preferred to go tracking with her father who taught her to ride and shoot.

But her mother despaired of what she saw in Tessa as a wild side that needed to be tamed. She argued with her husband about his misguided indulgence and she won. Tessa was sent to a boarding school in England. She had howled as the plane rose away from her beloved Africa and pressed her face to the porthole window, watching until the last bit of bush had disappeared. After five long years, troubled with homesickness and untamed by the boarding school, she went back to Kenya, determined she would never leave again.

With some reluctance, but to appease her sister, she had agreed to meet the stranger Lizzie had set her up with. She had scanned the restaurant for the possible Ralph Somerton when they had arrived. A man at the bar with sandy coloured hair, handsome in a rugged kind of way, had been holding court to the people around him.

'Who's that?' she'd asked, but she'd known the answer even before Lizzie had replied.

'That's your date,' and Lizzie had swept Tessa across to meet Ralph Somerton before she'd a chance to change her mind. She'd stood on the edge of the group, in a state of nervous apprehension, and wondered why on earth she had allowed Lizzie to talk her into coming. Her date was regaling the group with stories from the past and she thought he hadn't noticed her until he suddenly downed his drink, said goodbye to the others and swept her off to dinner. He was better company than she had expected and, when he took her straight home after the meal, she had felt a moment of disappointment. He'd punched her number into his phone and said he would call her. Six months later they were married.

The driver stopped to collect Sophie, Tessa's best friend. They'd grown up in Kenya together and Sophie was now part of the management team at The Norfolk hotel. She kept Tessa amused with her hilarious tales about the guests and the people she'd met - dignitaries, movie stars and celebrities. Today she had some intriguing news. 'Darling, you wouldn't believe who we've had staying. Only the dashing young Prince! Well, you know, he's been staying up north and he popped down here for a weekend.'

'Was he with anyone?' Tessa pried.

'If you mean the 'daughter', well they were both booked in but not 'together',' Sophie made quote marks in the air.

'Oh Sophie, you're such a gossip!' Tessa laughed and she gave her friend a huge hug. 'I've missed you and you're useless tittle-tattle.'

'Of course you have, darling. You've had nothing but ghastly guests to talk to.' Sophie pushed a mass of glossy black hair away from her face. She was tall and elegant with creamy coffee coloured skin and nut-brown eyes, the daughter of an Italian father and Indian mother. She wore beautiful silk saris tailored into long dresses or flowing trousers, which enhanced her slim figure.

'They're not ghastly!' Tessa protested. 'Well, not all of them.'

Sophie pulled a face. 'Oh, you're too generous, darling.'

'Just having guests, ghastly or otherwise, would be good.'

Sophie shook her head at Tessa and threw up her hands in mock despair. 'I'm sorry, but there will be no doom and gloom talk tonight. You've got to forget about it all, just for this evening. I promise I'll be around tomorrow and the night after, and the night after that if you like and you can pour out your heart to me, but not tonight. We haven't seen each other for months and we need to have fun, fun, fun.'

Tessa hugged her again. 'Don't worry. I've already made up my mind not to think about it.' She pushed aside her negative thoughts and focused on the evening ahead.

The club was quiet when they arrived, and it was a good time to sit and chat and catch up on Nairobi news and gossip, before more friends arrived and the music grew louder.

Looking around her a bit later on, Tessa noticed a group of people in the corner and spotted Alexia Sackville from the new camp, Nyara; the new camp that Ralph seemed so resentful of. Tessa and Alexia had passed each other on a bush track not so long ago; they had waved and called a greeting, but they had not stopped to speak. Tessa had been meaning to go over to the new camp and introduce herself, but it was hard to find a spare moment when Ralph was so often absent. She wanted to meet Alexia and her husband James and, despite Ralph's reservations, Tessa would rather have them as allies than rivals. She should arrange for them all to meet for dinner one night, in Nairobi. Yes, she'd sort that out soon.

Her friends were not, under any circumstances, going to allow Tessa to dwell on anything other than fun and vodka cocktails, and she was soon joining in the laughter at some of the stories that were being passed around. Then the dancing began. Sophie and Idi, her boyfriend, were raving it up on the dance floor and they looked so happy and easy together. If only she and Ralph were still like that, Tessa thought ruefully. After her whirlwind romance she had been pitched straight in to the busy life of running a safari camp and it was as if after that they had never found the time to really explore each other and grow together.

Tessa looked at the drinks in front of her and baulked. Her time away from the camp was too precious to blow it all and lose a day to a hangover. Making an excuse about going to the cloakroom, Tessa stopped at the bar for the real reason - a large glass of water. She caught sight of Alexia again and decided to gatecrash her group and say hello.

Alexia regarded Tessa with a quizzical look as she approached.

Tessa put out her hand, 'Hi, Tessa Somerton, Chui Camp?'

'Oh yes, of course. How nice to meet you,' Alexia enthused. 'How's it all going?' She pushed her long streaked blonde hair behind her ears and her almond-eyed smile was wide and warm.

'Good, thanks,' Tessa lied. 'What about Nyara? Is it all going well for you?'

Alexia pursed her lips. 'It's hard work, but every bit worth the effort. James and I are loving it.'

'It looks wonderful,' Tessa said. 'I've been meaning to come over to see you. We passed on the airport track a little while ago but I've been too busy I'm afraid.' It was not quite the truth, but she didn't want Nyara to know they were struggling.

'Yes, I remember,' Alexia nodded. 'I thought the same thing but, like you say, we're just so busy with clients coming and going. I don't seem to have much time to myself at all.'

'That's safari bush life for you.' Tessa paused before adding, 'I'm not sure how long you are here, but I was wondering if we could find a time to meet up whilst we're all in Nairobi – with our husbands. I'd love to offer you both dinner.'

'Oh yes,' Alexia said with genuine enthusiasm, 'that would be lovely, but we're only here for about a week and a bit pushed for time.' She reached into her bag and handed Tessa a business card.

Tessa took it and tucked it inside her own bag. 'I'll be in touch with some dates. Nice to meet you, Alexia.'

She rejoined her group but somehow she just couldn't get into the evening any more. Tiredness overwhelmed her and she longed for bed. 'Sorry darling,' she said to Sophie, 'I'm worn out – my body can't believe it's not on stress level ten anymore. Think I'll get a taxi home.'

Sophie threw her arms around her friend. 'I can't bear it if you go. Please stay, just for a little while. It's so long since we've done this.'

Seeing the disappointment on Sophie's face Tessa relented. 'Okay, I'll stay a bit longer, but I can't take any more drinking, and if I fall asleep don't say I didn't warn you.'

Sophie threw her hands up in despair and waved over a waiter. 'A large glass of sparkling water for my ageing friend, and a martini for me.' Then she took a long hard look at Tessa. 'You, my girl, are in danger of forgetting what it's like to relax and have fun. What happened to Tessa the dancing queen?' Tomorrow we are going to spend all day talking. There's a lot going on in there that I need to know about,' she said leaning forward and tapping Tessa's head.

'I'm tired because I have relaxed,' Tessa protested, 'and let's make that the day after. I have a feeling you will be sleeping most of tomorrow.'

Sophie shook her head. 'You can't pull the wool over my eyes. Why don't you stay at mine tonight? We can go out for brunch after we've both had a good lie in.'

'I'd love to but Ralph's due to fly up to the camp tomorrow and I want to make sure he goes. I know,' she said, seeing the disapproving look on Sophie's face, 'but I can't help worrying about it. Somebody has to. If you're up for it we could meet for a late lunch somewhere.'

'All right, it's a deal, and no reneging,' Sophie warned. 'Text me when you get home so I know you're okay.'

The house was in darkness when Tessa arrived back. The taxi driver flashed the guard who opened the side gate for her. Then she spotted a glow from a small light in the study at the back of the house. The door was open a crack and she could just see into the room. Ralph was sitting at the desk on his computer.

'Tessa?' he said, swinging the chair around. He was half hidden by the shadows in the room and she couldn't see his face.

'I thought you'd be asleep, its almost two - you've got an early start.'

'I know, but I wanted to make sure you got back safe and sound. Did you have a good time?'

Was it the truth? It was a surprising mood change and she was wary in her response. 'Yes, it was fun. Would you like coffee?'

'God no,' he said, 'I won't sleep.' He yawned and rubbed his chin and stretched his arms wide towards her. 'Bed I think.'

Tessa felt an overwhelming sense of emotion. She wanted so much to believe that Ralph was still the man she'd fallen in love with, the big warm-hearted man with courage and conviction and someone as safe as houses to be with. Against her better judgment she went to him. 'What were you looking at on the computer?' she asked as he pulled her onto his knee.

'Flights to South Africa and places to stay; how does ten days in Cape Town sound at the end of the month?'

'Very nice,' she said, which it would be, but then the thought of spending ten days away with Ralph brought her back down to earth. His moods were so random and besides there was the financial issue. She stood up and went into the kitchen to make herself some coffee.

'Can we afford it?' she called out.

'Stop fussing and let me be the judge of that.'

It made her wonder that if they had the money for a trip, why then didn't they have money to spend on the camp? But she bit her tongue and changed the subject. 'By the way I met Alexia this evening from the new camp, Nyara. I thought it would be nice to meet up with her and her husband for drinks or dinner.'

She heard Ralph draw breath before he asked, 'what was she like?'

'Young, attractive, smart and there was a genuine warmth about her that I liked,' Tessa said, coming back into the room and sitting down on the sofa with her coffee.

'Sounds like you've fallen for her charm already,' Ralph said with a hint of cynicism.

'I haven't fallen for anything. I'm just saying that I liked her. If they come to us for dinner then you can judge for yourself.'

'I don't know if we'll have time. You said yourself we've got our work cut out.' Now he sounded petulant, blaming his excuses on her.

'We'll make time,' Tessa replied with determination. 'I think it's important to get off on the right footing with them.'

'I'm not so sure if I want to dine with the enemy.'

'Oh Ralph, they're not the enemy,' she sighed, 'they are just another camp trying to make a living.'

He shrugged. 'That's your opinion, but I can see you're not going to give up on it.'

'I'll arrange a date.'

'Don't expect me to be polite,' he warned.

5

NAIROBI

April

While Ralph was away at Chui, Tessa got to work setting up meetings with the tour operators. She was determined to do something about Chui's decline and she used her time to visit the Kenyan Tourist Board and some of the operators that had Chui Camp on their books. First of all she browsed through their websites to see how they were portraying Chui as a destination. It was advertised as: *A step back in time but with modern comforts. This is a traditional bush camp, where you can experience your safari as it used to be. Sit out under starlit skies with tales around the campfire and dine in the light of hurricane lamps, whilst elephants feed nearby and lions roar around you.* Not so bad, she thought, almost romantic, but then she turned her attention to the reviews. They followed the same pattern: great staff, great game viewing but the camp and the tents are a bit tired and shabby, and we couldn't charge any of our gadgets. It was what Tessa kept trying to tell Ralph and, with a camp like Nyara as their closest neighbours, they had to pull Chui into the twenty-first century.

'Charging their mobile phones,' he'd roared, 'there's no signal anyway!'

'More and more people use the camera on their phones these days to take photographs,' she'd tried to explain, but he'd stormed off, muttering again about how ridiculous it all was.

Tessa wanted to show the tourist agents that she was doing everything in her power to make Chui Camp a better place for their clients. She had taken photographs of the updated tents before they closed up camp, of the new white bed linen, soft wool throws and cushions and mirrors she had found in the Karen Dukas. The bathroom areas also looked much more appealing with large copper water jugs and stone washing bowls, ladder racks to hang new towels, woven mats and lantern lighting. She'd hung batik-patterned cloth along the inside of the tent walls, hiding the patches of worn canvas. Now the overall effect looked so much more inviting in the photographs that were put up on the tour operator websites but, of course, it was just a cosmetic overhaul. What the camp really needed was new tents, new furniture, and better toilet and shower facilities provided by re-cycled water and solar power; more powerful generators to provide the power to charge up phones and cameras, despite Ralph's refusal to even consider it.

Working on that imperative, the first place that Tessa made an appointment with was Karibu Africa Tours, not just to meet the operators, but also to collect Alexia's contact details. She wanted to get to know their neighbours who were not, as Ralph seemed to think, the enemy but healthy competition and an asset they needed to harness to their side. If they could convince the Sackville's they were serious about smartening up then perhaps they would help by suggesting Chui when their own camp was too full to take any more guests. Of course she knew Ralph would view that as taking second place and they had to create their own guests too, but Tessa wanted to work with Nyara rather than against it. He told her she was being naïve trying to engage the opposition, but Tessa believed it was the only way for them to survive.

A meeting had been called in Nairobi with the Wildlife Services for those who ran the safari camps. On the agenda was the drought from late rains, and also the excessive flooding that followed caused by the drought impacted hard ground. There was also a new and added concern, regarding attacks on tourists on safari. Protection from wildlife was one thing, but dangerous people quite another.

The meeting started with coffee in the lobby of a downtown hotel.

'Hello,' said the tall, handsome young man in shorts and safari shirt standing next to Tessa and he shook her hand. 'I'm James Sackville. I don't believe we have met before.'

She smiled at him in delight. 'Hi James, Tessa Somerton. I met your wife at the Mercury Lounge the other evening.' She couldn't help but notice how self-assured he seemed, nor not admire his thick dark hair and blue eyes.

'Yes she told me,' James seemed unaware of Tessa's admiring scrutiny, 'and she mentioned your idea that we should all have dinner together.'

'I do hope so, but I appreciate how busy you must be.'

'It is hard finding time to socialize,' he agreed, 'and we are only in Nairobi for a short visit, but I hope we will. So, what do you make of this meeting? As if we haven't enough to worry about without the potential for attacks on our camps.'

Tessa grimaced. 'It's not something that is happening on a regular basis but the fact that it has happened at all is a harsh reality we must all face. What are your thoughts?'

James considered it. 'No matter how remote the threat seems, I think we should be vigilant. Are you contemplating employing more security?'

'I don't know. My husband thinks it's all scaremongering and something we shouldn't get worked up about. I suppose he's thinking about the cost too. I feel it's a good investment but Ralph and I never seem to be in the same place at the same time to have a proper conversation about these things.' She looked away, realizing she might have said too much. She didn't want James to think there was trouble between them. 'Do you trust all of your staff?' she asked to change the subject.

He looked thoughtful. 'I like to think I do. I treat them with the respect they deserve and I expect their loyalty. It's all one can do really.'

Tessa smiled. 'That's all any of us can hope and do.'

'I like to believe that by giving them responsibility and respect and paying them what the job deserves then perhaps they will remain loyal.'

'That's a fair assessment,' said Tessa. My husband would do well to take your advice, she thought. She put a hand in her bag and brought out a business card. 'I didn't have one to give to Alexia the other evening, but it would be good if we could all have dinner.'

James nodded. 'I agree. I'll get Alexia to get in touch and

arrange a date with you.'

Tessa put her coffee cup down and held out her hand, 'it was nice to meet you James and I wish you well with Nyara.' She picked up her bag. 'It looks as though the meeting is about to start.'

They made their way into the auditorium and took their seats.

Tessa was determined that they should meet up with the Sackville's for dinner and she made the arrangement without delay, calling up Alexia and setting a date for the end of the week.

'God, do we have to?' Ralph yawned when she told him, the morning after his return from the Mara.

'Yes we do. I want you to meet them and get over your preconceptions. It's important that we get along with them for all our sakes.' Why couldn't he just accept it?

Ralph gave her a withering look. 'For your sake you mean. I don't care if we get along with them or not and I don't suppose they do much either.'

'I think they do. Please try and reserve judgement until you've met them. You may even surprise yourself and like them.'

'Oh for Christ sake, I'll be the model husband,' he snapped and flung himself out of bed and into the shower.

'I've asked Esme to stay and help with the cooking and washing up that evening,' she said when he emerged, dripping from the shower, with a towel slung around him. 'She and Yahzid could do with the money.'

'The boy has no job, I presume,' Ralph snorted, 'too busy wasting himself down at the changa'a shack and then trying to rob innocent people like me.'

'You don't know for certain it was him in the forest,' Tessa said, but even she knew that Yahzid was wasting his life away. She felt sorry and concerned for Esme who was working to keep them both, often at the expense of her own education.

'Oh I'm pretty sure it was him,' Ralph growled. 'Well if it was him, then all the more reason to do something to help him find work. If only we could help to get him away from the influence of the crowd he's drifted into. Esme is so worried about him. She said the boys he hangs around with are much older than he is.'

'I can't promise anything,' Ralph relented, 'but I will ask around. He needs someone to take him in hand that's for sure.'

6

NAIROBI

April

Staring at the bottom of his empty glass at the bar in the Norfolk Hotel, George Stephenson was reviewing his miserable situation and thinking about the stoical way in which his wife, Mary, had accepted their ruin. It was all such a bloody mess and he could see no way out of it.

The only other person in the bar, sitting at the other end, raised his glass and George returned the gesture.

'Would you like another?' the man asked.

George nodded. Why not? He was glad of something to distract him from his depressing thoughts. 'Thanks,' he said and moved to a vacant stool.

'Hi, George Stephenson.'

They shook hands.

'Ralph Somerton.'

'Do you live in Nairobi, or are you a visitor?' George asked.

'I own a camp in the Mara.'

'Ah. Which one?'

'Chui Camp, it's based in a reserve in the north. It

belonged to my father. It's a mobile camp and rock solid authentic and it's in one of the best areas for wildlife.'

George detected a defensive tone.

'Then, all of a sudden,' Ralph continued his eyes gleaming, 'the tour operators don't want authentic, they want modern, contemporary with all mod cons. Now the clients aren't happy to take a bucket shower. They want all singing, all flushing bloody luxury, in the bush!' He downed the drink in his glass and called to the barman to bring him another, 'and I'm in danger of going out of business.'

George was a little taken aback by Ralph's outburst but he acknowledged the irony of their situations. 'Welcome to the club,' he said.

'You're not a camp or lodge owner are you?' Ralph scanned George's face.

George shook his head. 'No. I'm an engineer. I had my own business until my Kenyan partner died and left his share to a son, Malik, who had no interest in the business whatsoever. He was more interested in politics and because of that he cost me my business!' George banged his empty glass down on the counter to emphasise his frustration.

Ralph looked at him with interest. 'Ouch. An opposition guy I'm guessing.'

'Yes,' said George. 'An imprisoned opposition guy and even though I have nothing to do with politics myself, never have done, never will do, his actions have ruined us and they are punishing me for his damned beliefs.' He took a slug of drink. 'He was seized at an opposition meeting and not long after that my government contracts were frozen along with the company bank accounts and financial assets, all without further explanation. I protested about it but I was warned in no uncertain terms against making a fuss unless I wanted to join Malik in prison.'

'Sorry old chap.'

George grimaced and took another slug of his whisky. 'I opted for silence. I thought that if I kept my head down and waited the business would be restored, but weeks and months have gone by and, nothing. Every day I traipse down to the government offices trying to set up a meeting with the business minister or at least someone from his department. Every day it's the same. All the doors are closed. In the meantime there are unfulfilled contracts, angry phone calls and messages, creditors, debtors. The place my wife and I had come to know as home has become a hostile environment.'

They downed their drinks together in silence.

George looked up at Ralph as a memory came to him. 'You know I'm pretty sure my wife and I have been to Chui Camp – it must be getting on for fifteen plus years ago though.'

'That far back it's more than likely you were in Chui when my brother, Geoffrey, was running the camp.'

'Is it just you now?'

Ralph gave a hollow laugh. 'Yes. Geoffrey was trampled to death by a bull elephant while out tracking poachers.'

'How dreadful,' George exclaimed.

'Hazards of a bush life,' Ralph shrugged, 'but safer than the city in my opinion.'

George was not quite so sure, despite his current circumstances.

'So what do you plan to do, about your predicament?' Ralph asked.

George shook his head. 'I don't know. I sold the house

41

we had in Malindi to pay off some of the broken contracts, but I still owe money and I envisage things getting nasty. I can't sell the business and I can't take money out of the bank because they've frozen my accounts.'

'Look's like we both need help,' Ralph said. 'Have another drink on me George, you've earned it.'

'I should go home, Mary will be waiting,' George replied, but part of him wanted to.

'Oh come on, one more for the road won't hurt George, and it sounds like you could do with a good chat.'

The man was very persuasive, and perhaps one more wouldn't do any harm. It was good to talk things through, even with a stranger. He didn't like to do so with Mary because he knew how much it upset her. 'Just one then, thank you.'

'Have you got any sort of plan about what you could do?' Ralph asked.

George shrugged. 'I can't go back to England. The authorities insist I stay in Nairobi and I'm hoping they'll unfreeze one of the accounts if I ever get an appointment with someone to ask. Until then I don't know what I'm going to do.'

'Typical government officials,' Ralph snorted. 'Are you scared?'

'I think I am, yes. It's the first time in all my years in Kenya that I've felt this way. I've never involved myself in anything controversial - just kept my head down and got on with it and the people. I employed local people, contributed to the economy and helped this country but now it seems I have to take the rap for what my so-called 'business partner' is doing? I should think his father is turning in his grave. He was a good man, Asif, but I curse him for leaving me with his son.'

'It all goes tits up in the end, mate,' Ralph said gloomily.

'What are you going to do, about your own problems?' George had talked enough about his own and thought he owed the man the courtesy of listening to his.

Ralph shrugged. 'My wife agrees with the tour operators view that we have to invest some money in the camp to bring it up to date. She bangs on about it all the time. I blame our damned new neighbours who were sponsored by a consortium to build a permanent camp, and my God you should see it. It's a bloody five star hotel in the middle of the bush with a canvas covering, so they can still call it a tented camp. It's got a swimming pool and a hot tub and Christ knows what else. It's only been operating for just over a year but it's never empty. I hear it's just what the punters want and the tour operators call the shots on that decision. So this young couple have been taking my clients and coining in the money whilst we've been sliding towards bankruptcy. I call that dishonest competition.'

It just sounded like business to George but he didn't say. It was obvious Ralph Somerton was feeling very hard done by. 'So what can you do about it?'

Ralph looked down at his glass then he shrugged, 'Maybe I could think of a way to get them discredited.' He drained his drink.

George stared at him. 'Discredited? What do you mean?' It sounded a bit drastic to him.

'Oh don't mind me,' Ralph said, with a dismissive wave of his hand, 'it's just the drink talking.'

George got off his bar stool. He was feeling a little bit

queasy and uncomfortable, and he wanted to go home. 'I'd better be off,' he said, 'my wife will be wondering where I am. Thank you for the drinks.'

Ralph clapped a hand on his shoulder. 'Pleasure to meet you old chap. Let's stay in touch.' He handed over a card and George put in his pocket but he didn't plan on seeing Ralph again.

7

NAIROBI

April

Tessa couldn't help staring at Alexia as she climbed out of the car in an ankle length dress of deep blue silk - simple but stylish - with a silver wool wrap draped across her shoulders. When Tessa tried the same look she reckoned it made her look more like a gypsy. Alexia's long streaked hair cascaded over her shoulders like a lion's mane. The girl was stunning. Tessa's hand reached up to her own short blonde hair and she pushed it back with her fingers. Stop it she told herself, you have nothing to be jealous of.

'Hi you two, welcome, come in,' she said, kissing them both and directing them into the living room. Ralph was there to greet them and Tessa could not help noticing his double take at Alexia. Well, maybe she would be the catalyst that helped the evening along, coupled with the champagne that Ralph had already opened and indulged in.

'Hello, I'm Ralph,' he said, putting his hands on Alexia's shoulders and kissing her on both cheeks. He took hold of James' hand and pumped it up and down with enthusiasm. 'Let me get you a drink. Thought we'd start off with some champagne.'

'Thank you,' James said. He looked around the room. 'What a lovely house you have.'

Tessa smiled to herself. That's a good start. Ralph loved talking about his family home and their past.

'Goes back a long way,' Ralph said, handing James and Alexia their glasses, 'it belonged to my grandfather.'

'So it's been a family home for quite a few generations. What did they do here?'

Ralph gestured to them to take a seat. 'Two centuries ago my great-grandfather made a home at the foot of the Ngong Hills, just like Isak Denesen, or Karen Blixen as she was known. Back then the area we call Karen was remote, not like the sprawling suburb it is today. The family had a fifteen thousand acre cattle farm. Life was hard but profitable enough for my ancestors, an elite and tough-minded group of people who had landed in a unique environment where sudden death was not so unexpected from disease, poisonous snakes and dangerous wild animals.'

'Real pioneers,' James remarked.

'Yes but like all pioneers, back then, they could lose everything in a heartbeat.'

'Did that happen to your family?' Alexia asked Ralph, with a small frown on her beautiful face.

He grimaced. 'I'm afraid so. They had a run of extreme weather and resulting financial problems led to the failure of the farm. Coupled with playing too hard in the social environment, and by that I mean my great-grandfather enjoyed gambling, the family fortune was eroded away.'

'Ouch,' said James. 'Did they ever recover?'

Ralph held his glass out towards a photograph on the

wall, a sepia portrait of a man in safari gear holding a gun. 'Thanks to my grandfather, yes they did. He was far more a businessman and he realized that the future lay in big game camps, shooting camps back then of course, but with regulated licenses. He sold a big area of land and used the money to fund his enterprise. He was a member of the East African Professional Hunter's Association, founded in the thirties by a group of like-minded individuals at the Norfolk Hotel. Family connections brought wealthy clients and even royalty. They were advocates of regulating what species and how much of them were hunted. Without such regulations unscrupulous people could shoot animals randomly wherever and whenever they liked and the Association were alarmed at the sudden decrease in wildlife. They were serious about doing things properly for the long term, rather than wiping out all the game in the short.'

'It's hard to reckon with that way of thinking these days, when the ecosystem and the survival of species they so liberally killed back then is so precarious, but it sounds like there was an integrity about your grandfather,' Alexia commented.

Tessa held her breath, expecting a backlash but Ralph regarded Alexia with reluctant surprise.

'Yes. Whatever you might say about people like my father and grandfather it is because of people like them that there were more species in survival than if they had not been in that business.'

'Except of course they were unable, in the end, to control people's insatiable appetite for trophies,' James intervened.

Tessa prayed Ralph wouldn't take his comment personally.

'True,' Ralph conceded, 'but we all make mistakes.' He drank the remaining wine in his glass before saying, 'so, your turn, tell me about your background.'

'I can't claim the Kenyan heritage you have; my family have been in business over the past twenty years in Mombasa. They were British expatriates.'

'Is that where you grew up, in Mombasa?'

'On and off; I was a weekly boarder at a school in Nairobi, and then I spent a few years learning the safari business in South Africa.'

'Oh I see,' Ralph said evenly, 'I suppose that makes you an expert.' He went to refill their glasses with more champagne, but both Alexia and James declined.

Tessa noted that Ralph, who had refilled his again, had consumed most of the bottle.

'I wouldn't say that,' James continued with his boyish charm, 'but it gave me a good start.'

'Why South Africa?' Tessa asked.

'My father's brother runs a safari business out of Johannesburg, with a camp in the Madikwe region. It seemed like a good idea to learn from him.'

'I love that area,' Tessa said. 'We've been there, haven't we Ralph?'

He chose to ignore her. He could be so ignorant sometimes but she tried not to let her irritation show.

'What made you come back to Kenya?' Ralph continued, 'I would imagine life was pretty good in South Africa.'

'I met a friend in Botswana, Paul Butler, and he was about to set up a mobile camp in a reserve in the Mara and suggested I join him. Which is what we did until...'

Ralph interrupted him with a flourish of his hand, 'you

found Nyara.'

'Yes,' James said, 'or rather it found me.'

'He was headhunted by the Monsoon Consortium,' Alexia explained.

'Oh,' Ralph said with a dismissive laugh, 'is that how people get safari jobs these days – by being headhunted? That's quite a pun, don't you think?'

Tessa gave Ralph a warning glare but he either didn't see it or he chose to ignore her and blundered on regardless.

'So based on two years in South Africa, two years in a bush camp, the Monsoon Consortium considered you the perfect man to run it?

'Ralph,' Tessa warned again. She turned to the Sackville's. 'Please don't take any notice of him, he's a plain speaker and he enjoys needling people, especially when he's been drinking.'

Ralph laughed, but it had a cynical sound to it. 'Yes, don't mind me, I'm just the drunk with a big mouth, but after being in the business for nearly twenty years I find it surprising that one so young and inexperienced would be headhunted for such a big project.'

James shrugged. 'I would concede that you are a man with more experience than most and could teach anyone a thing or two about running a safari camp.'

'Well that's very generous of you,' Ralph said.

Tessa detected the edge of sarcasm.

'I don't think Alexia and I have done a bad job,' James replied evenly.

'Not a bad job at all,' Ralph agreed, 'in fact you're so bloody good at it that everybody wants to go to Nyara.'

Tessa was mortified. Why oh why did he have to be so

aggressive?

'There are plenty of other full camps in the Mara. I'm not sure why you're targeting Nyara,' James challenged.

'Full?' Ralph said, 'well lucky old them. I wish I could say the same for us. You see, my point is that we've lost quite a bit of business since you and Nyara arrived.'

Tessa could have killed him. She watched James regard Ralph with a strong unwavering eye but no anger. That's the way, she thought; don't let him bully you.

'I'm sorry to hear that, but I'm afraid I can't accept that we are to blame.'

Tessa wondered if what he was actually thinking was that her husband was a complete prick.

'Ralph, please, can we leave it there?' Tessa said with a forced smile. 'You're plain speaking is bordering on the point of rudeness and you'll make our guests feel uncomfortable.' She saw James and Alexia exchange a small glance at each other and her heart sank.

Ralph opened his arms and dipped his head at the Sackville's. 'My wife is right and I apologise.'

James gave him a tight smile.

Was this the time to announce dinner? She hurried out to the kitchen to warn Esme and the cook.

'Let's eat,' she said, returning with a bright smile. The announcement was long overdue and what had started as easy conversation had now gone sour. She led the way into the dining room. She placed herself next to James and engaged him in conversation for as long as she could and left Alexia with Ralph. It seemed to be going well. Alexia was engaging and Ralph at least acted as though he was enjoying her company.

'What's your history?' she heard Ralph ask Alexia and, despite the fact that she was supposed to be listening to James, she couldn't help but eavesdrop on the reply.

'I'm fourth generation here in Kenya; my mother is part Italian and my father from Scottish ancestry. They had tea plantations up towards Mount Kenya,' she explained, 'I spent half my life growing up there and the rest between the Scottish Highlands and Puglia, in Italy. My grandparents went back to those countries, so my vacations were divided up.'

'Sounds very exotic,' Ralph commented. 'Did the plantations fail?'

'No, why do you ask?' She was looking at Ralph with a puzzled smile.

Tessa almost sighed. Why did he always drive a spike into a general conversation?

He shrugged, 'because most of them did. So where did you go to school?'

'My parents sent me to a government Kenyan school,' she said and gave a short laugh, 'they didn't want me to grow up with the wrong ideals.'

Tessa saw the surprise on Ralph's face. 'So you know how to handle and speak to the natives?'

Alexia shook her head, frowning. 'The point of going to the school was so that I don't see them that way. I was glad to be able to integrate into the Kenyan culture.'

'Just a figure of speech,' Ralph murmured.

'We live in their country and my father does not believe in the notion of the white Kenyan as the ruler, like some others do,' Alexia continued. 'I grew up with the children of my dad's employees and learned from them early on in my life how to track an elephant, how to stalk antelope, how to get close to lion, how to spot snakes. At the weekends I slept in a tent out in the bush with those kids, surrounded by the sounds of the African bush and the wild animals, so it became like second nature. I knew then that I never wanted to leave.'

'I'm willing to bet that the average Kenyan has never seen a wild animal up close or spent any time in the bush,' Ralph said, 'and your time in a tent is nothing compared to a night in a shack in a slum.'

'I appreciate your point, but I am not unaware of the inequalities that exist.'

'Well, how lucky for you that you met a husband with the same ideals,' Ralph said.

Alexia smiled not, it seemed, put off by Ralph's attempt at putting her down. 'Yes, but in fact he rescued me from Nairobi. I worked for a travel company – I wanted to learn all I could about how it works from the other end of the business.'

'Were your family ancestors here during Mau Mau?'

'Yes.'

'Any casualties?'

'I believe there were a few. I think that's why my grandparents went home.'

Tessa realised that James was watching her listening to Ralph and Alexia. 'I'm so sorry,' she apologised, 'that was very rude of me.'

'It's okay. I never tire of hearing her story,' he said with a smile.

Wow, he really was charming.

Tessa decided it was time to intervene, in case Ralph was

luring Alexia into a trap.

'How did you two meet?' she said, when there was a lull in the conversation between them.

'At a party,' said James, 'it was all a bit of fate. I'm afraid I don't like parties very much but my friends told me to lighten up and socialise a bit more so I agreed to go.' He looked at Alexia and smiled. 'Thank God I did because if I hadn't I doubt if I would have met Alexia.'

'Why don't you like parties?' Tessa asked.

'Too busy being serious about work,' James laughed. 'I spent all my time working or touting for business. Makes Jack a dull boy, I guess.'

Tessa looked at Ralph expecting him to comment but he was just watching.

'I escaped the roomful of people with a beer and wandered out onto the terrace. It was a dark steamy night packed with the sounds of crickets, the planes taking off from JK, police sirens and the constant roar of traffic. Not the sounds I prefer. Anyway out of the gloom came this gobsmacking beautiful girl who literally had me stepping back a few paces. She apologised for startling me but it wasn't that, she had simply taken my breath away and after the party I couldn't stop thinking about her.'

Alexia turned to Tessa. 'He didn't realise that he'd had the same effect on me, but we both left without exchanging phone numbers.'

'I managed to get hold of her phone number and the relationship grew, interspersed by periods of absence when I was in camp and our voices just a crackle on a camp radio. But the more time I spent with Alexia, the more I discovered the beauty and strength within her.' James gave her an adoring smile and Tessa saw Ralph rolling his eyes at them.

'How very romantic,' he said. 'By the way, do you think flushing toilets and baths filled by running water, in the bush, are a good idea?'

That spike again.

'Don't you care for romantic stories?' Alexia challenged.

Ralph shrugged. 'Not really, no, it makes me too aware of my own inadequacies,' and he gave Tessa a look.

'You were romantic yourself when we first met,' she returned.

'Was I,' he said yawning and stretching, 'it seems so long ago now.'

She coloured with embarrassment, also aware that Ralph had consumed not only most of the champagne, but also most of the contents of a bottle of red wine. No wonder he was being so obnoxious. The Sackville's, on the other hand, had politely declined more than a glass of champagne, followed by one glass of wine with the meal.

'If you're referring to Nyara again,' James began, 'I don't have a problem with it because we recycle all our water and provide solar-powered heating.'

'I bet the water you use on a daily basis is a walking week's worth for a Masai village,' Ralph retorted, 're-cycling or not.'

'And I bet it's little more than the amount you use in your bucket showers. Come and see for yourself,' James challenged, 'you and Tessa are very welcome at any time.'

'We don't have time for social visits,' Ralph said 'but thanks anyway.'

Tessa intervened. 'Thank you James, I would love to come to Nyara to see how you do things there.'

After that awkward exchange, the Sackville's declined coffee and politely called it a night.

'Well that went well,' said Ralph, pouring himself a brandy when they'd said their goodbyes and closed the front door.

Tessa turned to him shaking her head in disbelief. 'Went well? What part of that evening do you consider, 'went well'? You just couldn't help yourself, could you?'

'What do you mean?' he protested, 'I was just being honest.'

'No Ralph, you were being antagonistic and rude,' she snapped back, 'probably because you drank three times more than anyone else did.'

'Well, personally, I think they were sanctimonious and bloody goody two shoes about drinking. And they had a driver. Don't you see how full of themselves they are and I bet I'm not the only one in the world who thinks it? They needed taking down a peg or two. God all that romantic bullshit makes you want to heave.'

Tessa shook her head in disbelief. 'I thought it was charming and they neatly revealed you for what you are – jealous.'

'Don't be ridiculous,' he snarled, 'jealous of them - why would I be?'

Tessa sighed, 'you know why – they haven't gone out of their way to take our business, we're handing it to them on a plate!'

'Those people have no idea what it is to work hard at a safari business. They've had it handed to them on a plate by that bloody consortium,' he raged.

'When are you going to see sense? We need to adapt to

the clients needs, regardless of anything else,' Tessa insisted, keeping her voice even, but determined to make her point. 'It's not Nyara ruining our business, its you!'

He sneered. 'That old chestnut again; well my camp will never succumb to that sort of indulgence.'

'Then you'll have to accept the consequences.'

'And so will you!' he shouted back at her and stormed out of the room.

8

NAIROBI

April

Day after day George trekked to government offices in Nairobi, hoping to speak with an official about his situation. Hour after hour he waited in the corridors, grabbing coffee when he could from the local stand outside, or paying a boy to fetch some. Day by day he was promised appointments that never happened. He would wait right up to the time when the offices closed, and he was herded outside with other desperate souls like himself, as security locked the doors. Then he would make the laborious drive back home and sit in his car outside the house, sometimes for half an hour, before he felt composed enough to go and face his wife. For her he fixed a smile and told her that everything was going to be fine.

By the umpteenth unproductive day George couldn't stand the stuffy environment inside the building a moment longer. He decided to take a walk to the bank to see if there was any news there. On the way he caught sight of the man he'd met at the Norfolk – what was his name? Somerton? That was it, Ralph Somerton. George had not warmed to the man and the last thing he wanted was a conversation with him. He turned away, pretending to be on his phone, and hoped Ralph hadn't spotted him - but he had.

'Hey, George,' Ralph called out, 'fancy bumping into you. Have you managed to resolve the problems with your company?' He came hurrying over and grabbed George's hand to shake it.

George politely removed his hand and shook his head. 'No. I'm still waiting for an appointment with the minister of finance and the minister for commerce and industry and goodness knows who else.'

Ralph grimaced. 'Oh, bad luck. I'm in the same position. Well not with a minister, but with the tour operators, but I've got another plan up my sleeve. Fancy a drink?'

'Oh, no thanks,' George said in haste. 'I'm on the way to my bank. I must hurry. Murphy's law they'll call me the minute I'm away.'

'Understood,' said Ralph. 'Look, how about we meet up later, when they've closed up for the day?'

George felt awkward. He didn't want to go drinking with Ralph. There was something about the man that made him uneasy. 'Let me see how things pan out.'

'Okay, old man, that sounds like a plan.' Ralph clapped George on the shoulder. 'You've got my number. Give me a call. I've a feeling things will work out for you.'

It was not a sentiment that George felt able to share. The bank was crowded and he decided it was too risky to wait, so he hurried back to the government building. He took his place again in the crowd of people hanging around, people who were there day after day, just like he was, with the same look of despair on all of their faces.

Then, to his complete surprise, his number came up. A clerk informed him that he was to be seen by the minister in the commerce department during the afternoon. He progressed to the minister's waiting room, unable to believe he would actually step foot inside the department, let alone speak to a minister or his assistant, and quite certain he would still be there by the end of the day. But, within half an hour, George was called in. Pinching himself he walked through the door and sat down in front of the man he had waited for so long to speak to.

George, the minister informed him, would not be allowed to resume his business for the time being, but he would be given generous access to his accounts, in order to pay off some debts, and to help him with his personal struggles. The minister scribbled a signature on an official piece of paper that he was to present to his bank. The whole thing, for which he had been waiting days and weeks, took less than ten minutes.

He left the government offices in a daze, hoping to share his good news with Mary, but when he called home there was no reply. Wanting to celebrate with someone, George found himself calling Ralph Somerton. Somehow he felt he owed it to the man to let him know that his optimistic prediction had come true.

'George old boy, how's it going?' Ralph greeted the call. 'I can hardly believe it, but I got to see the minister this very afternoon, and I was granted limited access to one of my accounts. It seems your optimism paid off for me.' At the back of his mind, George wondered if Ralph already knew it would turn out well. But how could he?

'I'm very pleased to hear it, George. You watch, they'll

realize it's all been a big mistake and you'll get your business back in no time.'

'I'm not so sure about that, but at least I have something to live on and to keep the wolves from the door for a while. How about you?'

'I've been doing a bit of negotiating myself today with some success I think,' Ralph said with a grin, 'now what about that drink, it sounds like we both have something to celebrate.'

George hesitated – he ought to get home to tell Mary his news but she might not be there and perhaps a quick drink wouldn't do any harm, even with Ralph Somerton. 'Alright, would you like a lift?'

'Got my own vehicle, George, thanks very much.'

'Shall we meet at the Norfolk again?'

'Perfect,' Ralph replied. 'See you there.'

'How has your wife reacted to all of the problems?' Ralph asked when they were settled in a couple of chairs, clutching a cold tusker beer each. 'You didn't say much about her when we last met.'

'To tell you the truth I think it's been awful for her,' George said, and he found himself opening up to Somerton. 'Mary loves Kenya. I know it would break her heart to have to leave it. We came here on a whim and a sense of adventure for a couple of years, and ended up staying for more than twenty!'

'She sounds like a sensible woman,' Ralph commented.

'Oh yes,' George agreed.

'Children?'

George shook his head. 'We were never able to have a

family and it was a great disappointment for Mary. Our move to Kenya was part of the healing process and Mary, being Mary, found something to fill that hole in her life – an orphanage project for abandoned children in Nairobi. An American expatriate set it up and Mary joined forces with him. She was good at fund-raising and managed to get a lot of wealthy Kenyan's and expatriates, to cough up their money with lavish raffles and auctions. I helped in the construction of the buildings, including a school block and a dormitory. People from the local community were brought in to work and teach there, and the money needed to maintain the orphanage came from continued efforts to gain sponsorship and donations from all over the world.'

'It sounds like Mary found her niche in the end,' Ralph said, 'but all that work with deprived children must be exhausting and I bet she's seen her fair share of hard luck stories.'

'Oh yes,' George agreed, enthused by Somerton's interest, 'Mary has witnessed things I could never have imagined. Men and women who steal drugs from their own sick children to sell on the streets; children as young as two or three alone on the streets; abandoned babies. The orphanage was a huge and important part of her life but, for three weeks of the year, she put it aside to go to our place in Malindi. It was the only way she could cope. I felt so terrible about having to let it go.'

Ralph nodded in sympathy. 'It sounds to me like she needs a holiday, George, to take her mind off things.'

He shook his head, 'I don't know, we haven't really got the money for it…'

'Oh come on George,' Ralph pressed, 'you've just told

me the department have stumped up a good amount and now you have the chance to treat her.'

'I suppose so,' George relented, 'I'm sure I could use some of the cash for a break and, God knows, she deserves it. I would do anything to brighten her day.' It was true, he would do anything to see her happy again.

'What about a safari trip – the new season is coming up in June?' Ralph said.

It was a long time since they had done that – years in fact – and it was a tempting idea. 'Yes, maybe we could do that. We both love the Mara.'

'You should try Nyara Camp.'

George looked at Ralph in surprise. 'Isn't that the camp that you said was putting you out of business?'

Ralph shrugged. 'Well, whatever I feel about Nyara it's a bloody good place to take a woman to.'

'We'd be happy to go to Chui, if we went anywhere,' George said in a show of loyalty, although he still wasn't certain they would be going anywhere.

Ralph rubbed his hands together. 'I'm pleased to say, old chap, that Chui camp is full for the foreseeable future. I've had a bit of luck too, and I've got something up my sleeve that I think will solve Chui's long term problems.'

'Oh congratulations, good for you,' George said and, as they clinked their glasses together, he felt he liked Somerton a little bit better.

9

NAIROBI

May

Ralph took a Matatu to Kibera, the sprawling Nairobi slum lying west of the city centre on the edge of the Ngong Forest. Aptly translating to 'jungle' Kibera housed up to a quarter of a million of poverty-stricken people. He was on his way to Mashimoni, one of the twelve villages within the slum, where Esme and Yahizid had their home. A maze of narrow dirt tracks and footpaths ran between the densely packed single room shacks made of mud walls with corrugated tin roofs and dirt floors. These were often overcrowded and, Ralph knew, in some areas of the slum more than one hundred people had to share a single latrine. Young boys were paid to empty them and take the contents to dump into the river. During the rainy season untreated sewage overflowed from the ditches and the toxic mud was ankle deep. People walked a long way to the scarce standpipes, that the council had recently installed, for a bucketful of water, or they collected unclean water from the Nairobi dam. From time to time it caused typhoid and cholera outbreaks. An overhead chaos of power cables indicated electricity, but this was unpredictable and controlled by profiteers who saw fit to connect only those who paid their dues. Everywhere he looked someone was carrying something to sell – bundles of scavenged wood, bags full of old cans and bottles, shredded tyres. All these items were commodities and could make the supplier something to help them in their daily struggle for life. Young girls carried big plastic water bottles on their heads; boys kicked a football around a waste ground scattered with rubble and waste. How could anyone ever have a good life here, he wondered?

He was soon surrounded by a group of young children, holding out their hands for money, calling at him to come with them to buy something. Ralph stopped a while and chatted in Swahili to the boys, made them laugh, gave them chocolate he'd brought with him and discovered he was not far from the area where Yahzid and Esme lived. It took a couple more chocolate bars to find the exact shack. Nobody was in but, as he stood considering what to do next, he was aware that an older boy in a scruffy hooded top was watching him from the shadows. Ralph set off then he slipped into a narrow gap between two huts and waited. He heard the boy's breathing as he approached and he stepped out right in front of him. The boy jumped back in alarm and Ralph expected him to turn and run away. He lit a cigarette. 'Want one?' he said and held out the packet. The boy snatched one and retreated again. Ralph tossed over his lighter. The boy lit the cigarette and put the lighter in his pocket. Ralph smiled but didn't ask for it back. Someone coughed inside a shack nearby. The boy froze, poised to take flight like a frightened gazelle.

'Do you know Yahzid Adongo?' Ralph asked, before he lost him.

'Why?' the boy said and he took a deep drag on the cigarette as if his life depended upon it.

'So you know him?'

'I don't know him but I see him, yeah? I see him drinking the Chang'aa. He hangs out with the bad boys. I don't want trouble.'

'I'll pay you if you can take me to him,' Ralph said, knowing full well that it was money the boy was after.

'How much?' the boy kicked at the ground with the toe of his rubber shoe. It looked as though it had been cobbled together from an old tyre.

'Tell me where I can find him first?'

The boy shook his head. 'You give me the money and then I show you.' He took a last drag on the cigarette before grinding the butt out in the mud on the street. 'If that Yahzid find out I've been talking to you I'm a dead man.'

Ralph nodded. 'I understand but I need you to show me first. I'll pay you good money.' What he was prepared to pay was twice the average wage earned per day in Kibera, and he was pretty sure this boy didn't have a job. 'He won't know it was you.'

The boy pulled at his hood, trying to hide his face. He looked around, his body tight with nervous tension.

'There's no-one around,' Ralph assured him.

'There's a place, yeah, Yahzid he goes there to sell things – maybe things he's found, maybe things he's stolen, but that's how he makes enough money to buy the brew. I don't want no trouble for him, but I need money too, you understand?'

Ralph nodded. 'You show me where and I'll give you

the money. You're going to have to trust me like I'm trusting you.'

The boy kicked his toe in the dust then he turned and set off along an alleyway his feet squeaking with each step. Ralph followed, keeping a distance between them for the boy's sake, but mindful that he could be heading into a trap. They passed several people who gave Ralph a curious look. Soon the alley widened out onto a piece of wasteland. Children played there amongst piles of rotting rubbish. A long road ran to one side of it with market stalls. Men and women sat beside them looking bored and vacant.

'Over there,' the boy said, pointing but hanging back in the dark shadows of the alleyway. 'The shop with the tyres outside; now you give me the money.'

Ralph handed over the promised cash and the boy stuffed it into a pocket and ran back the way they had come. He guessed the boy would probably spend it on cheap drugs or glue for sniffing.

There were three men sitting around on grubby old plastic chairs as Ralph approached. They looked up at him, eyes glazed and yellow most probably from drinking changa'a. Ralph was not surprised that so many men succumbed to that deadly brew of poverty, including Yahzid Adongo. With half the population of Kibera out of work, and basically living in squalor, there was a lack of self worth. Changa'a helped to deaden that feeling.

Something was cooking on a brazier in front of the men and the air was thick with acrid fatty smoke.

'I'm looking for Yahzid Adongo,' Ralph said, and he lit up another cigarette.

One of the men shrugged, as if to say 'so what', but

Ralph saw his eyes linger on the cigarette.

'Here,' said Ralph offering the packet. They took one each without thanks or any change of expression.

'So, do you know him?'

The men looked at each other. 'What is he to you?' one asked, exhaling smoke.

'How much will you give us?' said the other.

Information, Ralph surmised, seemed to be the thriving economy around here. He asked them to name their price, heckled it down and waited.

One of the men spat on the ground then he disappeared into the back of the shop. He emerged a few moments later with another.

He eyed Ralph up and down. 'I don't know you,' he said and turned to go.

'I know Esme,' Ralph said, 'and you do know me.'

Yahzid turned on Ralph with a vicious glint in his eyes. 'What do you mean?' he snarled.

'She cleans for my wife and I,' Ralph said. Yahzid was no longer the boy he had seen at the house. Now he was a young man hardened with the years of his difficult life. He was unkempt with dirty clothes and his eyes were the yellow eyes of a changa'a drinker. For one moment Ralph felt sorry for the boy, for his loss of self-respect, but it was contempt that overwhelmed him. How could anyone resort to such low esteem, get into such a state? 'Esme told me about you. She said you were looking for work.'

The men laughed and Yahzid glared at them. He looked at Ralph for a moment then he pointed to the interior of the shop. 'We will talk in there.'

They stepped into a gloomy, windowless room. Once his

eyes had adjusted, Ralph made out a counter, a grubby old sofa, and a pile of rubbish in the corner. The room smelled of paraffin and was hot as a furnace.

'So?' Yahzid said.

'I've got a job for you if you're interested.'

He shrugged. 'What is this job? How much does it pay?'

Ralph explained what it was.

Yahzid stared at him, his eyes gleaming in the gloom. 'It's a dangerous job and it will cost you.'

'That's not your problem. I will pay good money to whoever does the job. Are you interested or not?'

'I might be.' He leaned closer to Ralph, his breath sour with chang'aa, 'but how do I know I can trust you?'

Ralph shrugged. 'That's for you to decide.' He could see the gleam in Yahzid's eyes through the gloom. He'll do it, he thought. He's desperate enough.

Yahzid let out a breath.   'Okay, I will do it.'

Ralph turned to walk out of the shack. 'I'll be in touch.'

'I'm doing it for my sister,' Yahzid called after him. 'Make sure she is well looked after when she works for you.'

Ralph turned and saw the gleam in the boy's eyes.

'Or I will kill you.'

10

NAIROBI

May

After the disastrous dinner with the Sackville's and the confrontation with her husband, Tessa sank to a low point. She felt beaten. What more could she do? It was clear that she and Ralph were never going to see eye to eye. They'd reached a stalemate, an impasse.

They passed, like ships in the night, at the house in Karen speaking when they had to. He told her he was visiting the tour operators trying to drum up business for the new season. Whether it was true or not she couldn't tell. When he was home he was more often than not talking on his mobile in the garden, then driving off without telling her where he was going. When he did come back he would disappear into his study, until the early hours, whilst she lay in bed wondering what he was doing. She began to think about their future, and it pained her to think that it might not be a future together. She loved the old Ralph, not the man he was now. She worried about the new season and whether he would be there or not. It was so difficult when he went away and she had to handle everything on her own.

The camp needed him there; she needed him there. Deep down inside she had some sympathy with her husband's feelings about the failings of Chui, but he had to recognize the changes that were needed if they wanted to keep the business going? How she was going to persuade him, she had no idea. He was stubborn and volatile but she had to keep trying.

One morning, when she was making coffee, he came into the kitchen from the garden.

'Would you like a cup?' she offered. Perhaps now was a good time to bring it up.

'What? Oh yes, coffee, thank you,' distracted he sat down at the kitchen table, staring at his phone.

She suppressed the irritation she felt because she knew he wasn't really listening to her, and carried on. 'We've both been so busy there hasn't really been time to talk, but I thought we could have a chat about the new season.' Tessa sat down opposite him with her coffee and pushed his across.

'Hmm?' he said, still looking at his phone.

'Ralph, the new season, we need to talk about it.'

'What's there to talk about? We've started a new season enough times before without having to talk about it.'

'This time is different. I need to know that you will be there for a start…'

'Of course I'll be there.'

'I'm only asking because you were away so much before and it's harder when you are not there. I miss you're presence.' She didn't want to sound needy or nagging; she just wanted him to know that she appreciated him.

He looked up at her frowning. 'I told you why that was – I was trying to do something about our failure to get punters to the camp, just like I've been doing over the past few weeks.' He sounded irritated but she had to persevere.

'I know, and I saw online how many slots have been filled. You've done well.' She tried to keep a balance between praising and patronizing. 'I've had some ideas about how we could make a few changes to make it more…'

He gave her a long hard look as he interrupted her. 'You won't give it up, will you?'

'Give up what?'

'Your stupid notion that we have to change.'

'No, I don't think I will, because we do,' she retorted. 'It's not a stupid notion, it's reality.' Why did he always get so angry about it and defensive?

He leaned towards her, 'I've told you, Tessa, I will not change anything because of that damned new camp. I resent from the bottom of my heart the fact that you feel we have to. I thought you at least would be on my side.'

Tessa's heart sank. 'I am on your side, Ralph, in fact I am on OUR side, but you have to stop blaming other people. We need to change because we do, not because of anyone or anything else.'

He stared at her for a moment with a hint of a smirk on his face. 'Well it's irrelevant, anyway, because I've sorted it.'

She frowned, 'what do you mean, sorted what?'

'I mean you don't have to worry any more. Things will get better and I don't want any more talk of change,' then he got up and strode out of the kitchen. After a few moments she heard him in his car tooting at the guard to open the gate.

11

NYARA CAMP

June

As the little plane lifted away from Wilson Airport and skimmed over the vast Nairobi slum of Kibera, Mary looked down on the acres and acres of tin roofs and imagined all the children down there struggling to survive, enduring poverty, hunger, thirst, abuse and hard labour. Her heart ached for them and for the orphanage she felt she had abandoned. She had her reasons of course, but that was the secret she carried. The trick was to be positive, to be as brave as the orphaned children were. She reached out a hand and put it on top of George's. He turned to smile at her and, with her sun glasses, on he couldn't see the gleam of sadness in her eyes.

'We need this break, George. Thank you so much for organising it.'

'You don't have to thank me,' he replied. 'You deserve it.'

'We both do,' she said. Mary had been more than a bit surprised when George had announced that they were going on safari. 'How can we when you owe people money?' she'd questioned.

'The government have given me access to an account with enough money to pay off the creditors and some left over. I thought a holiday would do us good. God knows we've earned it, Mary.'

She couldn't help but agree with that sentiment, but she had also felt the need for caution. 'Shouldn't we put the money aside in case we find ourselves in need of it in the future?'

'Don't worry,' George had assured her. 'There is enough for this trip and I've taken the precaution of transferring funds to another account to keep our heads above water. I'm pretty optimistic about getting the business back soon.'

Mary had been carried along and swayed by his optimism. One thing you could be certain of in Africa was that life was unpredictable and, after twenty-five years of dedication to the place they called home, they had both found that out to their cost. On top of the business problems and the orphanage, Mary carried a secret that she had not yet shared with George. She just hadn't yet found the right moment.

After the sobering sight of Kibera, the flight into the bush soon turned into some breathtaking views. The suburban outskirts of Nairobi vanished into the edge of Nairobi National Park. It was a park in the loosest sense of the word - a unique wilderness full of wild animals, like lions and rhinos, cheetah and leopard, just a heartbeat away from the city. She looked down on a herd of zebra galloping below them, on gazelle and giraffe feeding. If you lived on the outskirts of the city you might hear the roar of lion and the cry of hyena in the night. She turned to tell George but he had pulled out the safety instructions card and was fanning himself.

'It's very hot in here,' he said, untwisting the cap on a bottle of water and drinking down the contents thirstily.

'We'll soon be there,' Mary said. She looked out of the window at the landscape below. 'It's easy to forget that Nairobi is surrounded by an endless wilderness when you live in the heart of the city. I'm so looking forward to spending time in the bush again.

'Do you remember the last time we went on safari?' George said. 'It must have been at least five years ago – when we were in Malindi and we flew to Tsavo for a weekend?'

Mary couldn't help but feel sad at the mention of Malindi and it must have shown on her face.

George patted her hand. 'I'm sorry Mary, that was thoughtless of me to mention Upepo.'

She forced a smile. 'It's all right. There's no good dwelling on it. We were lucky to have had the time we did have there.' But the lump in her throat took a while to dislodge, and she forced herself not to think of the house she had so adored. Upepo Mwanana, with its thatched roof, and whitewashed walls draped with bougainvillea; its echoes of the happiness and people from the passing years, was the embodiment of the words it translated to, *gentle wind*. It stood in the shade of tall palms and at night the 'shush' of the wind and rush of the surf on the beach lulled them to sleep, instead of the whine of police sirens and the constant hum of Nairobi life. There had been nothing better than spending a weekend there, where she could cleanse her dusty Nairobi-stained body in the sparkling Indian Ocean and curl her toes in the pure white sand of the beach.

A little while later the plane landed, like an airborne bush bus, dropping off and picking up new passengers, who were going back to Wilson. They remained onboard, waiting for bags to be loaded and unloaded.

Two stops later they landed at their own bush destination airstrip where a tall gracious Masai, Silas, greeted them and carried their bags to the truck. It was a forty-five minute drive to Nyara and Mary couldn't believe what they managed to see on the way: elephant, zebra, wildebeest and antelope all together as far as the eye could see. They stopped to watch a cheetah sitting upright in the grass, it's eye on an antelope herd, and then Silas's own eagle eyes picked out the peeping fluffy head of a cheetah cub hiding in the grass, cheeping like a little bird for it's absent mother.

As they approached Nyara, the pale grey canvas that was the camp blended into the rocky landscape that surrounded it. In the distance Mary spied a river, a gleaming ribbon cutting its way through the heart of the bush.

James and Alexia, the camp managers, came out to greet them as they drove into the camp and, after a chat about bush drives, dietary requirements and any other comforts they might require, they were taken by a member of staff to their tent.

It was a tent, Mary realised, in the loosest sense of the word. This tent had sliding glass patio doors, built in wardrobes and an en-suite bathroom, a toilet cubicle and a large shower area. Outside of each tent individual drums of re-cycled water were heated by solar energy which meant hot water was always available, and David their tent butler announced with pride: 'there is enough water for two showers each a day if you wish, or one bath.'

Despite the re-cycling it still seemed an embarrassing

luxury to Mary who imagined that where David came from there was unlikely to be any fresh water provision at all apart from a river, or a well that might be kilometres away and must be fetched on foot. 'One will be enough,' she said. 'More than enough, thank you.'

Outside a deck ran down one side of the tent where they found a big bamboo sofa with large soft cushions, a table and chairs.

'It is safe to sit outside during the daytime,' David assured them. 'Lunch will be served in about half an hour. Please come first for a drink and to meet the other guests.'

They left for early morning drives when the air was sharp and cool, hugging soft blankets around them as they sped down towards the river to cross into the reserve on the other side. As the sun rose higher the land began to warm up. The spreading sunlight pushed back the shadows of the night and the grass stood golden as far as the eye could see. Sometimes they found a lion pride still feeding on a kill, or on its way to a rocky mount where they would settle down in the shade of overhanging boulders for the rest of the day. Then Silas would park the vehicle nearby and they would speak in whispers, and take discreet photographs so as not to alarm the animals. Large breeding herds of elephants trekked across the plains, mothers, daughters, sons and babies all travelling to new feeding ground, waterholes or the river to drink and wallow. Near the river they sometimes stopped for breakfast on an outcrop of rocks, eating egg and bacon rolls and looking down on the hippos basking in the muddy waters of the river. Just a little further down crocodiles lay on the sand and waited for an antelope to come along to drink, or a young giraffe spreading its legs to reach down to the water. It was then that the giraffe was most vulnerable to attack.

Back at camp they had lunch followed by a rest for a few hours before they set off again on the afternoon drives. In the evenings, before dinner, the guests gathered around a campfire eating plantain chips with their sundowners, talking about what they had seen that day and catching the hum of the Masai singing at their boma in the distance.

'This has been a wonderful time,' Mary said to George, on their penultimate day. They were relaxing outside on the deck before the afternoon drive.

'It's certainly helped to take my mind off other things,' he said, looking up from his book with a smile.

But Mary knew, from the weary frown he wore, that all his worries were still weighing him down. 'It's so unfair when you worked so hard to achieve what you did and then to be so let down.'

George shrugged. 'I'm sure it will all come right in the end. I've made some progress. I'll get the business back, one way or another. At least I have the ear of someone at the government department now.'

'I should think so too,' she said, but guessed there would be a price to pay for that ear. 'They can't continue to hold you responsible for Malik's actions and political belief can they?'

'Who knows what they can do,' he said, and put down his book. 'I'm feeling a bit tired Mary, do you mind if I duck out this afternoon and rest up for the evening?'

She went on the afternoon drive alone leaving George to rest. Her secret she had almost managed to forget about, and she had made up her mind that the camp was not the place to tell her husband. It would be such a shame to spoil these precious moments together.

As the day wore on, Mary watched in wonder and joy at the deep red colours of the sunset and the big shining ball of sun as it settled down on the horizon, a sight that the regular dust and pollution over Nairobi often obscured. There is no sky as big as the sky that stretches over Africa, she thought. They sat on the truck and watched the dark silhouettes of animals against the reddening sky as they wandered across the landscape. She inhaled the musty smell of elephant, and the pungent scent of acacia and said to Silas, 'I think I've found a piece of Heaven.'

'Yes, Kenya often has the appearance of Heaven,' he agreed, then he added with solemnity, 'but sometimes there is a little bit of Hell thrown in too.'

On the last evening, after Mary had returned from her drive, she and George joined the guests around the campfire for the usual pre-dinner drinks at Nyara. It was a black, moonless night but the sky was clear with a canopy of glittering stars. Mary lay back in her chair to get a good look at them and, when she saw a shooting star, she wished for an end to her husband's anxiety.

After supper the Masai men, from the nearby village, came to dance and sing. It was a spectacle of wonder, through the smoke and sparks of the crackling fire, as they jumped like gazelles in rhythm to their humming voices, spears in hand, each trying to outdo the other with the highest leap. The night air resonated with their shouts and laughter. Then they left, melting into the bush, their laughter trailing behind them all the way back to the village.

'Do you mind if I slip off to bed now, I'm feeling rather tired?' Mary said to George, when the dancers had gone. 'You stay and enjoy the rest of the evening.'

'Are you sure?' he said, as Silas refilled his wine glass.

'Yes, quite sure, I'm just feeling a little tired, that's all.' In fact she was looking forward to some time alone to reflect on her secret and the impact it was going to have.

An Askari escorted her back to the tent and saw her safely inside. She lay for a while reading and pondering. It seemed there was every chance that she might have to leave a country she had come to love, for all it had thrown at them. She'd grown used to the way things stumbled into place, was fond of its madness and aware of its dangers. It was impossible to imagine she and George trying to settle anywhere else, but the possibility that they might have to always lay at the back of her mind. But her biggest regret had been the heartbreaking decision to leave the orphanage and its children and staff. It had broken her heart and theirs when she had come to say goodbye. Sadly there had been no choice. The secret had seen to that.

Long after George had returned to their tent and was snoring in a deep slumber, Mary lay awake listening to the sounds of the bush beyond the canvas walls of their tent. She heard the distant roar of lion on the plains beyond the river, rising above the cacophony of cicadas and the whooping cry of the hyenas. Something was munching on grass close by the tent and she climbed out of bed to peek through the mesh window, to see what it was. But there was no moon that night, just a canopy of stars. Even the solar lights along the path were out and there was no sign of the usual dying embers where the campfire had been. She shivered. It was hot by day but cool by night. Putting a fleece and her tracksuit trousers over her pyjamas she wished she could just step outside onto the veranda and become part of the African night – to lie back on the sofa and watch the stars again without fear of being taken by a leopard or trampled by elephant or hippopotamus. Instead she took a book over to the far corner of the tent so as not to disturb George, and used her head torch to read for a while. She moved part of the curtain covering the sliding glass door to one side and peered through the glass. Stars glittered in the dark sky amongst a head of heavy clouds and she wondered if they heralded the long awaited rains. Then the book absorbed her again and it was an odd sound towards the back of the tent that made her break off from reading; a sound that didn't quite sit right with the African night. She assumed it was the Askari prowling around and she twitched the curtain edge back into place. As she did so the book slid from her lap and clattered to the floor. Mary held her breath, expecting to George wake up but he didn't. She climbed back into bed and closed her eyes, feeling sleepy now. A little while later a hand clamped across Mary's mouth with a cloth steeped in a pungent liquid, and another held her down. Whatever it was did its work quickly, silencing her, so she had no chance to struggle or cry out.

12

NYARA CAMP

June

In tent number six George was woken by something that sounded like gunshot. He lay for a moment, trying to make sense of what he had just heard, wondering if it was a dream.

'Mary, are you awake?' He reached out an arm then began patting the space beside him where his wife should have been. It was empty.

'Mary, where are you?' he called, but there was no reply. He fumbled around for the torch on the bedside table and switched it on. He got out of bed and crossed the room to the bathroom area.

'Mary, are you in there?' There was no reply and he pushed open the door, searching inside with the torch beam. The bathroom was empty. He went in and pulled back the curtain to the shower area. In the torch beam he could see the canvas flapping in the breeze. On closer examination it looked as though it had been slashed from top to bottom.

George staggered back into the bedroom, frowning at the muzzy feeling in his head. Had he had that much wine last night?

'Mary?' he called again, shining the torch around the room. Where on earth was she? There was a sudden loud knocking on the patio door and George nearly leapt out of his skin. A voice called, 'sir, it is Silas here, please unlock your door, there is an emergency and we are evacuating all the tents.'

George opened the door and grabbed him by the arm, 'I can't find my wife. I don't know what to do. The canvas in the bathroom – it's been slashed and I think someone has taken her!' He knew he was gabbling but he was desperate to explain what had happened, to get them to act.

'Please sir, you must calm yourself. Sit down and I will fetch James.'

When James Sackville appeared, George leapt up from the chair: 'someone has kidnapped my wife! We must look for her.'

James stared at him. 'Kidnapped?'

'Yes. Something woke me, I think it was gunshot, and I thought Mary was still in bed, but she wasn't. I went to the bathroom but she wasn't there either. The canvas in the shower area had been slashed, with a panga or something. Someone must have come in and taken her!' George registered that the men had rifles in their hands. 'What's been going on here? Was it you firing shots that I heard?'

'No,' James told him, ' I'm afraid it was someone to us. It appears the camp was under attack. They fired shots into the air to scare us off.'

'Under attack?'

'Yes. Our Askari stumbled on two men when he was patrolling around the camp. They knocked him unconscious.

He raised the alarm when he came to. They must have heard him and fired their warning shots.'

'But my wife has gone missing. They must have taken her,' George panicked as the realisation of what had happened sunk further in.

'Perhaps she was scared and ran away into the bush,' Silas suggested.

George shook his head with impatience. 'No, Mary wouldn't do that, she's far too sensible. I told you the bathroom tent has been slashed. Come and see for yourselves.'

In the bathroom area Silas confirmed that a panga had indeed slashed the canvas. 'There are also footprints in the muddy area around the soak-away and look,' he said, pointing his torch to the floor and following the trail, 'mud prints going to the bed and back again.'

'On Mary's side,' George said, sitting down on the bed and putting his muzzy head in his hands. 'I can't believe I didn't hear anything, but I've always been a deep sleeper.' He looked around the tent and gulped when he saw Mary's slippers. Then he noticed that his camera and mobile telephone were still on the bedside table. 'Look, they didn't even steal anything. It seems as though they just wanted Mary. You've got to do something!'

'We'll take you to the lounge tent, where everyone is gathered. The rangers are being notified and the police. They will decide what to do from there,' said James.

'But they won't be here for ages,' George said.

'I'm sorry, Mr. Stephenson but it's the best I can do, at the moment.'

George detected the anxiety in his voice and, as they hurried him to the lounge tent, he heard James speak quietly to Silas.

'Who the hell are 'they'?' he whispered.

'I don't know – maybe militants or bandits who were frightened away,' Silas whispered back. 'Gone now. I think the shots were to stop us from following.'

In the lounge tent, where Alexia was trying to calm the gathered guests, George looked around, praying Mary would be there, but she wasn't. He was given a cup of tea whilst James explained to Alexia the facts surrounding the missing guest.

'I think we have to face the possibility that Mrs. Stephenson might indeed have been taken. Samuel and I heard a vehicle leaving, the solar path lights were all out, the lanterns standing at the edge of the tents were out and the fire embers had been doused with water.'

'Sabotage,' Alexia commented. 'Do you think someone inside the camp might have been responsible?'

James shook his head. 'I don't know. The Askari patrolling the camp, who was knocked unconscious, was the one who raised the alarm. So not him.'

'The police will get to the bottom of it, I suppose,' she said then she turned to George. 'I'm so sorry about your wife. We will do everything we can to find her.'

James gave Alexia a helpless look, that didn't escape George. He felt sorry for them, for what had happened, but finding Mary was more important.

'The Stephenson's bathroom tent has been slashed, most probably with a panga,' James said, 'so it does indeed look as though she was abducted.'

Alexia shuddered. 'Whoever it was took her from right under our noses.'

'Actually from under mine,' George said, 'I still can't believe I slept through it.'

'I'm so sorry Mr. Stephenson, I can't imagine how you are feeling,' she said putting her hand on his shoulder.

'Do you have any idea why she might have been taken?' James asked.

George shook his head. 'No. I lost my business because my deceased partner's son was involved in opposition politics. Perhaps it's something to do with that.'

'I assumed they came to rob the camp, but your wife missing puts a different slant on it,' James mused, 'especially as nobody else appears to have been affected.'

Silas and Masigonde came back. They had made a thorough check in and around the camp and they showed James a cloth they had found with a pungent acidic smell to it.

'What is that?' said James.

'Do not put it to your face,' Silas warned, 'it is a strong inhalant, I believe.'

'Do you think they drugged Mary with it?' George asked.

'It is a possibility.'

'Dear God,' he said, and began to shake. Alexia took his rattling teacup and saucer from him and gave him a glass of brandy. He downed it in one gulp. 'Please, we must go and search for my wife.'

'As soon as it's light Silas will go out on the truck, but to try and track whoever took her now, in the dark, will be too difficult.'

'But every minute lost,' he wailed, unable to bear the thought of what she was going through, even though he understood that it would be fruitless going out in the dark.

'I understand your anguish, Mr. Stephenson, but we must put it in the hands of the police.'

Not long after daybreak the police arrived from Narok. James came to the lounge tent after he had spoken to them, and explained that everyone would have to be questioned. Some, George noted, took it better than others.

'I want to leave right away,' a woman said, 'I'm not hanging around with people like that in the vicinity.'

'They might come back,' someone else wailed.

'I doubt it,' James reassured them, as best he could. 'They will know that the alarm has been raised and the police and rangers will already be tracking them.'

'I want to go back to my tent and pack,' a woman said, and others murmured in agreement.

'I understand,' James reasoned, 'but I think it's better if you stay here for the time being.'

'But you said the intruders had gone, so why can't we go back?' the woman pressed.

James remained resolute. 'The police want to question everyone before they leave and it is easier for them if you are all in the same place.'

'But we don't know anything,' someone retorted. 'It's nothing to do with us.'

'When can we leave the camp?' another demanded.

'The police will explain everything to you.'

George sat huddled in the corner, listening to James trying to keep order and the anguished chatter of the guests, whilst he tried to make sense of what had happened. Why had they taken Mary and who had done such a thing? He had no money so how was he supposed to pay a ransom? A sob rose up in his throat again. Mary, what have they done to you? Why did they take you instead of me?

13

CHUI CAMP

June

Ralph shook Tessa awake. 'Nyara Camp was attacked last night. I just heard it over the radio. Apparently a woman has gone missing.'

Tessa stared at him in horror. 'Oh my God, that's dreadful news! Poor James and Alexia...'

'They must have appalling security,' her husband interrupted with a yawn.

Tessa frowned. 'Let's not make assumptions about that.'

He shrugged, 'the news speaks for itself.'

'Can we do anything to help?'

'We could drive over later and offer a place to their clients, if they want to continue a safe safari, and I can help in the search for the woman.'

'I suppose so,' Tessa said, although she felt a bit uncomfortable at the thought of driving over to see if they could get any guests out of the unfortunate circumstances. 'Do you think she might have run off into the bush, to escape from the attackers?'

Ralph stretched his arms over his head. 'I don't know,

but I don't expect she'll come to much harm.'

'Not come to much harm?' Tessa exclaimed, 'she could be wandering around in the bush at the mercy of goodness knows what!'

'Whatever the answer, it'll take a lot for Nyara to recover from this once word gets out and I'd still question the adequacy of their security.'

'Is our camp any more safe against a gang of attackers descending upon us? Tessa questioned.

'I bloody well hope so. I pay the staff enough to make sure of it,' was his stinging response.

They called Nyara late morning and, although Alexia said there was no need to bother going over, Ralph insisted. 'Us camps must stick together at times like this,' he said.

It was about an hour and a half drive to Nyara from Chui, across the lush green savannah, renewed by the rains, alongside feeding zebra and antelope and a herd of elephants heading for the river.

They crossed the airstrip road where trucks were arriving to collect their new guests, and others bringing those who were leaving. Tessa felt a pang of envy and, she had to admit, she too had a sense of unfairness that Chui had fallen out of popularity. Every time a new camp appeared, or a camp brought something more unique to the table, everyone else had to compete with that or find some new uniqueness of it's own. The business was tough and competitive.

Her cell-phone rang. It was Sophie. 'I've just seen a newsflash on TV of an attack on a camp – they didn't say which one it was. Are you both okay?'

'Gosh that news got out quickly. Yes. We're fine. It

happened at Nyara, the new camp. As a matter of a fact we're on our way over there now, to see if we can help in any way.'

'Was it militants?'

'Nobody knows. We heard there is a woman missing but she may have wandered off, in the mayhem of the attack.'

'You're not on your own are you?'

'No, Ralph is with me. He's going to help in the search for her, and we've offered to take any clients who want to continue their vacation.'

'Well, keep safe and keep me posted.'

As they approached Nyara they passed the Nissan huts where the camp workers lived, the vegetable gardens, the carport and its mechanical workshop and then Nyara itself, the extent of which took her breath away. The main communal tents were vast, like circus big tops, and either side of them bedroom tents panned out. The pale canvas colour blended in well with the bleached rocky outcrops that surrounded the area. It was, she thought, quite magnificent. She'd been looking forward to visiting the camp for a long time, but never expected it to be under such awful circumstances.

Alexia came out to greet them looking pale and drawn. She took them to the office tent, sent for coffee then she went over what had happened. 'It was a terrifying experience for us all. The guests are still in shock, but at least no harm came to them and they were not robbed. A group of them left a bit earlier to catch the plane back to Nairobi.'

'Was the woman, who has gone missing, staying here on her own or with someone else?' Ralph asked.

'She was here with her husband.'

'Poor man, where is he now?' he said, and Tessa saw him

looking around as though he might be there.

'Oh, he's gone with the police to Narok. He was reluctant to leave but we assured him that we were doing everything to try and find her. All our guides and trackers are out looking for her, if indeed she's out there at all.'

'Why, is there another explanation?' Ralph probed.

'There is a strong possibility that she has been abducted.'

Tessa was shocked. 'That's terrible. Who would do that?'

Alexia shrugged. 'We have no idea.'

'Do they suspect that the husband might have been involved?' Ralph asked, 'I mean taking him off to Narok seems to indicate they want to seriously question him.'

'I don't think so, just routine questions,' Alexia said, 'I hadn't really thought about that possibility. He didn't want to go, but the police were rather insistent.'

Ralph pursed his lips. 'Oh well, I'm sure they'll get to the bottom of it.'

'I'm so sorry this has happened to you,' Tessa sympathised.

Alexia nodded. 'Made worse by the disappearance of Mary Stephenson of course.'

'Is he a wealthy business man, the husband?' Ralph asked. 'Has there been a ransom request?'

'I don't know about his personal life,' Alexia replied, 'but, as far as I know, there has not yet been any contact from anyone asking for a ransom.'

'Then perhaps it wasn't a kidnapping,' Tessa remarked. She hoped it wasn't, even though the meeting she had attended had warned that it could happen anywhere in Kenya.

Alexia hesitated before saying, 'the thing is all the signs point to it.'

'What sort of signs?' Tessa and Ralph said, in unison.

'First, the tent canvas in the bathroom area was slashed, most probably with a panga. Second, there are footprints in the mud outside and to and from the bed and third, there are signs outside of the tent that something heavy was dragged away. It all points to a strong possibility of an abduction.'

Tessa frowned. 'If she has, then by whom and why?'

'Who knows?' Alexia said. 'Maybe an extremist group – we've been warned about militant activists.'

'But that's happened further north; to come into a private reserve this far south…?' Tessa said, unnerved by the thought of it.

'These people will do anything for money. They're fanatics,' Ralph remarked.

'If that's the case then why hasn't there been any contact? It seems odd that the camp was attacked yet there was no robbery, just a missing person.'

'Yes, doesn't it?' Alexia agreed with Tessa, 'which makes it even more likely that the missing woman was a pre-meditated target. Her husband did mention to James that he had problems with an ex-partner of his business who was involved in oppositional politics.'

'Well there you go, I expect that's the answer, but we could discuss the why's and wherefore's all day. I'd like to get out there to help in the search for her,' Ralph said to Alexia.

'It's very kind of you to offer your time, Ralph. I'll take you to James and you can discuss it with him. He's been talking to Monsoon, the consortium who own the camp, and he'll be going to Nairobi for a de-briefing.' Alexia looked downcast. 'This will have a serious effect on the business.'

'Ah, the consortium,' said Ralph nodding his head, 'I bet

they're concerned. It will take a long time for you to recover from something like this, once the news gets out.'

Tessa gave him a warning glare. Why did he have to be so blunt?

'The police want to close us down for the time being. It will be disastrous if they do, but I appreciate the situation is an absolute emergency.'

'Yes it is and you know what people are like, with social media at our fingertips these days your guests are more than likely to post their accounts of what happened on any number of sites. I wouldn't want to come, would you?' Ralph blundered on ignoring Tessa.

'Oh for goodness sake, Ralph,' she snapped, 'give Alexia a bit of hope.' He was acting as though he had come to gloat, not help.

He pulled a face back at her. 'Sorry, I'm just being pragmatic, but I'm sure Alexia and James already know that they need to face the facts, not pussyfoot around them.'

'Even so,' Tessa said, embarrassed by his insensitive onslaught.

'Unfortunately I have to agree with your husband,' Alexia said, 'but I can assure you we are not just 'pussyfooting around.'

Tessa caught the edge of irritation in her voice but she knew Alexia was too polite to say anything rude. 'I'm so sorry for you and I hope the police don't have their way.'

'As for the rest of your clients, we've got some space if any of them want to come to a safer camp,' Ralph said, 'I mean after what's happened here,' he added.

Tessa rolled her eyes. Was there no end to his tactless jibes?

'That's a kind offer. I'll put the question to them now and you can come with me to find James,' she said to Ralph. It sounded polite, but Tessa saw her tight lipped expression and she felt embarrassed by her husband.

Alexia returned to Tessa about fifteen minutes later. 'None of the guests want to continue their safari here or anywhere else. I suppose you can't blame them. I'm so sorry you've had a wasted journey.'

'We would have come anyway,' Tessa said, 'just to offer you some support.'

Alexia sank into a chair. 'Thank you, you are very kind. I hope the attack doesn't have a bad effect on other camps around us, including Chui. We shall feel so responsible.'

'The attack wasn't your fault, it could have happened to any one of us,' Tessa reassured her.

'I suppose so, but the more I think about it, the more I'm beginning to think they targeted us because of the woman who was taken. But who took her, and why?'

'Let's hope the police and the rangers can solve that mystery as soon as possible.'

Ralph returned around mid-afternoon and they headed straight back to Chui, wanting to arrive before nightfall. There had been no signs or clues of the missing woman and due to the many criss-crossing tracks over the plains from many camp trucks it was impossible to single one out to follow.

'I've sent out a news alert about the attack to other camps in the Mara,' Ralph told her, when they were getting ready for bed.

Tessa looked at him aghast. 'Oh Ralph, why did you do

that?'

'They all have a right to know that they might be in danger if the attackers are still in the area,' he retorted. 'You can't keep news like that to yourself.'

'It might also have been better to have kept it quiet until the police had made their own statement. It will panic people unnecessarily, and it could ruin things for Nyara.'
'Tessa, a camp has been attacked, a woman has been taken and, as you reminded me, it could have been ours or any other camp in the area. Wouldn't you want to be warned so that you could be on your guard? Nyara will just have to deal with it.'

'It won't help their situation?' she persisted, but she had to agree with him.

'Maybe not, but it doesn't alter the fact that people have to be aware of what happened.'

'Do you think it could have been militants?' she said.

'Militants?' he mused, 'why not, it's happened before.'

'And what if it wasn't militants?'

'What do you mean?'

'Supposing it was someone who just wanted to cause trouble for the Sackville's.' 'Well they certainly got trouble,' he retorted. Then he turned away from her.

She lay awake long after he was asleep thinking it all over.

14

NAROK

June

'I can't tell you anything more,' said a weary George, after he had been questioned for two hours at the Narok police station. 'I woke up and discovered my wife had disappeared, taken by the people who invaded the camp.'

The interviewing officer sighed. 'You keep saying that your wife has been taken. How do you know for certain?'

'Look, I don't know for certain but all the evidence, the slash in the tent, the tracks outside, surely they point to it as being the most likely explanation?'

'Why do you not accept that she might have wandered away and got lost in the bush?'

'She would never have gone off alone into the bush. She knows how dangerous it is,' George insisted.

'People do irrational things when they are frightened.'

'Mary is not an irrational person. Please, you must send people to search for a clue as to where they have taken my wife,' he pleaded. Every minute that passed by, without them searching for her, was a minute too many for George.

He was so tired and he wanted time on his own to try and work it all out. Why wouldn't they believe him?

'If she did not run away of her own accord, why would someone want to kidnap your wife?'

George shook his head. 'I have no idea. I'm not a rich man and I am not important. My business collapsed due to the withdrawal of government contracts. I have debtors but my accounts are frozen by the state. The son of my deceased business partner, Malik, was taken for questioning by government people. He's an opposition guy and he is in prison. Maybe it's something to do with him.' George could not help but notice the look that passed between his questioners. 'Or perhaps someone I owe money to is angry that I haven't been able to pay up. Who knows? I don't.'

'Is there something else you are not telling us?'

He stared at them, puzzled. 'Like what? I've told you everything I know and remember.' His tongue swept around his dry mouth and across his lips. 'May I please have some water?'

The interviewing officer signaled to the man at the door and a bottle was brought in.

George drank it all down, realizing the extent of his dehydration. He could have swallowed at least two more. It was hot and stuffy in the room and there was a stale unpleasant odour – perhaps from previous nervous interviewees.

'Are you certain there is nothing else you can tell us,' the officer persisted. 'For instance did you arrange this whole charade yourself?'

'Me?' George said and he gave a small disbelieving laugh. 'Of course I didn't. I've told you, I'm not a rich man and anyway would I arrange for my wife to be kidnapped, and then ask myself for the money?' He was shocked by such a preposterous idea but, even though George had answered no, they kept on with that line of questioning, trying to get him to confess to something he hadn't done. It went on for at least another hour, trying to trick him into a confession, until he thought he would go mad or pass out with exhaustion. On top of that he was dealing with his anxiety about Mary. The hours and minutes of her disappearance were ticking by. What were they doing to find her?

At last they seemed to be satisfied, or as tired as he was, and they told him he could go, as long as he remained in Narok. He was surprised they hadn't kept him locked up.

He emerged from the police station into the steamy afternoon and found a modest hotel in the town where the rooms were small but fairly clean, and there was even a bathroom with a half-decent shower. After relieving himself of the grime of the past few days George lay on the bed exhausted, but unable to sleep, because of his own endless and painful questions that kept his spinning mind awake. Mary, where are you? What happened? Who took you? Why? And the more he thought about it, the more likely it seemed that she had indeed been taken. Nobody had been robbed which seemed odd. Why go to all that trouble to attack a camp if you hadn't intended to do anything? The only thing to come out of the attack was Mary's disappearance.

The following morning, when he returned to the police station, he was asked to make a statement and then he was surprised to learn that he was free to return to Nairobi, as long as he reported in at the Nairobi Police Station. If he did not they would regard him as a fugitive. The fact was irrelevant. George had no intention of leaving Narok until

Mary had been found.

15

MASAI MARA

June

A shaft of sunlight cut like a sword through the small window slit and Mary woke to the intensity of its glare. She was lying on a low platform that took up one side of the hut – a sort of makeshift bed. The smell of wood-smoke smothered the hut, and the room was hot and claustrophobic. Attempting to move, Mary discovered her hands and legs were bound again, but at least her hands were bound front of her. On the floor by her bed were several bottles of drinking water. She sat up and swung round so her legs were on the floor and, as she did so, her head swam and she felt nauseous. She leaned down to get hold of one of the bottles with her bound hands, opened it with her teeth, and drank thirstily. Looking down at her feet the rope knots looked impossible to undo, but Mary had to try. She persevered for a long time, with sweat pouring down her face, then at last the knot began to work free and soon it was loose enough for her to slip her feet out. She stood up, stretching out the stiffness in her hips and legs, and wiped the sweat away from her face with the edge of the bed fabric.

Her head was muzzy from the effects of sedation and there was a nagging headache over her eyes, but she had to ignore it. For a moment she tuned her ears to the world around her. She heard no sounds apart from birds - no voices, nor footsteps. As quietly as she could, Mary made her way along the short dim passageway. She took hold of the wooden gate at the entrance and lifted it aside. It was blinding daylight outside and its brightness stabbed at her already throbbing head. Doing her best, she waited for her vision to adjust. By the position of the sun and the white-hot glare of it she guessed it was around midday. She called out 'hello' a few times, expecting her captors to come running, but nobody did. It seemed odd that she was alone, but perhaps 'they' had not reckoned with the sedative wearing off as soon as it had. She took a tentative look inside a few of the other huts, but there was no sign of human life in any of them. The boma appeared to be abandoned. Beyond it lay bush-land for as far as the eye could see, stretching away towards the distant hills – a nameless, shapeless land. The Masai could sing it, the guides could drive it, but could she find her own way in it?

Mary considered her choices, fighting back a rush of fear and panic. It was important to stay calm. She could take her chances in the bush and run as far from the boma as she could, but to where? With no destination to aim for what was the point? The village was ringed with a thorny barrier to keep out predators; if she left its confines she would be putting herself at risk. But, if she stayed, her captors might kill her anyway. She felt weak at the thought of it. There was no escape, unless she dared to take a chance in the bush and risk the dangers lurking there.

Whatever she decided, she needed to get rid of the ropes binding her hands together. On a plank of old wood she found a rusty, but sharp, piece of nail securely attached and she started scraping the rope fibres against it. The job was hard work and made her arms ache and she had to keep stopping but, at last, the rope began to give and, with one final effort, she broke through the strands. Her wrists were chafed and she licked at them to try and ease the stinging.

She found some old crates and piled them on top of each other, then climbed up to take a better look at her immediate environment, beyond the thorny barrier. Just outside she could see a dusty track with tyre grooves ground into it. Could it lead to a road that other travellers or safari lodges and camps used? She was trapped and helpless unless she made a bid for freedom. Mary shivered, not from the cold, but from her own sense of desperation, then she made her decision. She would leave.

Back in the hut she found a packet of food containing bread, cheese and a small bar of chocolate. Together with the water it could keep her going for a day or so.

With a strip of material she tore from the bed cover, ripping it with her teeth to get the tear going, Mary tied three bottles of the water together and secured them around her waist. They were heavy, but she would need them. She ripped off another piece and wound it around her head as protection from the sun, then she ate the chocolate, which would soon melt and be useless, and stuffed the bread and cheese into the front pocket of her tracksuit top. Outside she found herself a stout piece of wood to use as a prop, and a weapon, then she climbed up onto the crates again to scan her location. The horizon was shimmering under the heat of the sun. Apart from grassland there were some thickets where animals may be hiding in the heat of the day, and which she would avoid. She walked around the perimeter of the camp and found a gate in the thorns, dragged it open, took a deep breath and stepped outside. This time of day was not the best time to be walking in the bush, but at least it was a time when predators were often full and resting, away from the heat. Mary began to follow the rugged track, hoping it would lead her to a road where she might encounter a safari vehicle, or another settlement. What have I got to lose she reasoned with herself - death in the bush, death by kidnappers? What about death from her secret? Whatever decision she took the chances of survival seemed about the same odds.

All around the horizon shimmered from the heat of the earth. Shapes were distorted – a tree stood like a giraffe, a bush like a rock, a rock like a lion. Come along now, you must be brave and positive, she told herself. Think of the children from the orphanage and their bravery; think of the children who were not so lucky and who walked for days in the bush, just to get water to make a pot of thin maize gruel.

She walked for hours, following the remnants of the dusty track, trying to pick out landmarks on the horizon, looking for signs of a moving vehicle in the distance. But there was nothing, just grazing gazelle and zebra and the occasional giraffe, and the trilling of birds in the bush. The sight of zebra made her feel nervous, as they were often in the company of dangerous buffalo. She had the stout piece of wood in her hand but it was not much of a weapon.

Mary rationed herself to a few sips of water, whenever

her mouth was too dry to swallow, but it was not long before she had emptied one of the bottles. She watched the sun move across the sky as the day passed, and knew how soon it would drop away below the horizon, leaving her to the dense blackness of night. In tears from fatigue and desperation she stumbled on, praying for the light of a camp, or the dust of a truck, or the sounds of a Masai village where she might find help and protection. But she saw nothing and, in the end, it was just Mary and the fast descending night, black and unforgiving. Then came the nightime sounds - first the chirping of crickets, the deep throaty rumble of a lion's roar and the hyena's laughing whoop. Wonderful sounds in the safety of a camp but now, quite terrifying. As she sat with her back against the trunk of an acacia tree and watched the huge bright globe that had beat without mercy down on her all day sink below the horizon, she thought of Silas' last words to her: *Kenya often has the appearance of Heaven, but sometimes there is a little bit of Hell thrown in too.* To comfort herself she imagined taking a walk on the beach in Malindi, where the fishermen set their nets and pushed their boats out through the surf with long poles as the sun went down, and the rolling sea turned pink in its light. She thought of the white muslin curtains in her bedroom, billowing in the sea breeze, and the sound of the ocean coming and going on the shore. She thought of George, cooking fresh caught fish on a fire in the sand and eating it as the stars came up. Dear George how worried he must be. She longed to feel his comforting arms around her and his shoulder to lean on. She peered into the dark night, her eyes still hoping to catch the flicker of a fire, or the glow of camp lights in the distance. She strained her ears for the sound of a voice, or perhaps the drone of a bush plane, but she saw and heard nothing like that. Where was everyone? All hope of finding someone, or being found, deserted her. Exhaustion took over and not even the rustlings and animal noises could stop Mary from closing her eyes. What could she do about it anyway? 'God help me,' she whispered and swallowed the remaining water. As the African night wrapped its arms around her, and crickets raised their cacophony; as the last drop of deep red in the sky vanished into the blackness, Mary thought of George.

The last thing she heard was a leopard's cough.

16

CHUI CAMP

June

Ralph was gone for two nights in Nairobi, without explanation. When he returned he took a truck and drove straight out to search for Mary Stephenson again. Despite the abruptness of his behaviour, Tessa was pleased with his dedication to trying to find the woman. There had still been no contact from potential kidnappers, and Alexia had told her that the police were beginning to doubt the abduction theory.

She heard his truck coming back just before sundown and went out to meet him.

'How did it go?'

'I didn't find her,' he said and hurled the truck keys at her. 'I'm going for a shower.'

She took his abruptness for disappointment.

He appeared for dinner and drank more red wine than was necessary and disappeared as soon as it was over.

Later, when the guests were back in their tents she went to look for him – to try and reassure him that it wasn't his fault. He was making such an effort to help, and taking each failure so personally. She saw the light from his cell phone on the perimeter of the camp, where there was a vague signal, and was about to call out to him when something he said, stopped her in her tracks.

'The package wasn't there, I tell you. Where the fuck is it?'

Tessa's heart missed a beat. What did he mean, 'the package, wasn't there?' What was he talking about? He sounded so angry.

'You'd better find out where it is and get back to me and, by God, she had better not have come to any harm!' he snarled. Shocked, Tessa shrank into the shadows as Ralph turned and strode past her.

She lay awake long into the night listening to the crickets outside and his words, turning over and over in her head. What package had he been talking about and had she really heard him use the word 'she'? What could it mean? There was an inkling of what it might be in the back of her mind, something dark and terrifying that she wished she didn't have to think about. Unable to bear the suspense any longer Tessa checked that Ralph was well asleep, he should be after the amount of red wine he had consumed, then crept round to his side of the bed and took his mobile phone. She went into the tented office area and began to go through his contacts. There were a couple of Swahili names that made her suspicious, and then she gasped at the next name that popped up on the screen. It was a name she had never expected to see in connection with Ralph, and then another. What could it mean? She went into his messages folder but, any messages that might have been between them had already been deleted from those threads. She quickly scribbled down the contact numbers for the people she found, then crept back into the bedroom and replaced the phone.

The next day, after he disappeared back to Nairobi yet again, without explanation, she called the only person she could trust.

'You sound stressed my lovely, what's up?' Sophie asked with concern.

'Oh God, Sophie, I don't know where to begin. It's all such a mess.'

'What are you talking about?'

'I have a horrible feeling that Ralph is somehow involved in the attack on Nyara camp.'

'What on earth makes you think that?' Sophie exclaimed. 'Why would he be?'

'I don't know but his behaviour – it's been so odd since the woman first disappeared.'

'In what way?'

'He insisted on coming to Nyara Camp to help in the search for her.'

'What's odd about that?' Sophie said, 'he's just the right sort of person to have around in those circumstances.'

'Sophie, I appreciate that I may be losing you here and not explaining things very well but I have a real gut instinct about it. The night before last I heard him talking on his mobile to someone. He said something about a package that had disappeared. It was after his second return to Nyara to search for the woman. Something just made me think the two are connected.'

'But he didn't actually say it?'

'I heard him refer to the package as 'she', at least I think I did, but…' she broke off, unsure of herself now and what she really had heard.

'Are you sure? He could have been talking about anything,' Sophie tried to reason.

'I know but somehow I just don't think so,' Tessa paused, unable to explain it any further.

'Oh come on Tess, it all sounds a bit far fetched?'

'Does it? He offered to search for her and seemed so confident that she would be found. Why? Why would he want to help the Sackville's when he hates their camp?'

'Okay, fair point, but you need more evidence than that.'

'Sophie think about it. Ralph has been bad-mouthing the camp for weeks, months even and then, out of the blue, this happens. Doesn't it seem a bit of a coincidence?'

'I suppose it has all fallen into place rather well but still…'

Now she had her friend a little bit hooked, Tessa pulled her in a bit further. 'He told me, a while ago, to stop worrying about everything because he had it all sorted. What did he mean by that?'

'Again it could have been anything,' Sophie reasoned, but Tessa could not accept it was anything other than what she suspected.

'I think he had it in mind to try and discredit Nyara camp,' she ploughed on, 'they are our nearest opposition and Ralph has had a thing about them from the start. He hates the idea of a camp with modern luxuries, but won't see that it's the clients who are putting pressure on the camps to provide it. I just have this dreadful feeling that he's gone a step too far.'

'But it doesn't make sense that he would arrange for a woman to be kidnapped?'

'Why not? It's the ultimate way of getting a camp closed down for a while,' Tessa urged, 'and, if he did plan it, I don't think he was ever going to ask for a ransom because he was going to find her. It was never about the actual kidnap, it was about the reason for doing it, to ruin Nyara. It explains why he was so keen to go looking for her.'

'You have no proof...' Sophie reminded her.

'I'm not sure if you can call it proof but I had a look through Ralph's mobile phone and there was a name that bothered me. It was Mary Stephenson's husband George.'

'Now that is odd,' Sophie conceded, 'and I wonder how Ralph and George know each other?'

'Exactly. Ralph has never mentioned any connection with the man before or since the attack? Do you think the husband was in on it too?' She thought back to Ralph's same question about that, on their visit to Nyara, the day after the attack. She had scoffed at the thought then, but now she wondered.

'I suppose it's a possibility.'

'It seems he had also been in touch with Yahzid, Esme's brother, just a few days ago, but I have no idea why.'

'You mentioned to me that Ralph had talked about trying to help the boy and find him a job,' Sophie reminded her.

'Yes but what if that job...'

'...involved the kidnap of a woman?' Sophie finished.

'Yes.'

'It's a sobering thought.'

'It's a terrifying thought,' Tessa said, feeling faint from

the fact that it might be true.

'Is Ralph there at the moment?'

'No, he's back in Nairobi again. He's been up there so often I don't know why he bothers to come back.'

'I hate to think of you at Chui on your own. Would you like me to come and be with you?' Sophie offered.

'Thanks for offering but I'll be fine.' Tessa paused before asking, 'do you think Ralph's capable of doing something like this?'

'Ralph is an unpredictable and volatile character, that's for sure,' was Sophie's candid reply.

'Yes, he is,' Tessa sighed. 'I was...I was wondering..."' she hesitated.

'What?' Sophie prompted.

'I wondered about having Ralph followed. I know its spying, but I'd like to know what he's up to and who he's meeting in Nairobi, but I've no idea how to go about it. I need a bit more solid evidence or proof before I can go to the police.'

'Consider it done,' said Sophie. 'I'll ask Idi if he can drum up a private investigator – his brother works in security so I'm sure he can find someone. Gosh, Tessa, I hope you're wrong.'

'So do I but somehow, with the evidence I have and his recent odd behaviour, I'm not too optimistic.'

'I'll do my best to find out,' Sophie promised. 'Try not to worry darling and remember: *innocent until proven guilty.*'

'I hope so, Sophie. God I hope so. I don't know what I'll do if I'm right, apart from go to the police of course. I'm desperate to come back to Nairobi, but with Ralph away there's no chance of that.'

'Why don't I come up to you for a few days, just to give you some support,' Sophie offered again, 'it won't be any trouble.'

'It's very sweet of you, but I'll see what happens over the next few days and, if it is as I suspect, I may have to shut up camp and come back anyway. If there is solid evidence I'll have no choice but to go the police.'

'I'm so sorry Tessa. It's a nightmare situation for you,' Sophie sympathised. 'I'm on the end of the phone for you at any time. We'll sort out what needs to be done.'

'I don't know what I'd do without your help,' Tessa said.

'What else are friends for, sweetheart?'

To take her mind off the recent events and the possibilities of what Sophie might find out for her, Tessa took herself off on a drive to see how the landscape was coping with the drought. She would also scout around herself for signs of the missing woman. The thought of her being at large in the bush was worrying and if indeed she was being held somewhere, then where? Another alternative was that she'd been taken across the border into Tanzania. It was odd that no ransom had been called for. Why not? Why take someone if you did not intend to demand something for their safe return? She had tried to talk to Ralph about it but he had dismissed it as a pointless conversation. He still seemed convinced that she would be found. At least, she thought, he was being positive about it. Perhaps her negative feelings about him were wrong. How she hoped they were.

The sun was high and white hot in the clear blue sky and there was still no signs of the heavy storm clouds the sky should be gathering together. Large cracks were appearing all over the parched earth. The rains had fallen sparsely during the long rain season and, with the lack of water in the waterholes and the river dropping lower and lower, the animals were beginning a fight for survival. Dust flew up behind her, engulfing everything as she drove across the landscape, heading for the river. A herd of elephants filed along on a slow walk heading, she guessed, for the same place. Little ones trotted along close to their mother's legs. She wondered how long they would survive if the rains didn't come. As she reached the bank of the river she slowed, hoping to catch a glimpse of the leopard whose territory it was, up in a tree feeding or stalking along the bank waiting for a gazelle to drop its guard.

There were wildebeest zebra and antelope along the banks opposite feeding on the sparse grass and popping down for a drink every now and then. The river was low and Tessa took some detailed photographs to send up to Nairobi, to the authorities that were monitoring the problem.

She put her camera and binoculars down on the seat beside her and opened a thermos to pour a cup of coffee. Jackson had packed her a bacon roll and she munched on it, savoring the taste, listening to the hippos grunting in the muddy waters and the call of the birds in the bush. Her feelings of anxiety began to ease. That's what she loved about the bush - the way it wrapped her up in a feeling of great serendipity that nowhere else on earth could manage to do in quite the same way. As the sun began to arc into its downwards trajectory to the west, the plains were imbued with a golden shimmering haze hovering above the heated ground. A group of impalas feeding on the dry grass on the other side of the river lifted their heads to stare at her, but did not perceive her as a threat. She sat still staring back at them and absorbing a moment of utter peace. Then, quite suddenly and with brutal finality, the peace was broken. A smell, a sound, something, had put the impalas on full alert. Out of the corner of her eye Tessa caught a glimpse of an animal moving low in the grass towards them. It was the leopard. The impalas twitched, heads raised, nostrils flaring and then two of the group broke into a run followed by the rest and then the last one, slower off the mark, brought up the rear. They flew like the wind and the leopard followed, bounding and powerful swatting the last impala, slowing it enough for the leopard to hold it tight and pin it down. Tessa heard its pitiful cries as the leopard strangled it with its powerful jaws. Then the warning cacophony from the birds and a stampede of wildlife resided - the bush resumed normal sound and, further along the bank, the remaining impala group began to feed again.

The leopard lay on the grass, getting its breath back and Tessa waited, hoping to see the leopard drag its kill along the bank to a tall acacia tree. She had her camera at the ready and after several minutes or so it began to move with the kill anxious, she guessed, to get it up into the tree out of reach of scavengers – hyena, jackal and lion. She took her photos as it began its climb, the kill clamped in its powerful jaws and hauling it up with strong shoulder and legs, until it reached a fork in the trunk high enough off the ground. There it wedged the dead impala and lay along the branch, panting with the effort. It was an incredible feat of strength and the impala was a relatively lightweight prey compared to the zebra she had seen the leopard drag up the tree in the past. She knew they were capable of dragging prey three times its own weight, into the canopy. Of all the big cats in the Mara, it was the leopard she had the greatest respect for and the one she feared the most, even more so than lion. Because of their solitary nature leopards did not announce themselves as lion did. The most you might hear of them was a male leopard's repetitive rasping sound, not unlike the sound of a saw on wood, which advertised his presence to a mate. They were unpredictable, furtive and, because of this, what she had just seen was a rare moment.

As she drove back to camp, Tessa could not help but compare Ralph to the leopard, for his own furtiveness and solitary nature. She was scared, for what he could be capable of and, for the way in which he seemed determined to bring down his own prey – those he perceived as his rivals.

17

NAROK

June

He woke in the gloom of his hotel room to the sound of somebody banging on the door. He groaned and would have ignored it but a voice called out, *'sir you must come right away, the police are here to see you.'* It was the voice of the hotel manager.

With a sigh George swung himself out of bed and rubbed at the stubble on his face. He dressed in clothes that were now three days worn, splashed some water onto his face and went down to the lobby.

'Mr George Stephenson,' said a man rising out of his chair as George appeared.

'Yes?'

'I am Detective Mwbani. We have come to speak to you?'

'Is it about my wife?'

'Yes sir.'

His heart jumped.

'Please sit down Mr. Stephenson, we have some news for you that is not altogether good news.'

It was a novel way of presenting bad news. George sat down in the chair, expecting the worst.

'I will come straight to the point, sir. A body, a female body, has been found in the Masai Mara and has been taken to the Mortuary, here in Narok.'

George gasped and closed his eyes.

'Are you okay to continue, sir?'

He nodded his consent.

The policeman continued. 'The body is that of a white female and it is possible that the remains are those of your wife.'

'Remains?' George looked up. 'What do you mean by that?'

The policeman took a moment to answer. 'I am afraid to tell you that the body in the mortuary has been badly mutilated by wild animals.'

It was more than George could bear. He clenched his knuckles and forced them into his eyes to try and shut out the hideous images that were forming in his imagination. A strangled sob escaped from him.

'I am very sorry to bring this bad news sir, but we must ask you to come with us to make an identification.'

George shook his head. How could he?

'You are the only person for this job, sir. We are sorry to have to ask you.'

He did his best to try and recover some composure. It was not yet a certainty that it was Mary, and he must hold on to that sliver of hope. He looked up at them. 'Yes, I'll come,' he whispered.

He had never in a million years envisaged himself in a

mortuary let alone identifying a dead body that might belong to someone so dear to him. Who did? The place was cold, damp and uncared for and, even though he knew it was irrational, he hated the thought of poor Mary, if it was her, being left in such a dreadful environment.

He stepped into the room where the remains of the body he was about to identify, lay on a slab beneath a grubby looking, white sheet. A mortician stood to one side and he the other. One of the detectives had kindly accompanied him. He guessed it was because they were already aware of the horror of what he was about to witness.

'Are you ready sir?' said the mortician in a low voice.

Ready? No I'll never be ready but I know I have to do this. He closed his eyes and swallowed. Dear God, what was it that lay beneath that sheet.

'Sir, are you ready?' the mortician repeated.

'No,' he said, coming to a conclusion and shaking his head. 'I'm sorry but I cannot do this. If it is my wife's remains, God only knows what they must look like and I do not think I can stand it. Is there some other way? Do you have any identifiable items that were left on the body?'

The detective nodded to the mortician who put down the edge of the sheet he had been about to remove.

'Yes we have one or two items – clothing material, a ring and part of a bracelet. We also have a lock of hair and some photographs. Will you be able to look at those?'

George turned to him, 'if the remains are that of my wife, then the ring is platinum, with one diamond inset into the band. It is inscribed: G to M 1982. The bracelet is a gold bangle. I don't know about the material until I see it. Yes, I will look at the photographs.' At least there would be some distance from the actuality of Mary's condition if he saw it only through photographs.

'Come with me sir,' the detective said and guided him out of the room.

They went to the mortician's office and a plastic bag, containing the items taken from the body, was removed from a safe and placed on the table.

'They are exactly as you described them,' said the detective, taking them out of the bag with gloved hands.

George swallowed, 'yes, those belong to my wife.'

'What about the fabric, sir?' he said, holding up some grey material.

'My wife had a grey track suit, but I don't know what she was wearing that night because she was already in bed asleep when I returned to the tent.'

'Perhaps we can safely say that it is material from your wife's garments. She was still partly clothed and the identification notes described it as a track suit, as you have said.'

'What about the photographs?' he asked with some trepidation.

The detective removed a large brown envelope from a tray and reached inside. He pulled out a handful of black and white photographs and displayed them on his desk.

George steeled himself to look. In one photo he could make out tooth marks, on what remained of the body, and some hair, stiff with dirt and blood. The worst of it was the missing bits – an arm, part of a leg, other things yet, despite the mutilations, there was something there that resembled his wife, and the images made him cry out in horror. Thank God he hadn't been forced to view the real thing.

'Oh goodness, I am sorry sir, for your distress, but I am obliged to ask you: can you identify the remains in these photographs as those belonging to the body of your wife?' The detective was visibly distressed by George's horror and anguish.

George choked back another sob. 'Yes, yes, I am certain that is, or was, my wife.'

So that was it. The remains were of Mary. There were no more slivers of hope to hang on to. Mary, his beloved Mary was dead, killed in the most horrific of circumstances. George leaned down and grabbed the waste bin beside the desk, into which he vomited.

The police took him back to his hotel where he gathered his stuff, paid his bill and then they dropped him off at the bus station. Some hours later, after a long hot and dusty bus journey, during which time he stared out of the window forcing himself not to think of the photographs but turning the words over and over in his mind, *Mary is dead, Mary is dead,* George arrived back in Nairobi.

He turned the key in the front door and entered a house very different to the one he had left. Then it had been a home for two and now… he went into the bedroom and sat down, exhausted, on Mary's side of the bed. The pillow still had an indent from where her head had last lain there. A book she had been reading, spread open at the last page, lay on the bedside chest with a packet of half-used painkillers lying underneath it. A photo frame held a photograph of the orphanage children. It was only now that he wondered why Mary had decided to leave the orphanage. It hadn't occurred to him to ask her before – he had been too wrapped up in his own problems. He lay down, too tired even to weep, and fell fast asleep.

When he awoke, sometime later, it took a few moments to register where he was, then he remembered and he let out a protracted moan. He sat up but he didn't have the strength to go and make himself tea or coffee, even though his mouth was dry and he felt parched. He wanted answers still. Why had this happened? Why had she been taken from the camp? Who had taken her? Was it the government? Someone he owed money to? Revenge? Who? Who? Who? He choked back a sob and then he opened the drawer to her bedside chest and started looking through it, as if he might find the answers there, handling the familiar contents: a spare pair of reading glasses, cotton wool balls and her cleansing lotion, some broken African beads and a bracelet, an old watch that had stopped, a pen and a notebook. He looked inside but there was nothing of interest written down apart from lists of shopping requirements, and a reminder to call a Mr Payne. The name didn't ring a bell with him but he surmised it was something to do with the orphanage. She often received calls from would-be donors and it was quite likely Mr. Payne was one of them. He pushed his hand to the back of the drawer and felt a smooth flat cardboard folder that he pulled out and opened up. It was a travel document holder and inside was a ticket to London. He stared at it, confused. Why did Mary have such a ticket? She hadn't said anything to him about going back to London. Then he saw the date of departure. Mary had been due to fly a few days after their return from Nyara. George pondered this new mystery. Why was she going back to England without telling him? Was she leaving him? Then he noticed that beneath the ticket there was an envelope. He hesitated. The envelope was addressed to Mary with Private and Confidential written on it, but she was no longer here to read it and this was an emergency. It could hold a clue about her disappearance. He opened it up and pulled out a letter. It was from a hospital in London – an oncology department. He read it through. Oh dear God. Mary had breast cancer and she was going home for treatment. The letter sign off was from Mr. John Milton Payne, Consultant Oncologist.

'Why didn't you tell me,' he wailed, 'we could have dealt with it together?' But George knew very well why she hadn't confided in him. Mary whom he loved so dearly had kept it all to herself, rather than bother her husband who was too preoccupied with his own problems. It was all a disaster – an utter bloody disaster. He lay back on the bed and sobbed.

18

CHUI CAMP

June

It was a nail-biting wait for Tessa to hear back from Sophie. What would she find out and did she really want to know?

'Have I got news for you,' Sophie announced, when at last she called. 'Are you sitting down?'

Tessa's heart sank. 'Yes, as it happens I am, catching up on paperwork.'

'I'm sorry to be the bearer of bad news but it seems you were right to be suspicious of Ralph.'

'Oh,' said Tessa, her heart beating a bit faster. 'Go on.'

'Well, Idi asked a favour of his friend in security at the Golf Club and he arranged for Ralph to be followed. I didn't say why, just indicated it was a domestic dispute. Ralph was tracked to Kibera…'

'Kibera,' Tessa interrupted, 'what on earth was he doing there?'

'I'm trying to tell you darling,' said Sophie, 'if you'll let me.'

'Sorry.'

'Ralph went to Kibera to meet a man,' her friend continued, 'an African. He went to the area known as Mashimoni.'

'I'm guessing it was Yahzid,' said Tessa, 'Mashimoni is where Esme and Yahzid live.'

'It does seem as though it was.'

'Perhaps he went to see him about Esme,' Tessa said, clutching at straws even though she didn't believe it.

'I don't think it was a family matter,' Sophie said gently.

'Then what?'

'The Private Investigator found a young man whom Ralph had apparently spoken to some weeks ago when he went there first asking about Yahzid. He said he heard that some men are angry because Ralph owes them money. The boy said the men Ralph owed the money to, are baying for his blood.'

'Why does he owe them money?'

'The boy didn't know, but he thought it might have been a job he heard some men discussing – a job for a white man.'

'Dear God,' Tessa breathed, 'did he find out anything else?'

'No. Look I know its not exactly incriminating evidence but if you put two and two together…'

Tessa's hands were shaking so much she had difficulty holding the phone to her ear. 'Oh my God.'

'Tessa I think you should come back to Nairobi right away. Have you guests?'

'Going tomorrow morning. Then we're empty. I'll come back on their flight if there's room.'

'I'll sort that, don't worry,' Sophie said. 'Just go to the strip with them and there will be a seat for you.'

'I can't believe this is happening,' Tessa said. 'What a stupid, stupid man my husband is.'

Sophie gave a harsh laugh. 'I can't argue with that sentiment.'

'He's somebody I just don't know anymore. I know it's not set in stone that he is part of it, the attack, but there are too many coincidences.'

'I don't have the answer to that,' said Sophie, 'but my concern is for you right now, not the inner workings of Ralph's mind. Just get yourself back to the city and I'll meet you at Wilson.'

Before she left Tessa got a call from Alexia with some shocking revelations.

'Tessa?' Her voice was flat. 'Have you heard the news?'

'What news?'

'The police called to say a body has been found in the Mara - a white female, or the remains of one, after it had been mutilated by animals.'

'Oh my God,' Tessa whispered. Could the news get any worse? 'Is it Mary Stephenson?'

'Yes, the poor husband had to identify it. He had waited in Narok, hoping she would be found alive of course. I feel so awful for him,' Alexia's voice broke.

'I'm sorry Alexia,' Tessa said, and her voice was firm and positive, 'it's going to be tough for you, for all of us, but you can get yourself through this. I'm going back to Nairobi, but if you need to talk just call me at any time.' She didn't feel she could possibly tell Alexia about her suspicions, not at this early stage.

'There's something else.'

'Yes?'

'I'm sorry to have to tell you about it but I do think you should know.'

Tessa felt a knot at the pit of her stomach. 'Okay, but it sounds ominous.'

'It is. James received permission to travel to Nairobi from the Narok police. The Consortium insisted he travel to Nairobi so that he could contribute to a tactical plan to deal with the impact that the attack would have on Nyara. Later on when he was driving back along the Langata Road, he spotted your husband. He was surprised to see him in Nairobi; it was only the day after he had been to Nyara to help search again. He wanted to speak to him but Ralph had got into a taxi and, on impulse, James decided to follow him.'

Tessa felt a sinking in the pit of her stomach. 'Okay.'

'The taxi turned off left at a T-Junction about half a mile on. A few miles further on the taxi stopped at the Langata cemetery and Ralph got out. He went through the gates and disappeared. James carried on past and parked a bit further along. He got out and walked to the gates where he glimpsed Somerton ahead. He saw him, amongst the tombstones, and he thought maybe Ralph was at the cemetery for a burial and he was worried that he was intruding on a personal mission, but something told him he wasn't. James decided to keep following. Suddenly he heard voices and he ducked down behind a large bush. The voices were raised in argument and he could just make out what they were saying.'

'What were they saying?'

'James heard Ralph say: *You will get the money when the package is found,*'

That phrase again.

'James heard an African voice answer: *the men want their money now.* Apparently your husband said: *why the hell should I pay for a job that has not been properly done?*'

'What job was he talking about?' Tessa said but she knew, didn't she?

'James heard the African say: *then you must be prepared for the consequences. These men are not good men and they do not agree with you.*'

'Your husband replied: *they have lost the package and not fulfilled the job.*'

Then the African warned your husband. He said: *'I am telling you, they are not good men and they will make trouble for you unless you pay them.'*

'I'm sorry but could you stop for a minute, I'm trying to take it all in but it's going too fast.' Tessa was finding it hard to breathe.

'I'm sorry Tessa, but I thought you should know.'

'Yes, I appreciate it, but as you can imagine it's quite shocking to hear.'

'Do you want me to carry on?'

'Yes.'

'Then James heard him say something that made his blood drain. The African said: *and where were your scruples when you asked for the woman to be taken?*'

'Oh God,' Tessa gulped.

'Your husband replied: *it was just a ruse to get the bloody camp discredited. A prank that went wrong. For the woman it should have been a harmless little adventure. Unfortunately it didn't turn out like that and you and the other two men are responsible for what happened to her, not me.*'

127

'No!' Tessa cried, 'he couldn't have said that.' She could hardly take in what she was hearing. Dear God what had he been thinking?

'I'm sorry Tessa, but I don't think James was making this up, and he managed to record some of the conversation. He missed the crucial part when they used the words: *'the woman'* though. He heard them carry on talking about a money exchange and Ralph insisted that he would only pay half of what was owed. He said they could have the rest when the goods were delivered safe and sound.'

'But they weren't,' Tessa burst out, 'she's dead!'

'Yes,' Alexia said, 'and I told James to go straight to the police.'

'Then I must do the same.'

'Why you?'

Then Tessa revealed to Alexia her own suspicions about her husband.

She called Ralph to tell him that Mary Stephenson was dead. She wanted to hear his reaction. Unless he'd already heard of course.

'Christ almighty,' he said, 'are you sure about this?'

'Yes I am. Alexia called to say that the husband, George Stephenson, had positively identified it.'

'I don't believe it,' Ralph muttered, 'it just shouldn't have happened.'

'What do you mean, it shouldn't have happened?' Her heart was beating so loud she was sure he would hear. She wanted to ask him about how he knew George Stephenson, about the conversation in the cemetery but she held back, wanting to push him a bit further.

'Well it shouldn't,' he said,' nobody deserves to die like that.'

'Of course they don't but Ralph, please tell me what's going on? Did you know the husband?'

'I don't know what your talking about, and how do I know what's going on?' he snapped.

'Your actions, your reactions, It's as if...' but she tailed off, unable to put into words the accusatory thoughts she was having about him.

'I don't know what you're talking about and I've got far too much on my mind to argue with you over this trivia.'

'Trivia!' Tessa exclaimed. 'I don't call a dead woman trivia.'

'It's not my fault the stupid woman is dead,' he shouted.

'Isn't it Ralph?' She wanted to ask him about the men he owed money to but she couldn't get the words together. She didn't want to hear the lies he might tell.

'How dare you!' he said through gritted teeth. 'What the hell do you think you're doing, hurling accusations like that around?'

'I just want you to tell me what is going on? You have to admit your behaviour is odd – rushing to and from Nairobi, making secret phone calls...'

'Secret phone calls?'

She bit her lip knowing she might have said too much. 'I've seen you going off after dinner at Chui, to call someone or another. Who were you calling? Was it George Stephenson?' She was pushing and pushing.

'Of course it bloody well wasn't George Stephenson! You know the phone signal is only good enough at the edge of the camp - and for your information I was probably calling

Anders about a flight.'

'But why do you need to be in Nairobi' she persisted. 'What are you doing up there?'

'Trying to save our fucking camp!' he yelled at her.

Something snapped inside. He always tried to turn the tables on her. 'I know you're involved,' she hurled back, 'I found some things out. A conversation overheard in Langata cemetery. What do you say to that? You owe money to men because of a plan you hatched to attack a safari camp. It was Nyara wasn't it? And I heard you talking to someone on your phone about a missing package, it was the woman, I know it was?'

In reply the line went dead. She sat down, shaking and nauseous. Deep inside she knew he was guilty – of planning the attack, of Mary Stephenson's death. Well, if she couldn't get the truth from him, she was sure the police could.

She had no choice but to put it into their hands now.

19

NAIROBI

June

'For fuck's sake, what the hell happened?' Ralph yelled down the phone at Yahzid. 'You promised I would find the woman safe and sound at the abandoned village but she wasn't there and now she's dead! What the hell were you thinking? You've ruined everything!' He could still hardly believe what had happened, since Tessa had told him. He needed to cover his tracks, stop anyone from talking. What stupid, stupid idiots those men were to leave her unattended.

'It was not my fault, not anyone's fault that this woman managed to get free.' Yahzid shouted back. 'I had nothing to do with it. All I did was find the men to do your stupid job.'

'Christ almighty! What a mess,' Ralph snarled. 'Why was she alone? Someone was supposed to be taking care of her. I told you she was not to be harmed in any way and that someone should be with her all the time and now I hear she not only escaped, but died in the process.'

'They told me she was tied up.'

'Clearly she wasn't as tied up as you thought,' he snapped

back.

'I do not want to be involved any more in this but the men want their money,' said Yahzid, 'like I told you at the cemetery.'

'They didn't fulfill the bloody deal! There is no money for people who fail.'

'You must understand. These men are desperate. They want their money.'

Ralph let out a breath. 'I told you before, I will give them half the money for half the job done, to keep their silence, but you'd better warn them this could turn out to be a murder case.'

'They won't accept it,' Yahzid persisted, 'and it is a murder case of your making.'

'I will pay them half,' Ralph repeated, 'that is my final offer.'

He sat after the telephone call, heart and mind racing. He couldn't believe the woman was dead. God knows why it had gone so wrong? He had never meant her to come to any harm. He was supposed to find her. What was he going to do? Ralph gave a thought to George Stephenson. It was too bad for him, but there was nothing he could do about it now. He punched another number into his phone. For the umpteenth time it went to answer-phone. It happened each time he attempted to get in contact with Tessa. He'd left countless messages but she had not responded to any of them. He had to know what she was planning to do.

As a safety precaution he went to ground in his lock up, near Wilson airport, where he kept various things he needed as he went to and from Chui – private supplies, parts for machinery and other bits and pieces. There was a camp bed there too - he sometimes used it when he had an early flight - a camp stove and a kettle. It was unlikely that Yahzid or his cronies would find him in a hurry and it might buy him time to think.

Then he drove to Kibera and waited for Esme to come out of school.

She was surprised to see him of course but he made a show of being delighted to see her and to gain her confidence.

'Hello Esme, how are you? Mrs Somerton asked me to pick you up.'

'Okay,' she unhitched the heavy school bag from her shoulder.

Ralph reached out a hand, 'here, let me take that for you.' When they got to the car he put it onto the back seat. 'Are you okay about coming with me?'

She nodded and he opened the door for her. They got into the car. 'Look,' he said, 'I'm sorry to be the bearer of bad news, but your brother has been involved in an accident and Mrs Somerton wants me to take you to see him at the hospital. She is waiting for us.'

Her eyes widened in alarm and she put a hand to her mouth.

'It's okay, his injuries are not life threatening, so don't be alarmed. Put on your seatbelt and let's go.'

As she turned to pull it across her, Ralph pricked her arm with a dart tipped with a mild animal sedative. It took seconds to work. By the time they were on the highway she was drowsy and her eyes were closed. He drove as fast as he dared to the airport lock up, where he got her inside and onto the camp bed. Then he spent some time working out his current predicament. Esme was collateral damage, a bargaining tool with Yahzid perhaps, but he was also taking her for her own protection. If the men were as desperate as Yahzid had made out, then she could get hurt. Better to have her in a place of safety and under his control.

Later he got on the phone to Yahzid again. 'Okay, I'll pay them, in return for their silence.' He'd decided not to mention about Esme just yet. He'd see how things panned out first and the less people who knew where she was, the better. If he had to leave Nairobi in a hurry, then he would tell Tessa where the girl could be found.

'You are making a wise decision my friend.'

'I'm not your bloody friend,' Ralph growled.

'Bring the money to the Ayani bus station tomorrow in a plastic bag and wait by the ticket office. Be there by eleven o'clock. Someone will collect it from you,' Yahzid instructed.

'Who will collect it?'

'You don't need to know that information now. They know who you are.'

Ralph had no choice but to agree. 'I'll be there, but don't try anything stupid,' he warned. 'I've got someone watching where you live.' It was a lie but he wanted to scare Yahzid. In reply the line went dead again, leaving him steaming with frustration.

20

NAIROBI

June

Sophie got Tessa onto the flight and was waiting at Wilson. They drove straight from the airport to the house in Karen, where Tessa packed some things up to take with her to Sophie's. It was where she was going to base herself from now on. Ralph, to her relief, wasn't at the house but she hadn't expected him to be, not after their last telephone call. He'd probably gone into hiding already. She could not bring herself to speak to him, and his string of messages on her phone had been left unanswered. Her head spun day and night with questions, answers, nightmare scenarios and general hellish thoughts. Why in God's name had he done such a thing, was the question that played over and over in her mind. It kept her awake at night and distracted her from the things she was doing during the day.

She had a quick rummage through his desk but found nothing of interest and, as she expected, his laptop was gone. She removed personal items of sentimental value from the house and packed them in a separate suitcase - photograph albums, a couple of her favourite watercolour paintings of

African scenes, animals and birds, some precious old books. They joined a number of wooden and pottery ornaments she'd collected from around Africa and the world, and some jewellery; nothing of particular value except for its sentimentality. She guessed that if and when the police turned up, they would pretty much ransack the place for evidence.

'Do you mind if I clutter up your place for a while with this stuff. I don't want it damaged or to go missing?' Tessa said, dumping the suitcase and bag by the front door.

'Of course you can.' Sophie shook her head in wonder. 'Your husband has a lot to answer for.'

'You can say that again. I can't begin to imagine how my life is going to change.'

Nairobi Central Police Station on the edge of Moi Avenue was an intimidating destination. The reports by those who had been held there made frightening media news, but Tessa told herself that she was not going there as a prisoner, she was going as… oh God, it made her feel queasy just to think of it - she was going as an informer against her husband. Feeling all of a sudden as though she might throw up she clutched at Sophie. 'I don't know if I can do this,' she muttered, 'please stop the car.'

Sophie pulled over to the side of the road and handed Tessa a bottle of water.

Tessa drank deeply then she sighed. 'It's too difficult, even though I'm shocked by Ralph and what he's done, it's such a hard thing to do. I'm hurt too.'

'Hurt?' said Sophie.

'Yes. Apart from causing the death of someone and

ruining the lives of everyone who was a part of that, he's destroyed every thing he and I worked for. All that effort was for nothing. I knew he was going off the rails and being impetuous about things, but nothing could have prepared me for the fact that he was capable of doing something like this,' she turned to Sophie with an anguished look, 'but turning him in? I know I talked about my moral duty and all that, but at the end of the day he…'

'…caused the death of another person,' Sophie finished for her, 'if what we believe to be true, is true. He didn't murder her, but he carelessly put her life in danger without a thought of the consequences.'

'I was going to say: but at the end of the day he's still my husband.' Tessa looked at Sophie. 'Is there the remote possibility that we've got it all wrong?'

'Oh darling, I wish I could say yes, but we know what we know.' She reached out and took hold of Tessa's hand, 'we have almost rock solid proof of his actions and you are doing the right thing. I don't think there is any remote possibility at all.'

Tessa's eyes filled with tears. Sophie was right but still it was so difficult. Then her mobile phone began to vibrate and buzz.

They looked at each other, both thinking that it was Ralph, but when Tessa answered it, it turned out to be James Sackville.

'Hello Tessa, look I thought it only right to call you and let you know what I've done. It's a long story but I think I have proof…'

'It's okay,' Tessa interrupted him, 'I already talked to Alexia and she told me everything, about the conversation you overheard at Langata Cemetery.'

'I'm so sorry,' he said, 'this must be hell for you, but I thought you should know.'

'Thank you, the thing is I'm also on my way to the police station to give evidence about Ralph,' she said. 'It seems we both have some proof.'

'Oh, I really am so sorry Tessa.' She could hear the genuine concern in his voice. It was so kind of him. After all it was her husband, who had gone all out to ruin his camp!

'Don't apologise James, please, it's me who should be apologising to you and it's becoming clear to me that I don't know very much about my husband at all. At least not the man he is now. Our business was failing and I suppose he thought that if he could do something to get your camp discredited it would help. It's impossible to believe he could do something so stupid and so damaging, but now I have to face up to the fact that he has.'

They ended the conversation and Tessa looked at Sophie in despair. 'Why has Ralph done this?' It was a question that she knew nobody had the answer to.

Sophie shook her head. 'I don't know. I'm as bewildered by it as you are.'

Tessa felt utter horror at the thought that the man, her husband, could dream up, let alone commit, a crime that had now led to the worst of circumstances.

The air was heavy with humidity and foreboding when they reached the central police station. The entrance was just a short walk away. Tessa looked through the fence at the building with its distinctive red orange and blue stripes, its row of many windows and the Kenyan flag fluttering above the entrance. People were milling around outside. She swallowed and said in a small voice, 'I'd better get this over with.'

PART TWO

CHASE

21

NAIROBI

June

Nairobi lay under a black cloud. The late rains that had started earlier in the day now had the streets awash. Those who had prayed for the rain were wishing it away again. Drenched through from the deluge, after just a few steps from the car to the inside of the police station, Yahzid Adongo waited for his details to be written up by the duty police receptionist, shivering as water pooled on the floor at his feet. The police had tracked him down and arrested him in Kibera, where he had just entered the Chang'aa shack about to drink himself into oblivion, afraid for his life and afraid of being arrested for his part in the death of a woman. He had heard grim tales of treatment at this police station and he was expecting to be beaten. After all, he came from a notorious slum and many people believed nothing good came out of that place. Now, sober and terrified, he was waiting to be interviewed by police officers. How could he have been so stupid to allow himself to be talked into Somerton's plot? He knew it was because he had been high at the time, and then got drunk to get himself through it. One thing for sure now was that if he was going to go down for the crime, then that white man was going with him.

He was handcuffed and taken to a dimly lit, cold and bare interview room and pushed onto a chair.

Across a table two detectives were appraising him with narrowed eyes. One was overweight, breathing heavily and sweating in profusion. The other was tall and sharp as a spear. A Luo and a Kalenjin.

'Do you know why we have arrested you?'

'No,' he replied.

'There have been serious allegations made against you. What do you have to say – and speak up?'

Yahzid looked back at them, 'I don't know what the allegations are. How can I answer you? I want to see a lawyer.'

The man like a spear stood up and leaned across the table, up close to Yahzid, staring at him with his bloodshot eyes. If it was meant to intimidate him it was working. He was scared but he forced himself not to flinch.

'It has been alleged that you were involved in the murder of a white woman,' he snarled. 'You had better start talking.'

'I want a lawyer.'

'Tell us what we want to hear and we will make arrangements.'

Yahzid shook his head and stood his ground. 'No. I am entitled to a lawyer.'

They glared back at him but still he held his nerve. Then, one of the detectives got up and went out of the room. He returned a few minutes later.

'Okay, a public prosecution lawyer is on his way. We'll speak to you again after you have seen him.' Then they got up and left him alone, agitated and fretting in the airless, stuffy room, wishing he had some Chan'gaa to drink all the fear away.

The lawyer arrived about an hour later and after he had taken details from Yahzid and advised him on his rights, the police interview resumed.

'My client has something he would like to tell you,' the lawyer advised.

'About what?'

'Let him speak and he will explain.'

They nodded at Yahzid to proceed.

'I have some information that could be very useful to you if you want to get hold of the man who masterminded the plot.'

'Don't get smart with us boy. You will strike no plea bargains here,' the fat detective warned.

Yahzid was silent. He was trying to help but he wanted something in return. He could feel the warm breath on his neck of a police guard standing behind him. It wasn't a pleasant sensation and he broke out in a sweat.

'My client wishes to co-operate with the police and the information he has could be important to this case. Will you listen to him?'

'We don't do plea bargaining?' the detective repeated.

'Let us say this is more a matter of give and take,' said the lawyer.

The two detectives spoke quietly to one another then one said: 'What man are you talking about?'

'A white man,' Yahzid said, his voice shaking.

'Who is this white man?'

'I have a younger sister who will suffer if I am not here to help her,' he told them. 'Some people may try to harm her. I want to know that she will be okay.'

They ignored him. 'Tell us about this white man, boy,' spearman demanded.

Yahzid did not reply. The policeman behind him smacked a truncheon hard onto the table beside his right hand and Yahzid jumped. He shook from his shoulders to his feet, he was really scared, but he had to hold his nerve and force their hand. His lawyer warned them to refrain from harming his client.

'It will be the worse for you if you don't co-operate with us,' they warned.

Yahzid took a deep breath. 'I will co-operate with you, I want to, but I am a desperate man for the sake of my sister.'

'You are a stupid man. Do you want us to beat everything out of you?'

Yahzid felt the hairs on the back of his neck rising where the breath of the man with the stick behind him was so close, but his lawyer was there and he knew they wouldn't harm him, not yet. 'If you beat me I want to know it was worth it for my sister,' he whispered.

The detectives sat back in their chairs and gave him a long hard look. He prayed for their compliance.

'What is your sister's name?'

'Esme,' Yahzid said, breathing out. Perhaps his prayer had worked. 'Our parents died five years ago. My aunt took us in and then she too died. So I brought her up myself and made sure she went to school. Now she wants to go to University.'

The detectives shook their heads and laughed. 'We're not interested in your life story, we just want the truth.'

'I am telling the truth. You must believe me if you want to catch the white man?' Yahzid insisted. 'It is why I got involved with his stupid plan. I wanted the money for my sister.'

Spearman leaned towards Yahzid again. 'What is this man's name?'

'His name is Ralph Somerton. My sister works for him and his wife as a cleaner at their house in Karen.'

The detectives exchanged glances.

'Do you know where this man is?'

'No, but I know where he will be tomorrow.'

The detectives exchanged glances again. 'Are you playing a game with us?'

'No,' Yahzid said. 'It is the truth. I know where he will be tomorrow.'

'How do you know this?'

'Because I arranged it.'

Spearman got up and went round to Yahzid's side of the table. He leaned down, his face so close to Yahzid's that he could see the dirt in his pores. 'You tell us everything you know from start to finish and if we like what we hear then we might consider giving your sister a small concession for your information.'

Yahzid nodded. 'I have no alternative but to trust your words, but you must believe that my sister had nothing to do with this. She is completely innocent. I used her.' Then he went on to explain his part in the set up and, most importantly, the role of Somerton, who had masterminded the whole thing.

The detectives sat back regarding Yahzid and his story. He knew they were debating whether or not to believe him.

'And what of the two men who carried out the abduction? Who are they?'

Yahzid hesitated. He was very afraid of the two men and the people they knew in Kibera. 'I am afraid to tell you because of the danger my sister may be in.'

'You must tell us or we cannot help you,' they warned.

He looked at his lawyer who nodded. 'John Kamathi and Jomo Wangondu, for all the good it will do you when you try to find them. People will be covering from them as many live in fear of these men.'

'Let us worry about that. What else can you tell us about these men? What are their descriptions?'

'Wangondu is tall and muscular and he usually wears a black and grey baseball cap. He has a scar down the right side of his face. He is a Kikuyu. Kamathi is shorter and he is also a Kikuyu. I don't really know him so I cannot describe him much to you. They have both spent time in prison before.'

'Are you sure you are not making it up?' the detectives growled at him.

'No, I tell you it is true. I have not made anything up.' Yahzid looked at his lawyer in despair. 'It is true,' he repeated, 'you can check their records.'

'Let us to go back to the white man. You told us you know where this man will be tomorrow. How can you be so sure?'

'Because I know this man is scared.'

'Why is he scared?'

'Because those men I hired for his scheme are after his blood. You see he refused to pay them and they didn't like it, not one bit.'

'That still doesn't explain to us why you know where he

will be tomorrow,' the detectives insisted.

'He has agreed to pay them to get them off his back, and I have arranged for someone to collect the money from him. That person will be waiting for him tomorrow at midday, at the Ayani Bus Station, and even he does not yet know who to expect.'

'But you must tell us. Who is this someone?'

Yahzid's eyes gleamed. 'My sister, Esme.'

'You told us your sister had no part in this?'

'I told you the truth. Esme has no part in it. She does not know why she is doing this. I have used her. She is an unwitting pawn. You must believe me.'

22

NAIROBI

June

I t won't take much to spot me here Ralph thought looking around at the crowds of Africans coming and going from the multitude of buses at Ayani – a white man in safari gear. In his hand he held a Tuskys plastic supermarket bag, into which the money had been packed in re-sealed food boxes. Out of the corner of his eye he saw a group of tourists getting out of a private mini-bus, ready for their guided safari around the slums of Kibera. Ralph couldn't understand the attraction for that kind of tour, but he moved nearer to the group, catching the eye of one or two and he smiled and nodded at them as though he were one of them.

He had no idea who would be coming for the bag but he felt pretty confident that he had the upper hand of it, with Esme tucked away in the lock-up. Any funny business and he would let Yahzid know he had taken her. He glanced around him again, searching the crowd for his likely contact. Minutes ticked by and still nobody approached him. Twenty more minutes and he began to feel uneasy. Why hadn't the person coming to take the money from him, shown themselves?

He looked around him, but all he saw was a sea of faces and none that he recognised. Unnerved by the no show, and half an hour late, he turned tail and disappeared into the crowds. Ralph knew it would not be wise to rush back to the lock up, just in case the two accomplices to whom he owed the money were following, so he jumped on a bus and took a journey into the centre of Nairobi, changing twice before leaving on another bus heading towards Westlands. He had no idea what he was going to do, but he was paranoid enough to believe that if he found himself out of a crowd, he would be set upon.

When he arrived in Westlands, Ralph hurried into a supermarket to lose himself in the throng of people shopping, before slipping out of a back door into the loading area where he climbed into a large industrial bin full of waste paper and cardboard. He listened to people coming and going in the yard, and then he heard the voices he had been waiting for.

'Someone saw him come through this door,' a man said.

'Then he must be hiding here.' His heart thumped like a drum as he listened to them walking around and searching, behind the bins and the stacks of boxes, raising lids and letting them fall back with a thud that almost made him cry out. He was sure they would find him.

'Look, the gate at the end. Do you think he could climb over it?' another voice asked.

'Desperate men will do anything.'

He heard footsteps hurry past the bin he was concealed in and the sound of metal being shaken.

'I think he escaped down that alleyway.'

'But we haven't looked in all the bins yet.'

Then Ralph heard one of the men exclaim.

'What is it?' asked the other.

'It was a rat, a big one.'

'Come on, let's not stay any longer,' the other urged. 'It's getting late and I think we have lost him.'

Ralph heard the sound of footsteps disappearing back towards the shop. He waited for what seemed like a long time, but the men did not return. Thank God for the rat. But it was not until well after dark that Ralph considered it safe enough to come out of hiding. He climbed over the fence the men had inspected and hurried down the alleyway to the main road, praying they were not there waiting for him. On the main road he hailed a taxi and returned to the lock-up, stopping on the way to buy some spit roast chicken from a market stall.

Esme was drowsy, but he forced her to eat and drink something, then she fell asleep again.

He knew it was only a matter of time before they were both discovered and Ralph knew he must get away. His plan was to make his escape across the border with Tanzania, under cover of the night. He still had his British passport and, if he could get to Mount Kilimanjaro Airport, he would buy a ticket there for Dar es Salaam. From the capital he could get out to England. Failing that he would make his way to the coast and find a boat to take him anywhere away from Kenya.

Some hours later Ralph took the small holdall he had stuffed with safari clothes, binoculars, a camera and a pair of walking boots, along with his toothbrush and shaving gear. He hoped it would make him look like a regular tourist on safari. Covering Esme with a couple of blankets and leaving her some biscuits and bottled water, Ralph hurried away to the outskirts of the city where he hired a car paying cash for it.

Tomorrow, when he had covered enough ground, he would let Tessa know where Esme could be found.

23

NAIROBI

June

He was back in the interview room, squinting in the glare of the bare light bulb dangling above his head.

'You lied to us,' the detectives said. 'You told us your sister would meet Ralph Somerton at the bus station, but she didn't show up.'

Yahzid looked at them in genuine surprise. 'I didn't lie to you. My sister was instructed to collect a package from Ralph Somerton and leave it at the left luggage office. I know because I arranged it myself.'

The detectives exchanged glances.

'I am not lying,' he insisted. 'I swear to you that Esme was supposed to be there.' He felt anxiety rising for his sister. 'Where is she?'

'All we know is she didn't show up and we followed Ralph Somerton, who led us a merry dance around Nairobi.'

'Did you arrest him?'

They ignored his question. 'Why did you tell us lies about your sister?' they persisted.

Yahzid shook his head. 'I did not lie. I don't understand why she wasn't there, and now I am concerned for her. She could be in danger.' He felt panic rise and sweat poured down his face. He mopped it with his sleeve.

'You had better be telling us the truth,' they warned.

'I swear to you, I arranged for my sister to be there to collect the money from Ralph Somerton. I don't know why she didn't show up. Please believe me.'

'You must tell us where these men are.'

Yahzid held up his hands. 'I told you, I don't know where they are – maybe the changa'a place, but they could be anywhere and they will be hiding. It is impossible for me to know where.'

'For your sister's sake you had better tell us where they are,' the detectives persisted. The man with the truncheon smacked it into his hand.

'I swear I do not know where they are and I beg of you to find my sister,' Yahzid pleaded. 'Even if you beat me I cannot tell you what I do not know.'

They left him fretting in the interview room, imagining the things that might have happened to Esme. He knew those men; they were desperate and would stop at nothing to get their money. The police, it seemed, were not prepared to listen to him, and the only person who might was Tessa Somerton. He asked to speak to his lawyer and begged him to find and speak to her and ask her to come and see him. To his surprise she did.

Through the bars dividing them, Yahzid told Tessa of his concern for Esme.

'Please try and find her,' he pleaded. 'I am very worried

for her safety.'

'You should have thought of that before you involved her,' Tessa reprimanded.

Yahzid hung his head in shame. 'I know, Mama Somerton. I was greedy for the money because I wanted to help my sister. I wanted to help her to go to university. Esme is a good girl and always does what I ask without any questions. I arranged for her to collect a bag of money from your husband at the bus station, but she didn't show up and nobody is interested in looking for her. I am worried that those men have taken her. If they have they will do bad things to her.'

Tessa promised to do everything she could to find Esme.

24

NAIROBI

June

Ralph planned to drive through the night, arriving at the Tarime Border Post with Tanzania at dawn. Once through he would go to a hotel in Arusha and board an early shuttle-bus taking travellers to Mount Kilimanjaro airport. He would buy a ticket to Dar es Salaam and, from there, a ticket to England.

In fact he didn't get any further than just beyond the lock up near Wilson Airport. The police had issued an alert at the airport, and an airport worker had spotted and recognised him, and called the police.

Ralph heard the siren before he saw the police patrol vehicle that pulled him over. One of the policemen got out and came to his car.

He wound down the window a fraction, feigning surprise and innocence.

'Good evening officer, how can I help you?'

'You are Ralph Somerton?'

'Why are you asking?'

'Please answer the question, sir. Are you Ralph

Somerton?'

'Yes, but...'

The officer waved a piece of paper at him. 'I have a warrant for your arrest. Please give me the keys of your car and get out of the car, sir.'

'Arrest, what on earth for?' he demanded, staying where he was.

'Get out of the car and give me your keys,' the officer repeated, 'or shall I break the window and drag you out.'

Ralph thought, for a moment, of zooming off. It would take them a few moments to start following him and he had a chance of losing them. His hand hovered over the ignition, but the officer lifted up the baton he had as if to smash it against the front window.

'Okay, okay, I'm getting out,' Ralph said, facing defeat, and he held up his hands. The second he was outside he was pushed face first onto the car bonnet and handcuffed. The officer grabbed the keys out of the ignition.

'What the hell is going on?' Ralph protested. 'Why are you arresting me, what have I done?'

'Ralph Somerton, I am arresting you in connection with the death of Mrs Mary Stephenson. You have the right to remain silent. Anything you say can, and will be, used against you in a court of law. You have the right to a lawyer...' Ralph listened to the officer reading him his rights. He said nothing. Then he was bundled into the back of the patrol car and taken to Nairobi Central Police Station.

The cell, where he had been sent to await his police interview, stank of stale sweat. Ralph had now been there for two hours, with nothing to drink, and the temperature was stifling. Sweat ran off him and he was beginning to feel faint from dehydration. He needed water. He banged on the door and called out, 'Can I have water, please,' but nobody replied or came.

After a long time someone did come and open the door, but it was not to bring water. He was taken to a dim, shabby room where two policemen were seated at a table. They read him his rights again and informed him they were going to ask some questions.

'I will not answer you until I have seen my lawyer,' Ralph declared. He had been allowed to make one telephone call and he had made that to Anders, who agreed to find him a lawyer, whom he was still waiting for.

'Where were you on the night of the attack on Nyara Camp?'

'I invoke my right to silence until my lawyer arrives,' he replied.

The grim-faced police officers were not happy. 'All right Mr. Somerton, play it your own way. In the meantime, you will remain here at the police station whether you are prepared to be co-operative or not.' They threw him back into the cell.

'I'm Jafri Ajulu. You've got fifteen minutes to tell me everything. Remember it's in your own interests to tell me the truth,' Ajulu warned. 'The police have arrested you because they seem to think they have enough evidence to bring serious charges against you.'

Ralph surveyed the man in front of him, the man who was there for his defence. He was a slight man, dressed in a well-worn grey suit, with shiny patches. He didn't look very inspiring but he had come with a recommendation from Anders. 'I haven't even made a statement yet. I have invoked my right to remain silent until I know what they are going to charge me with.'

Ajulu held up his fingers, 'There are several things they can charge you with: One - conspiring to attack a safari camp; Two abducting a woman; Three – her death; Four – absconding arrest; shall I go on? We could add withholding evidence to that list. Now, you must tell me everything and it must be the truth. If not it will make it difficult for me to help you.'

Ralph did not respond. He had made up his mind not to give anything away unless he had to.

'Do you understand the severity of the charges that may be brought against you?' Ajulu persisted. 'It is also alleged that you were found in possession of money you were going to hand over to two men, in payment for their part in the attack on Nyara Camp. The police already have a testimony, from an individual, alleging that you masterminded the entire crime.'

Still he remained silent, trying to work out his next move. He gathered they must have Yahzid in custody.

'A man has been arrested and interviewed and provided the police with a detailed statement that implicates you in the conspiracy,' Ajulu continued. 'I urge you to communicate with me.'

Ralph regarded the lawyer as his mind strove for another angle. 'I want to plead diminished responsibility?'

'That is only permissible in a murder case and I am sure you don't want to turn it into that,' Ajulu dismissed, 'and, unless you wish to proceed under that charge, I think you should start by telling me what you have done so that I can decide the best way for us to proceed.'

Ralph remained unresponsive, not daring to trust words to anyone.

'If you do not start cooperating with me you could languish here for months. You must stop playing games. You have one more chance or I shall leave and you may remain here, for posterity, awaiting charges. It could be weeks, months or years.'

'I will talk to you, but I still want to plead not guilty,' Ralph tendered.

Ajulu nodded. 'We will see but first you must tell me everything, Mr. Somerton, from the start to the finish, such as it is.'

25

NAIROBI

June

A call came for Tessa from the Nairobi Police. 'We have arrested your husband – he is detained at the Nairobi Central Police Station. A lawyer has been to see him.'

Despite the initial shock it was a relief to hear he was in police hands and had representation. 'Thank you for letting me know.'

'Your husband is asking to see you.'

She arrived at the police station for the third time, dreading what lay ahead. The police took her into a room and left her. Then another door opened and Ralph appeared in handcuffs.

Shocked she turned to the guard. 'Why on earth is he handcuffed?'

The guard shrugged.

'Apparently I am likely to abscond,' Ralph answered for him. He sat down at the chair on the other side of the table and put his cuffed hands in his lap.

She said, 'well you did try to evade arrest.'

He shrugged but made no comment.

To her relief the guard left the room, but he remained on the other side of the door, watching them through the metal grating.

Ralph looked up at her with a smile but she didn't return it. 'I'm sorry if they tried to keep you away.'

Tessa almost laughed. Nothing could be further from the truth.

They faced each other across the table.

'Ralph, I'm not here because I want to be. I'm here because you are going to be charged with conspiracy to attack Nyara camp, as well as the planned abduction of Mary Stephenson and her manslaughter, not to mention trying to run away.' She prayed he would not deny it.

'I had nothing to do with her death,' he said.

'I hope to God you didn't.'

'You don't believe me?'

'You have lied to me about so much, how should I know whether you are telling the truth or not. I am sure you did not desire Mary Stephenson's death, but I'm afraid that you were responsible for the circumstances that led to it.'

Ralph stared at her in disbelief. 'You're my wife and you should believe in me and stick by me. You know what I've had to endure these past months – the uncertainty of our future, the failure of our business.'

Tessa didn't, couldn't respond. Words failed her. It didn't seem to matter what had happened. It was all about him and his problems as it always had been. The plan he had staged was so awful, and the consequences so dire, that for a moment she wondered if perhaps he was insane. She had a sudden urge to leave the room, to run and run as far away as she could, so that she would never have to see or hear of him again.

'Tessa?'

She looked up at him. 'Why are you pleading not guilty?'

'Why do you think?'

Tessa shrugged. 'I don't know. God knows the police seem to have enough evidence against you.'

He did a slow shake of his head. 'After all I've been through, and you still don't get it, do you?'

'Get what, Ralph?'

'You're my wife, you should be supporting me.'

'I will only support the truth.'

He gave her a long cold stare then she jumped as he banged his hand down hard on the table in front of her. 'Guard, we are finished,' he shouted, 'we have no more to say to each other.'

Tessa tried one more appeal. 'Ralph, I beg of you, don't continue with this charade. Plead guilty to the charges and co-operate. If you do your sentence will be more lenient. To go through a court case will be dreadful for you and everyone else involved. I do believe it was not your intention, but there is the death of an innocent woman at the heart of this.'

But the guard had arrived and Ralph had turned his back on her.

On the way back to Sophie's apartment Tessa received another call, from a worker at Wilson Airport. He had been walking near the Chui camp lock-up and heard someone calling from inside. 'It sounds like a girl.'

'Thank you, I'll be over right away.'

'Shall I call the police?'

'No, no, not yet,' Tessa stalled. 'Let me come and see what it's all about first.' She had a feeling she knew who it would be.

'What happened?' she said to Esme, who was staring up at her in complete confusion. Tessa could see in her eyes how frightened she was. 'Don't worry, Esme, you're not in trouble.'

The girl began to cry. 'Mr Somerton brought me here. I didn't break in, I promise. He tricked me because he said Yahzid was in hospital, and then he said he had done so for my own good. He told me that some bad men wanted to harm me because of something that Yahzid had been involved in. He said, if I ran away, my brother would be in big trouble.'

'It's okay, Esme, the police have arrested my husband.'

The girl looked at her wide-eyed. 'Oh. What is it he has done?'

Tessa grimaced, 'a lot of things I'm afraid.'

'How did he know about Yahizid and what he was involved in?'

'Because, I'm afraid to say, my husband organized it.'

'What did he organise?'

'The attack on Nyara Camp in the Masai Mara, and the abduction of a woman from the camp, who died trying to escape from her captors.'

Esme gasped. 'I heard about this, but I cannot believe that Yahzid was part of it.' She started crying again. 'Oh my God, what has he done?'

'I'm sorry Esme, sorry for everything that has happened.'

Her words were inadequate but what more could she say.

'What about Yahzid? Do you know where he is?'

Tessa sighed. 'I'm afraid he has been arrested too.'

Esme put her hands to her face in dismay. 'The last time I saw him he asked me to collect a package, from your husband, at the bus station but I couldn't because I was here.'

Tessa felt her anguish and she put an arm around her shoulders to comfort her. 'You poor girl, I'll send a message to let Yahzid know that you are safe and well.'

'Will my brother go to prison?'

Tessa shrugged. 'If he has broken the law then yes, I expect he will, but perhaps they will take into account his co-operation with the police.'

Esme shuddered and Tessa put an arm around her. 'They need to see that you are safe and well. You must tell them Yahzid was telling the truth, about you going to meet my husband at the bus station, and you must tell them about being confined here.'

'Will they keep me in custody too?' she looked frightened.

'I think they will understand that you were not involved, other than being a pawn in your brother's plan.' Tessa was quite sure that Esme had nothing to do with anything that had happened.

'I don't want to get Yahzid into trouble,' she pleaded.

'I'm afraid it's too late for that. You must tell the police the truth and everything you know.'

'I don't know anything apart from collecting the package. Why did my brother involve himself in such a stupid and terrible thing?' Esme wailed. 'I warned him that he was mixing with the wrong people but in the end it was not them, it was your husband.' Her tone was reproachful and

Tessa could not blame her for it.

'I know, Esme, and I am so sorry. My husband should never have involved Yahzid. Your brother told me that he wanted the money to help you to go to university, so perhaps he is not so bad. He did the wrong thing for all the right reasons. Now we must try and support him as best we can.'

The girl shook her head. 'I am sorry. It is not your fault. Yahzid was going to fall in with the wrong people one way or another, whether it was your husband or with others. Whatever the reasons for getting involved, Yahzid must face the consequences of what he has done.'

They drove to the police station where Esme made a statement, then they returned to Sophie's apartment and insisted that she should stay there with them for a few days for her own safety.

Later that evening, Tessa turned on the television to watch the news. She was glad she had when the reporter made a surprising announcement: *In a strange and bizarre twist of fate, the Nairobi police report that two males, John Kamathi and Jomo Wangondu, whom they were seeking in connection with the mysterious death of the white woman, Mary Stephenson, are themselves dead. The woman went missing from a safari camp in the Masai Mara after it came under attack. Her mutilated body was found a few days ago, also in the Masai Mara. She had been wandering in the bush and was mauled by wild animals after, police believe, she tried to escape her captivity. Police say that they had been tipped off on the wherabouts of the two men after a reward was offered for information. The police went to a home in Kibera but the pair managed to escape. The police gave chase but Kamathi and Wangondu pushed a man off his motorbike and used it for their getaway. The police, who then commandeered a vehicle, continued to chase the men along Magadi Road. Soon they found themselves in Nairobi National Park. Night was falling and the going on the road in the park was rough and dangerous. Kamathi and Wangondu went further and faster into the park and then diaster happened. Their motorbike slammed into a tree and threw them onto the ground. They scrambled to their feet and ran into the bush. The policemen shone their headlights and saw a most unfortunate incident. Kamathi and Wangondu had run into the heart of a buffalo herd and they were trampled to death by the frightened animals. Their bodies were recovered this morning.*

'They have got their retribution,' said Esme.

'But Kamani has lost his key suspects,' Tessa added. Could there be a case to answer to now?

Then a photograph of Mary Stephenson popped up onto the television screen.

'Oh,' said Esme staring at it, 'that is the same woman who came once with another to Kibera. They came to take Yahzid and me to an orphanage.'

'I heard she was involved in an orphanage project,' said Tessa, 'so why didn't you go with her?'

Esme shrugged. 'I am sure she was only doing it out of kindness but Yahzid and I ran away and hid because, whatever you may say about Kibera, it is our home.'

'I understand,' said Tessa, 'but I'm sure she meant well. I've heard that the children who go to the orphanage she supported are well looked after, and given good opportunities for their futures. They are taught many skills by volunteers.'

Esme sighed. 'Perhaps it would have been better for Yahzid if we had gone there. He might have a job now instead of being in prison, and I'm sorry the orphanage has lost such a good woman.'

26

NAIROBI

August

George heard the news that Kamathi and Wangondu had been killed with regret, because they would not now stand trial. They were as much to blame for Mary's death as Somerton was. They had undertaken the crime for money, had been negligent in their duty of care to Mary whilst she was being held against her will. It was a travesty of justice that they had not lived to account for their evil crime.

In the meantime there was to be an Inquest into Mary's death, and George knew he was going to hear some hard and grim facts surrounding the death of his wife. The Narok County police had undertaken a full investigation of the circumstances. Their findings had been presented to the local magistrate who had read the police report and agreed, that the mysterious circumstances surrounding the death did warrant an inquest. Witness statements and testimonies had been obtained from those with direct involvement and knowledge of the disappearance of the victim - George, James, and the ranger who had found the body, the investigating police officers as well as the pathologist.

The pathologist concluded that, in his opinion, Mary's body had been mauled and mutilated by wild animals and there was no evidence to show that her death had been anything other than accidental. The magistrate ruled that the evidence was inconclusive and that, in his opinion, the poor lady had died from natural causes. This included exposure to the elements, dehydration and general despair for her predicament, as well as the unfortunate injuries inflicted by wild animals.

'I believe the matter of the alleged abduction and confinement of the victim calls for a different police investigation,' an observation to which the magistrate agreed. He recorded his verdict based on the pathologists report, the initial police investigation and testimonies of the witnesses. *'After assimilating and assessing all the evidence and information regarding this case, I find that I cannot attribute the injuries to anything but having been caused by wild animals mauling her already dead body. There is no evidence to suggest foul play and I must agree with the pathologist that the death of the poor woman was as a result of natural causes including dehydration and extreme heat fatigue after which her dead body was subject to the mercy of the wild animals. It is a terrible tragedy but my final verdict can only be that of: death by misadventure.'*

It was a relief to have the inquest over, but George was devastated by the magistrate's verdict. It was an injustice that nobody would be held directly responsible for Mary's death. His only concession was that his lawyer was still lobbying the police, and the attorney general, for further police enquiries into the matter of the abduction. Somerton and Adongo would continue to be held in custody, pending these investigations, whilst the police sought to find enough evidence to press charges.

In an effort to make some gesture for the memory of Mary, George visited the orphanage to face the people she had loved and helped. He knew it would be hard for them - they were locked in their own devastation and grief for the loss of their beloved friend. George hadn't paid much attention to Mary's work at the orphanage, apart from supporting her with monetary gestures, but now he wished he'd got more involved in her projects; wished he'd been more interested in the people who had meant so much to her, and who worked so tirelessly for the orphans of Nairobi.

He was humbled by their grief over her death, the warm way in which they welcomed him, the lovely people that they were. He allowed himself to be taken around to see the work that his Mary had done, and was overwhelmed by the children that he encountered. He sat with them and their workers and listened to the tales of those whose parents had died of Aids and other diseases, of those who had simply been abandoned and found by orphanage staff foraging in rubbish dumps and sleeping rough in the slums. Some had been abused and badly treated by the people who were supposed to be caring for them, and they had found their way to the orphanage and begged to be accepted. George was moved to tears by their stories and he promised himself that he would do something to help them, in the name of Mary.

He received the news that his wife's remains were at

last available for burial. He had already approached the authorities about having Mary cremated at the Kariokor crematorium and he knew where he wanted her ashes to lie – under the ground beneath a tree he planned to plant in the orphanage yard. It would be a fitting place for them.

A lot of people packed into the crematorium for the funeral service, not least the Nairobi press and media. Everyone attending had to run the gauntlet of flash photography, microphones and rolling video, before they managed to get inside. George had tried to keep it as low profile as he could, but word had obviously got around. People from the orphanage shielded George from the prying press and their questions, begging for respect and privacy for the funeral of his wife.

James and Alexia were also targets but they managed to push their way through.

'For God sake have some respect for the poor man and his deceased wife,' James begged, but nobody seemed to take any notice of him.

Eventually a couple of police officers turned up and moved the media back to a more respectable distance.

Inside George forced himself not to think of the grim remains that lay inside the coffin, but to focus instead on the picture of Mary, as she had been, on the front of the Order of Service. He sat among the people from the orphanage who had come to mourn the loss of their dear friend and patron. Behind him were children whom Mary had helped, who had grown and left the orphanage. Other rows held friends left in Nairobi - the attaché and his wife from the British High Commission; old colleagues and people he had known through his business and, he noticed gratefully, that

James and Alexia Sackville had come, along with another woman George didn't know. After the service they had all been invited back to the Muthaiga Country Club for refreshments

Although it was meant to be a celebration of Mary's life, the shock and grief for the way in which Mary had been so cruelly taken from their lives was obvious on people's faces. George had wanted to speak about Mary, but he knew he would be unable to see it through. Instead he asked a colleague from the orphanage to speak on his behalf. The woman told the congregation of all the good things that Mary had done, all the young lives she had saved. She was, she told them, a warm and courageous woman who would never be forgotten by those who had loved her and been saved by her. She ended by saying: *'Mary has just gone ahead to show us the way and she will be waiting when it is our time to join her.'* Then a group of children from the orphanage sang a beautiful Swahili farewell: *'Kwaheri, kwaheri, mpendwa, i matumaini sisi kukutana tena, Mungu akitaka, Mungu akitaka, i matumaini sisi kukutana tena,* which translated to English meant: *Goodbye, goodbye, loved one, I hope we meet again, God willing, God willing, I hope we meet again.* George, and many of the congregation, broke down as the beautiful young voices filled the crematorium.

After the service George stood by the door to thank everyone for coming. He did it with a smile, but it was the smile of a programmed robot. It all felt so surreal, even the finality of the service.

'Thank you for coming,' he said, over and over, and listened without listening in particular, to the kind words of whoever it was in front of him. He appreciated their concern and kindness but he was struggling with the whole concept of Mary's death and felt as though he walked every day in a nightmare. Then his attention was drawn to the stranger who had come with the Sackville's.

She gave him a rueful look and held out her hand. 'Tessa Somerton, Mr. Stephenson, I'm so sorry for your loss.'

'Thank you,' he said, and then he leaned closer to her and lowered his voice so that only she heard him. 'I hope your husband rots in hell, although I understand that you yourself knew nothing of your husband's involvement in my wife's murder.'

Tessa took a step back and he saw her visible shock.

'You're not welcome back with the others. It wouldn't be right,' George said and then he turned his back on her. When he looked round again she was scuttling away. He heard Alexia Sackville calling out to her. He couldn't understand why the Sackville's wanted to have anything to do with the wife of the man who had brought about their ruin.

He got himself through the rest of the day by pretending to be someone else; shaking the hands of his fellow mourners and making sure they had enough to drink and eat; nodding and shaking his head in obedient reply to their questions and condolences. The orphanage staff hovered around him like a protective ring of bodyguards, and he was grateful to them for fending off too much attention and concerning themselves with his own wellbeing. Yet the visible pain of loss on their faces made George feel all the more agitated about Mary's death. Not only had he lost a wife, but they too had lost a good friend and champion of their cause.

A short while after the funeral he visited Malik. He had been thinking a lot about his old friend's son and wanted to put some things straight with him.

Malik was not in the best of health when George got to see him. He was thin and unkempt and looked unwell and under nourished. George took him in bread and soup and watched as Malik devoured it. He told himself he had made the gesture for Asir's sake, not because he felt sorry for Malik. After all, Malik was at the root of all his problems.

'Thank you,' Malik said, 'you are very kind.'

'I did it for your father.' The flat statement indicated that it hadn't been for the son.

Malik nodded. 'I know how much you cared about and revered my father and he you.'

'Yes, it's a pity you are not even half the man he was,' said George. He saw how Malik was shocked by his words and it pleased him. He ploughed on. 'I think he would be very disappointed in you. Your actions cost me the business – the business your father and I built up together and it ended up costing Mary her life.'

Malik's eyes widened. 'Your wife is dead?'

George nodded. 'Yes, her funeral was last week.'

'I am sorry,' Malik said with sadness. 'She was a good woman.'

'Yes, she was,' George agreed, his voice hard and cold, 'but now she is dead and is not here to be a good woman anymore.'

'How did she die?'

George gave a harsh laugh. 'She was mauled by wild animals,' he said and gauged Malik's horror.

'That is a dreadful thing but I don't understand. How did it happen?'

'Then let me explain,' George said. 'There has been a chain of actions and consequences culminating in Mary's death. It began with your own actions that put my business, the business your father and I built up, in jeopardy. Of course you had no interest in that business, only in pursuing your own selfish and stupid ideals without thought of how this would affect Mary and I.' Malik opened his mouth to speak but George silenced him with his hand. 'No, let me finish. I lost the business and everything your father and I had worked for, which of course had given you the financial ability to take the risk that brought it to an end. Can you imagine the despair I was thrown into? Because of that despair I let myself be duped by another desperate man. His actions resulted in Mary's death because, like you, he was a selfish man who thought of nothing but his own desires. Mary was kidnapped from a camp, a plot this man devised to discredit another camp he saw as a rival to his own business. Can you imagine? But the plan went wrong and Mary escaped. She wandered off into the bush where she met her grisly end. So you see it all began with your selfish desires, if you care to trace it back.' He sat back exhausted from the effort and emotions of his rhetoric.

Malik, he saw, was shocked and struggling to find the right words to say. 'It is indeed a terrible sequence of events,' he managed to whisper, 'but we all have our principles and what I did was because I believed it was the right thing to do. The people governing our country are...'

George stood up, interrupting him. 'I don't care,' he said. 'Have a good life in prison, Malik,' and he turned his back on him and left.

Revenge did not sit easily with George, but he was discovering that it was good to make people face up to the consequences of their actions, and he was determined that, one way or another, Ralph Somerton would be the next to do so.

27

NAIROBI

August

She tried not to dwell on the shame and hurt that had overcome her as she hurried away from the funeral. She had wanted to pay her last respects to Mary Stephenson, but she had not considered how distasteful it might be, for George Stephenson, to have the wife of the person who had effectively caused her death, present at the funeral.

Tessa sat in her car and sobbed, for the dead woman, for George, for the Sackvilles, then she pulled herself together and called Sophie, who insisted they met for lunch.

'I imagine everyone is going to tar me with the same brush as Ralph,' Tessa said gloomily, 'and I can't say I blame them.' She gave a cautious glance to the other diners, expecting them all to be staring at her.

'Of course they won't,' Sophie said, 'look, I can understand George's reaction but, nobody else who knows you will also hold you responsible. It's not as if you were in on what Ralph was planning.'

'I know, but I still feel responsible,' Tessa said. 'I'm his wife and I should have seen what he was capable of.' She took a large gulp of wine.

Sophie shook her head. 'How could you possibly have known? What he did has nothing to do with you.'

'You're so sweet Sophie, but you know as well as I do that it's not that simple. I won't feel comfortable and however much people say they've forgotten it they won't have done, not really.' Tessa put down her knife and fork. 'I've got something to tell you.'

Sophie frowned, 'okay, tell me.'

'I've made a decision. I'm going to leave Kenya.'

Sophie looked at Tessa aghast. 'You're going to leave Kenya? Where will you go? What will you do? When did you decide this, just now?'

'No, I've been thinking about it over the past few weeks. I just don't see myself with a future here anymore and certainly not with Ralph. I'll either go to England or South Africa, or maybe both. I haven't quite made up my mind yet.' She had known her friend would be devastated but Tessa had to think of herself and her own future.

'What about Chui?'

Tessa shrugged. 'What about it? I'm closing it down. There's no way I want to carry on with it. Running the camp is over. My life here is over. I'll sell the apartment and hope that will pay off the bank debts.'

'Oh Tessa, I'm so sorry,' Sophie said. Then her eyes brightened. 'What if we ran the camp together?'

Tessa knew Sophie was clutching at any means to get her to change her mind, and stay in Kenya, but it wasn't going to happen. She shook her head. 'I wouldn't say yes, even if I knew in my heart that it might work. You see I have to get away, to move on, to put some distance between myself and Ralph and everything that will be hanging over us.'

'This shouldn't have happened to you,' Sophie said fiercely, 'really it shouldn't have, and I can't bear to lose you.'

Tessa was grateful for her friend's support, 'but it did and now I have to live with the consequences.' She gave Sophie a despairing look. 'When did Ralph become so angry and bitter? Perhaps it was my…'

'Don't you dare blame yourself,' Sophie fiercely interrupted her. 'Ralph is a complex man with a lot of baggage. He blows hot and cold and always has done. I think you've been a saint to put up with him.'

Tessa decided to approach Esme with her ideas and plans for the future. She and Sophie had tried to persuade the girl to live with them at Sophie's place, so she would not to be alone in the home she and her brother had shared, but Esme chose to stay in Kibera. She reminded Tessa that the slum was her home and, if she did not use the accommodation in Kibera, the right to have it might be taken away from her. Then there would be nowhere for her brother to return to, after he had served his sentence. Besides she had to go to school to finish her studies and sit her exams.

Tessa spent a lot of time making plans for her return to England, researching places to live as well as work on another project that she had been planning.

One afternoon she went to meet Esme from school and took her for an early supper.

'I thought we could have a chat about your plans for the future, when you leave school. You said you were hoping to go to University?'

Esme nodded. 'Oh yes, I very much hope to do this. I would like to be a teacher.'

'What training have you been offered or advised about?'

'At the moment I do not know where I will go. I have to pass my exams and then I hope someone in Nairobi will help me to find a college place somewhere.'

Tessa pitched straight in. 'Have you thought of trying for a place at a University in another country, in England for instance?'

Esme eyes lit up. 'I would like to study in England but I have never set my hopes that high even though my tutor thinks I am clever enough.' Then her eyes dulled again. 'But it is only a dream.'

Tessa smiled. 'What if somebody could help your dream come true?'

'It would be more than I could ever hope for. But I don't know anyone in England.'

'Yes you do,' said Tessa. 'You know me. I'm going back to England to live after Ralph's court case and I would like to help you to achieve your ambitions.'

Esme stared at her in surprise. 'You are very kind Mama Tessa,' she said at last, 'but I cannot accept this from you. It is too much.' She hesitated and then added, 'I know it is none of my business but why are you leaving Kenya?'

'There is nothing left to keep me here,' Tessa said. 'My husband is likely to end up in prison and even if he doesn't there will be no relationship left between us.'

'But you will want to visit him?' Esme persisted.

'I'd rather not talk about that. I'm more interested in what I can do to help you.' Tessa's broken relationship with her husband was not open for discussion.

Esme's eyes brimmed with tears and for a moment she was unable to speak. 'It is a very kind offer,' she said at last, 'but I don't think I can leave Yahzid here alone. He has nobody else who cares and I don't know what would become of him if I was far away.'

'I understand your concern, but it may be possible to arrange for someone to take him food and other things he needs and to keep an eye on his general wellbeing. I could ask the church and the mission hospital,' Tessa offered.

'I will have to speak to him about it,' Esme said, 'but he is protective. I don't think he will like the thought of me being far away in another country.'

'Let's hope he welcomes the opportunity for his sister's benefit and for her future.' Tessa was determined that he would not obstruct Esme's future and she would do everything she could to make sure that didn't happen. Yahzid would need reassurance, she understood that, and so she had to provide details of that reassurance to show him that she had nothing but Esme's best interests at heart.

Despite her resolve not to ever visit her husband again, Tessa knew she had no choice. It was her duty to tell him that she had disbanded Chui Camp and sold off goods and property to pay their debts.

'How dare you,' was his hissed response when she broke it to him. His words echoed around the grim room in the prison where they were allowed to meet.

Tessa gave a grim laugh. 'You left me with no choice. We have debts and responsibilities that you will not be able to fulfil. What did you expect me to do?' She forced her voice to be as cold back to him but inside her stomach was tied up in knots.

'That camp has been in my family for generations.'

'I haven't sold it,' she reminded him. 'You still have the rights to it and it can be resurrected, and you should have thought about the consequences before you embarked on your stupid plot.'

He shook his head at her. 'You are unbelievable. You still won't support me, will you? You were lucky I married you. Nobody else would have and look how you repay me.'

It was a vicious jibe. Tessa stood up to go. 'I don't want to hear any more. You are twisted and cruel and I shan't be coming again.' She shook her head in exasperation as he smirked at her. 'I won't change my mind Ralph. I'll see you in court and I hope you get exactly what you deserve.'

'Bail would be good,' he said, as if he hadn't heard any of it.

Tessa knew that every fortnight, since he had been in custody, Ralph had made a bid for bail but, so far, the court had refused on the grounds that there was nobody willing to stand the bail money for him and, because he was a risk as an absconder. Every fortnight she had held her breath praying that bail would be denied.

'How can I help you when you won't help yourself? I hear the Psychologist's assessment of your, so-called, diminished responsibility plea has ruled a negative. You were in your right mind all the time, weren't you?'

'You're my wife. You should be supporting me,' he persisted, ignoring her question.

She gave a disbelieving laugh. 'Wife? Help you? That's the last thing I want to do. I see nothing of the man I once loved.' Tessa left before he could see the tears that were filling her eyes. She hadn't even told him she was going to move to England.

28

MASAI MARA

August

With the decision made, there was nothing left but to pack up Chui and make her plans to leave Kenya. It was a sad, sad day when she had to break the news to the staff, those men who had been so loyal to her. Jackson, her headman was a particular sadness, and she promised to try and find him work in another camp. It seemed so ironic that Ralph's plot, and the purpose of it, had been to get Nyara camp discredited and shut down and, in doing so, he had only succeeded in getting that to happen to his own.

Over the days, weeks and months, that had passed, since the dreadful events in June, she had felt days of immense sadness and days of extreme anger, combined with confusion and wonder at what her husband had set in motion. It was true he had not yet been found guilty, but in her heart she knew he was. It was more than she could bear and packing up Chui was a painful task and it broke her heart.

When most of the pack up of the camp gear was completed,

loaded onto trucks and on its way back to the lock up at Wilson, Tessa drove over to Nyara to see how the Sackville's were getting on, and to give them her news.

'We heard on the bush grapevine that you were closing up,' said Alexia, 'and we're very sorry, Tessa. What will you do now?'

'I'm planning to go back to England and I want to leave here without debt, material commitments or worry.'

Alexia was taken aback. 'England? What will you do there? I'd heard you were thinking of South Africa.'

'No, England it is,' Tessa said firmly. 'I will rent a place, for myself and Esme, and then find a job.'

'Esme? Alexia said, with a puzzled frown.

'Yes, Esme, the maid we employed at the house in Karen. Her brother is Yahzid, Ralph's accomplice. I am worried about what will happen to her if Yahzid goes to prison, and I thought I'd try and help her to get a place at a college or university in England.' Tessa explained. 'She deserves a chance in life. That's why I've chosen England.'

'Lucky girl,' said Alexia, 'what a wonderful opportunity.'

'There's a lot of preliminary work to do before it can all be confirmed, but fingers crossed it will work out. At any rate we'll give it a good try.'

Alexia regarded her with a wry smile. 'If anyone can do it, you can Tessa. You are the most determined person I have ever met.'

'And what about Nyara, how are you managing?' Tessa asked, hoping it was going well for them.

Alexia shrugged, 'it's been a slow start but the bookings are trickling in, and we think we've managed to convince the tour operators that Nyara is safe enough to send their clients to. The reviews are positive, at least.'

'I'm so sorry, you've been through the worst nightmare and all caused by my husband and his stupid scheme.' Tessa felt so bad for them and the terrible setback they had suffered.

'You mustn't blame yourself Tessa. We know you had no part in it and your life has been turned upside down too.'

'Yes,' Tessa said with a rueful smile, 'but that chapter in my life has come to an end and I must face a new one.'

'Well, I know how I would feel. I simply can't imagine doing anything else than run Nyara and live in Africa.'

'I thought the same about Chui, but it just goes to show how life can change so suddenly, without expecting it,' Tessa said, 'and I certainly never saw this coming.' Not one bit of it.

'Poor you, it must be awful. When are you going back to Nairobi?'

'I leave Chui, for good, tomorrow morning.' It was a sobering thought, despite what had happened. Leaving the safari business was going to be hard but then she must harden herself to the future, and that future was to be in England, the place she had once vowed never to go back to.

'I'll see you next at the trial, I imagine?' said Alexia.

'Yes,' Tessa sighed. 'Until then I shall be trying to sort out the mess Ralph has left me with.'

29

NAIROBI

September

R alph lay on his prison cell bed wide-awake. He was still not used to the sounds of the prison, that he could sleep through them; men crying, moaning and calling throughout the day and night, doors banging, guards shouting. Thank God he didn't have to share a cell. He yawned, and ran his hand over the prickly stubble on his chin. The battery razor he was allowed to use was too blunt now to make his skin smooth. He'd sent a message to Tessa, asking her to send a new one. Despite the rift between them, Tessa still sent supplies to him in prison – cigarettes and clothes and food – all good stuff with which to barter his way around the rules and laws of the criminals, who presided as lords, inside the prison. Some of these men, hardened by their lives of crime, were cruel and heartless and he often heard the anguished cries of those who were suffering because they had nothing with which to defend themselves. He would definitely rather face a wild animal in the bush than have to deal with the abuse that was meted out to those poor fellows. It was the one thing that really freaked him out about prison. Yet, despite the fact that her supplies were a Godsend, he could not forgive Tessa for what she had done, for the fact that her last visit was to tell him that everything he had ever lived for was over; that Chui camp was finished. Something had snapped inside him and what Tessa had mistaken for fury was, in fact, utter despair.

He was glad his father had sent him to a Kenyan Government School, unlike his brother Geoffrey who had been packed off back to boarding school in England. His father didn't think Ralph was worth the money, but the local school had served Ralph well and it was the only thing he had to thank his father for. There he had studied alongside Kenyans and learned to speak fluent Kiswahili. He was as happy in their company as he was his own community, and he could converse in Kiswahili, as well as he could English. It was serving him well now in prison. Being able to communicate with his gaolers and fellow inmates was something of an advantage.

Ralph and his father had never seen eye to eye and his father had not favoured his second son. Because of it Ralph was the first to admit he had gone off the rails, living wild in Nairobi, partying and drinking and procrastinating about what he was going to do, whilst in fact doing nothing. He had no focus and his future was blurred so he just carried on doing what he did best – socialising. Then his father had passed away and Ralph's elder brother, Geoffrey, had taken over Chui. His brother, being a decent sort of chap, had tried to bring him into the business and Ralph had, after some resistance, found himself enjoying it, particularly as he wasn't shouldering the responsibility. If he felt like returning to Nairobi, then he would. God, even he would admit he had behaved like a brat. Then, after only a few years of running Chui, Geoffrey had died and Ralph found himself inheriting the responsibilities of the tented camp with its faded old photos, its battered leather sofas, bucket showers and a genuine pride for its old fashioned style. At first he planned to sell up but, with long-term bookings to honour, he agreed to run it to the end of the year and to his surprise, and to others who knew him, he had found himself working hard to make the business work.

Tessa had been the icing on the cake and in the early years they had made a good team. She was a gracious host and a good manager of the staff, better than he was being more tolerant and patient. He recognised that about her. She was also a competent safari guide with a wealth of wildlife knowledge, and she could handle a gun as well as he could. For more than a decade Chui thrived and swelled in reputation.

But then it all began to go wrong. The new camp arrived, the clients were stolen and he couldn't help but fall into despair watching his traditional camp fall from its gracious pedestal, through no fault of his own. It simply wasn't right and he had been determined to prove his point. He had expected his wife to agree with and support him, no matter what happened, but she hadn't.

Once a week his lawyer paid a visit to prep him for the trial, that was due to begin the following March. He was the only visitor who came on a regular basis. With each visit, Ajulu tried to get him to change his plea to guilty but Ralph was resolute in his refusal. Guilty of what he mused – of trying to save my business? He strode grim-faced and miserable around his cell, wishing he could address the people wanting to stay at a camp like Nyara and tell them what he thought of it.

PART THREE

KILL

(The following year)

30

NAIROBI

March

The day before the start of the trial of the Republic versus Ralph Somerton, Tessa drove west from Nairobi along the Ngong Road, towards the suburb of Karen. She passed things which, over the years of doing it so often, she had simply stopped noticing. Things like the big Carnivore billboard, the sign for the Masai Teachers College, Kerarapon, the water vendor beating his mule, the worsening potholes – how could you forget those! Now, with her impending departure from Kenya creeping ever closer, nostalgia got the better of her and there were tears, for herself and the mess that had become her life, for the mule, and for all she was about to relinquish. Leaving Kenya were words that she had never thought to think, let alone utter, and it would have been unthinkable a year or so ago. Yet now she was on the verge of doing just that. She had found a place to rent, of all places in the heart of London. Living in the countryside, she had decided, would be too difficult to bear without the familiar bush sounds to wake to, and the British dawn chorus a constant reminder of where she wasn't any more. The sounds of London would be the perfect antithesis until she had settled into her new life. Out of bad endings would come good beginnings and it was that hope that she clung on to – a new start in a new place.

Today, and perhaps for the last time, she was returning to Ralph's family home, a place that had felt like home in the early days of her married life with her husband. Now she drove there with a heavy heart, not looking forward to the emotional memories it would stir. The staff had long gone and the furniture would be draped with dustsheets. The house would be little better than a mausoleum.

As she turned a corner towards the house, Tessa saw that it was already under siege from the media – reporters and photographers gathered in front of the gates. She drew up a short distance away, and waited for Esme, whom she had arranged to meet.

To her delight, Esme had decided to take up the offer of trying for a place at university in England. They had met with the school authorities, and discussed what needed to be done to make an overseas student application for Esme, for a teaching degree.

They had both gone to see Yahzid to reassure him that his sister would be well looked after, despite the fact that she would be in the hands of the wife of the man who had encouraged him to commit the crime, the crime that now saw him held in the detention centre awaiting his sentence.

'I trust you in the hands of this woman,' Yahzid said, solemnly, to Esme, 'I know she had nothing to do with what happened and she has been nothing but good to you. I wish you were not going to be so far away, but I have come to realise that you deserve the best and I deserve my punishment. I promise you, sister, that one day I will do something to make you proud of your brother, just as I am proud of you.'

'You are a good man, I know it,' Esme responded, 'and one day we will put all of this behind us and we will be together again.'

Tessa had stepped away from the brother and sister to allow them time to say their farewells. She was going to make sure that help would be on hand to keep Yahzid on the right track. The church would send regular visitors to encourage him and he was going to learn a trade during his time in prison, a trade that might also bring him work when he was released.

Tessa spotted Esme walking down a dusty road opposite where she was parked, under the heavy-leafed trees that lined the street. She wound down the window and called to her.

Esme came hurrying across and got into the passenger seat.

'I'm afraid the house is surrounded by the media,' Tessa explained. 'Keep your head down as we drive through, the photographers will be snapping away.' She began to drive towards the house, pressing a button to lock all the doors from the inside, and a remote to get the gates opening. Someone spotted the car approaching and the group whirled round to face them. She drove with an unwavering purpose through the crowd, dispersing them either side of the car as they shouted their questions and thrust their cameras to the car windows. As the gates opened Tessa wedged the car in the entrance. As they started to close behind her she inched forward until the gap behind them was narrow enough to prevent anyone trying to follow. They shut with a satisfying snap and automatically locked. Tessa let out a sigh of relief.

'Okay?' she said, turning to Esme. The girl nodded. Tessa released the door locks and they both got out of the car. The reporters were shouting through the gates for their attention, asking about Ralph, but they ignored them and went straight into the house.

Esme opened the metal window shutters in the kitchen and living room to let in some light and fetched her old cleaning box. 'It is very dusty in here.'

'Oh don't worry about cleaning, Esme. It's going to get a lot worse over time.'

'It will give me something to do,' Esme insisted.

'I'm sorry about the people out there,' Tessa apologised, unloading milk, bread and something to eat later on from a paper shopping bag.

Esme shrugged. 'It is not your fault they want a story.' She turned to face Tessa and said, 'I am sorry for you, and for what my brother did. It makes me feel ashamed.'

'You have nothing to be ashamed of, Esme. It was my husband who involved your brother in the first place, so you see we both have things to apologise for.'

'My brother was a stupid boy. He wasted his life drinking and getting involved with the men who think they are so clever. All they think of is robbing and doing other crimes to get the money for that drink. I pray that Yahzid will not go back to that life when he comes out. It is that which worries me most about him,' she faltered before adding, 'and if I am not here, he will have nobody to keep him on a better path.'

'I'll speak to someone about helping him to make a better life when he comes out of prison,' Tessa reassured her. She didn't want Esme changing her mind now about going to England with her. 'There are church organisations who may offer him counselling and he is at least learning a skill in prison. Do you think he would respond to something like that?'

'I am not sure. I know he is very sorry for what he did and now, without the drink, he is listening to what I say, but there may be people who want to send him back on a bad path and he is vulnerable.'

'I will do everything I can to make sure that doesn't happen.'

They got on with the work they had come to the house to do. Esme cleaned and tidied, and Tessa packed boxes with her belongings to be shipped to England. She put the stuff she didn't want into other boxes to be sent to the orphanage via the Church. Tessa had a feeling that George might not want them to accept charity from her so she was sending them anonymously.

A little while later she made some coffee, opened a packet of biscuits and invited Esme to join her.

'I don't know what to expect at the trial,' Esme confided. 'I am very nervous about it.' She hunched on the sofa rubbing her arms.

'You'll be fine. When it comes to giving evidence you must just tell the truth.' Tessa tried to ease Esme's apprehension, but she was experiencing similar emotions.

She woke at five and made herself a cup of tea, sitting alone at the kitchen table, trying to combat the churning apprehension. The dilemma about giving evidence against Ralph had taken its toll of her. She was sleeping badly, woken at night by bad dreams and feelings of anxiety, when her heart would miss a beat or race ahead and she had to get up and splash her face with cold water and take some deep breaths to get herself back to normal. There were days when she could have taken a knife to Ralph, and killed him, and other days when she tried to rationalise what he had done with the deep despair he had over their failing business. Yet nobody in their right mind would have gone to the lengths that he had done, surely? He was not yet proved to be guilty, but in her heart she knew that he was. She showered and dressed in preparation for the day at court, just as she would do over the many days in the future, for as long as it took until a verdict was reached. At least she would not have to return to this house again. From this day on she would be back at Sophie's.

There were only a couple of reporters at the house gate when she and Esme came to leave. The rest, Tessa surmised, had gone downtown to cover the trial.

The air was stale and hot in the courthouse from the intermittent competence of the air-conditioning units. It was packed with court officials, witnesses, counsels, reporters and clerks. Beads of perspiration peppered Tessa's face as she scanned the room for a familiar face with Esme, at her side poised like a frightened gazelle, ready to take flight. She caught sight of Sophie waving and pushing through the mill of people to join her and hugged her in relief.

'How are you doing?' Sophie asked.

'Not brilliant.'

'Don't worry, you'll be fine,' Sophie attempted to reassure her, but they both knew it was far from the truth.

The prosecution counsel clerk sought them out

andushered them through the throng, to where Kamani and his witnesses were gathering for the days briefing on the trial.

'Do you know the defence counsel? James asked him. 'Do you know his style?'

'Yes,' he said, 'Ajulu will be tough and clever with you, and he will try to trick you so must be prepared to stand your ground on the truth you are telling him.'

Esme shuddered and Tessa put a protective arm around her shoulders. 'You'll be fine,' she soothed.

'But I am so scared.'

'We all are,' Tessa confided.

Half an hour later they were ushered into a witness waiting room. It was going to be a long and frustrating wait every day with the trial going on and they unable to observe until they had made their own appearance in the witness box.

31

NAIROBI

March

In the courtroom the trial was declared open and Paul Kamani stepped up for the prosecution with his opening statement. Ralph steeled himself to listen.

'Good morning ladies and gentleman of the court, my name is Paul Kamani and it is my pleasure to represent the people of the Republic. In May of last year the defendant in this case, Kamani paused and pointed towards Ralph, *'set in motion a conspiracy to attack a safari camp, the said Nyara camp, to cause panic and mayhem during which time an innocent woman was abducted from this camp and taken to a place where she was held against her will. A few days later this woman was found dead in the Masai Mara where she had been attacked and mauled by wild animals during an apparent effort to escape her captors who had left her unattended in an abandoned camp. The attack on the camp was allegedly instigated by the defendant and carried out by two men who had, allegedly, been recruited in Nairobi by a second accused man who has pleaded guilty and is being held in Kamiti Prison, awaiting the outcome of the trial and sentencing. The said two men subsequently tried*

to escape capture and were trampled to their deaths in Nairobi National Park. Ladies and Gentlemen, this case is about a defendant who became so obsessed with his own business failure that he could not see straight. All he desired was to get even and he went to extraordinary lengths to achieve his desire.

When he was arrested the defendant even pretended to be insane to avoid being held responsible for his own actions.

Ladies and Gentlemen, the prosecution will call the following witnesses to the stand. We will call a representative from the Narok Police who investigated the crime that took place at Nyara camp and for which the defendant faces charges. We will call James Sackville, manager of the camp, Nyara, who will testify to the events during the attack. We will call George Stephenson, husband of the deceased victim, Mary Stephenson, who will testify that the defendant befriended him with intent to mislead him and beguiled him into taking his wife to the camp that was attacked and from which she was abducted. We will call the wife of the defendant, Mrs Tessa Somerton, who bravely reported her suspicions about her husband to the Nairobi police, and will give evidence against him. Last, but not least, we will call Miss Esme Adongo who was drugged and abducted by the defendant, and held against her will in a lock-up near Wilson Airport.

You are going to hear over the course of the next few weeks much evidence from prosecution witnesses in the trial of Ralph Somerton, the defendant, who stands accused on three counts - one count of culpable conspiracy for master-minding an attack on the safari camp, Nyara. A second count of culpable abduction of the deceased Mary Stephenson from the aforementioned camp, and a third count of actual abduction of Esme Adongo, a maid in the defendant's employ.

You are going to hear the defense's side of the story and, you are going to hear, no doubt, a sad story about the defendant. You are going to hear that he was a victim of circumstance and the defence wants you to feel sorry for him and to believe that his crimes were justified in light of the circumstances under which he committed them, because they had made him mentally unstable. I would ask you to think of the victims, in particular the deceased Mary Stephenson, an innocent woman, who took a trip to Nyara Camp with her husband believing that, after all they had been through with their own circumstances of bankruptcy and loss of income and home, she was going to enjoy some time with her husband on a relaxing safari. Instead she was cruelly taken from her husband, bound and left scared and alone in an alien environment, the African bush, where wild animals roam freely killing for food wherever they can get it. The victim, Mary Stephenson, a woman who had set up an orphanage in Nairobi and worked tirelessly for the abandoned children of our nation, Ladies and Gentlemen, thought to escape her imprisonment in an abandoned Masai camp and subsequently died, scared, dehydrated and alone. God forbid she was still alive when attacked by wild animals and suffered a terrifying and horrifying death.' Kamani paused then, for effect, and looked around at the people gathered in the courthouse. *'The man who committed this, by his culpability, and other heinous crimes for which he has been charged, is sitting in this courtroom behind me. He committed these crimes to solve a grievance, to get even; a prank that went horribly wrong — indeed it did at the reckless cost of a woman's life.'*

I intend to prove, Ladies and Gentlemen, beyond all reasonable doubt, that the accused is guilty of all the charges made against him. These are serious crimes that have had serious consequences. I hope you will ensure that justice is done at the end of this trial because at the end of the day the accused broke the law not once, not twice, but THREE times. He knew what he was doing and be in no doubt that the accused is GUILTY of all the charges he stands accused of. Thank you.'

Almost before Kamani had sat down Ajulu was on his feet, ready, with the defense statement.

'Good morning Ladies and Gentlemen, my name is Jafri Ajulu, defense attorney, and it is my pleasure to represent my client the defendant, Mr Ralph Somerton, in this very important case. You have heard the prosecution explain what he hopes will be proven, but the prosecution did not tell you all the facts. For instance, the fact that the defendant is a man who has no history of previous criminal activity, in fact he is an honourable man, of great integrity, who contributed a great deal to help the economy in our illustrious land of Kenya, and for this he has been much admired. Ralph Somerton has an impressive family history spanning more than a century in Kenya. His fore-fathers who came here, two centuries ago, built up businesses that embraced the employment of people in their local communities, brought wealth to the country through their products and their export value, and helped to establish the wonderful national reserve that we know today as, the Masai Mara. The defendant himself has worked tirelessly throughout his time at Chui Camp, to preserve the conservancy area where the camp is located. He provided excellent viewing facilities, second almost to none in the area, and ensured that his clients were given the best natural experience of the bush they could have ever imagined. With his wife he built up an impeccable reputation throughout the industry, and he employed local people, from the Masai to Kenyan's, based in Nairobi. But, Ladies and

Gentlemen, within one year my client's camp had almost failed and was on the brink of bankruptcy. Why? Because of the greed and power of a consortium that put money and profit before the livelihood of people like Mr. Somerton; a consortium of people who put money into projects like Nyara Camp, but had, most probably, never even visited the place. They did not care that the placing of their camp severly affected the business of my client's and impeded upon the viewing areas that my client had used and enjoyed for more than a decade. My client was a victim of their greed and he was brought to the brink of despair and severe depression. No wonder he was depressed. No wonder he was at his wits end. No wonder his mental condition was in question. This is a fact, Ladies and Gentlemen, despite what the prosecution may say to the contrary.

Ladies and Gentleman the defense will call only one witness, Mr. Anders Snyman, a pilot, who has known the defendant for many, many years and who will testify to the unblemished character of the accused; he will testify that the defendant is a person of honest character and great integrity, and has never acted against the law before in his life. He will also testify to the financial difficulties that my client was facing, which was clearly causing him much anxiety.

We would ask you to keep an open mind and listen to ALL the evidence in your consideration of a verdict of 'not guilty'. Thank you.

In the defendants box, Ralph closed his eyes. The opening statement by his counsel had been strong and moving and he had high hopes for himself.

32

NAIROBI

March

Kamani began his questioning by calling to the stand, the Askari who had been knocked unconscious during the attack on the camp. The Masai guard was clearly uncomfortable about appearing in court. He stood in the dock, a bright figure in his red cloak and coloured bead bracelets, against the dark suited officials and clerks and the magistrate and his assessors.

'You have sworn to tell the truth,' Kamani began.

'Yes.'

'You are employed as an Askari, a guard at Nyara Camp in the Masai Mara?'

'Yes.'

'You were guarding the camp on the evening in question when Mary Stephenson was allegedly abducted from that camp?'

'Yes.'

'Please tell the court your own recollections of what happened that evening?'

'I was patrolling the camp, sometime after midnight, and I noticed that many of the solar lights that usually shine outside the tents, were broken. In fact, every one of them.'

'What did you think about that?'

'I thought at first that it must be an animal, but then I saw that the campfire embers had been doused and stamped out. Usually the fire smoulders all night and I sometimes warm my hands there.'

'What did you do?'

'I was suspicious and I went to alert Silas, the headman. I had a feeling that something bad had happened.'

'What happened next?'

The Masai put his hand to his head. 'On the way, somebody hit me hard on the head and I was knocked out.'

'I'm sorry to hear that. How long were you knocked out for?'

'I don't know exactly, but when I came to I remembered what had happened and I shouted out loud and blew the whistle that I wear around my neck, to try and alert somebody.'

'Did somebody hear you?'

'Oh yes, Silas, the headman, he came running with his torch and I signalled with mine so that he would know where to find me. I told him somebody had attacked me.'

'What did he do?'

'He helped me up and we both went to alert Mr. Sackville. I went to the office tent and Mrs. Sackville came to have a look at my head. A large bump was forming and she put something on to soothe it.'

'And afterwards?'

The Masai shook his head, 'I didn't see anything, but I heard shouting and then some gunshot fire. A little while after that, everyone was taken from their tents to the living area for their own safety. That is all I know about the incident.'

'Thank you, your evidence has been most helpful.'

The magistrate asked Ajulu if he would be cross-examining the witness, but Ajulu declined.

'It was clear to me that the tent canvas had been deliberately slashed…' James Sackville was now in the stand after the morning break, and explaining how they had found the Stephenson's tent on the evening of the abduction.

'Objection, sir, the witness is surmising,' Ajulu objected.

'Sustained.'

Kamani shook his head. 'On the contrary, the witness is basing his reply on the evidence that has been corroborated by the police.'

'Ask the question again, counsel,' the magistrate suggested.

Kamani changed it with undisguised cynicism. 'Mr. Sackville was it usual for you to your client's tents slashed?'

'No.'

'Your staff and other people did not go around wielding pangas and slashing canvas for the fun of it?'

'No, of course not.'

'So, the tent canvas had been slashed, possibly by someone using a panga, but the important point is that it had been deliberately slashed.'

'Was there anything else of interest that you noticed on the night the intruders came to your camp?'

'There were footprints in the mud outside and drag marks that could have been made by a body…'

'Objection,' called Ajulu again. 'Speculation.'

The magistrate pursed his lips. 'Sustained. Please be more specific in your questioning of the witness Mr. Kamani.'

Kamani continued. 'In the police investigation report, it is stated that the solar lighting around the camp had been smashed?'

'Yes, most of the lights had been broken.'

'In your opinion could this have been sabotage?'

'Objection,' called Ajulu, 'the prosecution is putting ideas into the witnesses head.'

'Sustained.'

'What did you make of so many broken lights?'

James shrugged. 'It seemed strange that all of them were broken. It could have been an animal, although because of the position of some of the lighting, I believed that it was unlikely. In the end I came to the conclusion that it had been done deliberately.'

'Objection sir, without proof of what happened there could have been a number of explanations.'

'No sir,' Kamani said, addressing the magistrate, 'the police investigation concluded that because every single light had been broken, it was most likely a deliberate act of vandalism, committed by persons unknown.'

'Overruled. Thank you counsel.'

Kamani turned back to his witness. 'Was there anything else that caught your attention, after the attack?'

'Yes. When we went into the tent occupied by Mr. and Mrs. Stephenson, we found muddy footprints going from the slashed canvas area of the bathroom tent, through to the bed and back again. I thought that was unusual, and so did the police.'

'Anything else, Mr. Sackville?'

'Yes, the gunshots; these were shots were not fired by anyone in the camp. Therefore, we concluded that they had been fired by intruders.'

'Thank you Mr. Sackville, for your detailed account of the events of the night in question.' Kamani leafed through his documents.

'Have you finished your questioning, counsel?' the magistrate enquired.

'No sir, I would like to continue, if I may?'

'You may. What line of questioning will you now be pursuing?'

'I would like to question the witness about an overheard conversation in Langata Cemetery.'

Ralph drew in a quiet breath.

'Very well,' said the magistrate.

'Mr. Sackville, you have testified in your statement to the police that you overheard some incriminating evidence against the defendant in the cemetery at Langata. Is that correct?'

'Yes it is.'

'Can you tell the court why you were there?'

'I followed the defendant to the cemetery.'

'And what happened when you got there?'

'I followed him in and I overheard him talking to an African gentleman.'

Ralph coughed and Kamani glanced over at him.

'Could you identify the African gentleman?' Kamani asked returning to James.

'No sir, I could not.'

'Can you tell the court what it was that you overheard?'

'They had a conversation regarding a job that had not been fulfilled and a package that had gone missing.'

'Objection,' scoffed Ajulu, 'a missing package is not incriminating evidence.'

'Overruled, prosecution please continue.'

'Did you discover exactly what the package was?'

'I heard the African say: *those men want their money now,*' and Mr. Somerton, the defendant replied: *'why should I pay for a job that has not been properly done?'*

'Objection,' said Ajulu, 'this could have been about anything and it has no meaning.'

'On the contrary it means a great deal and I would like to have the opportunity to prove it. All will become clear if I am allowed to finish,' Kamani appealed to the magistrate.

'Granted. Defense Counsel, please allow Mr. Kamani to make his point.'

Ajulu sat down with a scowl.

'What else did you hear?'

James faced the courtroom. 'I overheard the African, to whom the defendant was talking to, distinctly refer to the package as a woman. He said, *'and where were your scruples when you asked for 'the woman' to be taken?'*

The defendant replied: *it was just a ruse to get the bloody camp discredited. A prank that went wrong. For 'the woman' it should have been a harmless little adventure.* You and the other two men are responsible for what happened to her.'

Kamani turned to speak to the courtroom. 'There you have it, ladies and gentlemen, and I quote from that last piece of evidence, *for 'the woman' it should have been a harmless little adventure.* Those two words, **'the woman'**, are crucial to this evidence. I am left in no doubt that **'the woman'** referred to was Mary Stephenson and it was an adventure that ended up costing **'the woman'** her life.'

Ralph shifted in his seat, uncomfortable from the sweat that soaked his body and the last piece of evidence. What a sanctimonious bastard Kamani was.

'Thank you Mr. Sackville for your very concise evidence.' Kamani turned to the magistrate, 'thank you sir, I have no further questions.' He sat down and took a handkerchief to wipe his own face. The soaring temperature in the courthouse was affecting everyone.

'Will you be cross-examining the witness,' the magistrate asked Ajulu.

'Yes, sir, I will.' He turned to James and said: 'Did you see Mrs. Stephenson taken from the camp?'

'No, but...'

'Thank you, 'no' will suffice and by your admission of 'no', I believe you mean that you cannot be sure of what happened to her? That is a statement of fact, I require no answer from you.'

James looked down and Ralph guessed it was to hide his irritation. He smiled - Ajulu was doing well.

'You said that you and your staff found footprints at the victim's tent outside the bathroom area?' Ajulu continued, and he looked up at James with a questioning expression.

'Yes.'

'Does any of your staff walk in that area, for any reason, perhaps to check the solar panels or the water recycling systems...?'

'Yes, but...' James began again, but Ajulu interrupted him for the second time.

'Then the footprints you encountered might well have

belonged to any one of those people?'

'It is possible.'

'Then the footprints cannot be taken as a positive identity of intruders,' Ajulu established. 'Therefore your opinion and the flimsy evidence it is based upon is, as I questioned earlier, unreliable. Is it not?

'I don't agree,' James said, 'the prints...' but Ajulu interrupted him yet again.

'I didn't ask if you agreed with me Mr. Sackville, I asked a question that requires a simple yes or no answer.'

'Can you repeat the question please?'

'I asked you whether the footprints outside the tent had been positively identified as those belonging to the intruders?'

'No, but there were footprints inside the tent that had not been made by either the staff or the Stephenson's, so a logical conclusion was drawn not only by me, but also by the police.'

Ajulu raised his eyebrows. 'Have these prints been positively linked to anyone?'

'I concluded that as they did not belong to the staff, or the Stephenson's...'

'But have they been matched to anyone specifically?' Ajulu persisted.

'I don't know the answer to that question but I'm sure you have the police...'

'I can tell you that, in fact, they have not been positively identified or related to any of the suspects, despite your so-called conclusion.' Ajulu looked down at his papers dismissively.

Ralph looked across at James. Frustration was written all

over the man's face. Good.

'Let us move to the alleged conversation you say you heard at Langata Cemetery, between the defendant and an unknown person,' Ajulu announced. 'Did you not, in fact, make the whole thing up, fabricating a story to implicate the defendant?'

James looked at him aghast. 'That's ridiculous. Of course I didn't make it up and I am not in the habit of lying.'

'But it is your word against nothing. Nobody else heard this conversation?'

'No, but I managed to record some of it, so surely that confirms that a conversation took place?'

'I'm afraid that recording is not permissible in a court of law as it cannot be satisfactorily proved who the two people conversing are or were. It could have been anyone, anywhere, perhaps a recording made up by you.'

James stared at Ajulu for a moment with a frown on his face, then he replied, 'well it appears that you are correct.'

Now it was Ajulu's turn to frown. 'In what way do you mean that I am correct?'

'You are correct in that it is my word against the rest of the world. However, I repeat that I am not a liar and the conversation and its content did take place. I contacted my wife on the spot and relayed it to her, almost word for word, and she in turn relayed it to the defendant's wife.'

'Quite a game of consequences,' Ajulu said cynically, 'and we know how that game often ends up, with quite a different meaning from the one that was originally intended.'

'I heard what I heard, and this consequence ended up as true at the end as it was at the beginning,' James replied with defiance, 'I will not be doubted, and I have sworn to tell the truth under oath.'

The magistrate turned to James, 'be careful not to overstretch yourself,' he warned.

'I apologise sir, but I am not a liar and everything that I have said, regarding the alleged conversation between the defendant and his accomplice, is the truth.'

Ajulu leafed through his papers again before replying, 'you may not be a liar, Mr. Sackville, but there are many elements of your testimony that are shaky and unreliable because you cannot prove anything that you have told the court. Let me just recap on this. One, you did not see the victim taken from the camp, that is based on assumption. Two, you cannot positively prove the identity of any of the footprints you or the police found outside the victims tent, and three, you have told us a long convoluted story about a so-called conversation, that you overheard in a cemetery. It all sounds a bit far-fetched to me Mr. Sackville.'

A faint murmur of responses passed around the courtroom. Ralph turned his ear to try and catch what they were saying.

'Everything I have said has been corroborated by the police investigation. That is why we are here today,' said James firmly, 'and, at the end of the day, a woman lost her life because of it.'

'You are an emotional man, Mr. Sackville, but you are without substance in your arguments. No further questions,' Ajulu concluded and ended his cross-examination.

Kamani jumped up and addressed the magistrate. 'With your permission, sir, I should like to question my witness again, to re-establish his good name.'

The magistrate sighed, 'as you will, but please make sure

you are quick.'

Ralph guessed the magistrate wanted his lunch.

'My learned counsel,' Kamani said, of Ajulu, 'seems determined to raise doubt about the case for abduction of the victim, Mary Stephenson, despite the fact that my client has given information that ties in with the police investigation and for which the defendant is here today standing trial.' He turned to James, 'Mr. Sackville, I ask you again, can you please confirm your reasons for concluding that an abduction had taken place?'

James cleared his throat. 'One, we could find no other reason for the fact that the solar lights all over the camp had been smashed; two, we found, again for no logical reason, that the tent canvas had been slashed; three, not only were there muddy footprints outside the tent but they were also inside it, leading from the bathroom area to the bed on the tent on the victims side and back. It was confirmed that none of these belonged to either the staff, the victim or her husband, and it was concluded by ourselves and the police, that in all probability they belonged to unidentified persons, and four, tyre tracks were found on the perimeter of our camp in the bush.'

'Thank you, Mr. Sackville, and now can I just reiterate a couple of facts about the alleged overheard conversation in Langata cemetery, which you say, quite rightly because you were there, took place between the defendant and an unknown African gentleman. Can you confirm, under the oath that you made here today, that the conversation that you told the court you heard was not only the truth but was, word for word, the same conversation that was in the statement you gave to the police?'

'Yes, I can confirm that is the truth,' James agreed in a strong and unwavering voice.

Kamani turned to the magistrate's bench. 'It is a known fact that liars have difficulty in maintaining a consistency in their so-called truth and testimonies but my client, on the contrary, has not wavered at all no matter how many times he has been asked to repeat his testimony. It is my own unwavering belief that my client is telling the court the absolute truth.'

He turned back to face James. 'Is that correct, Mr. Sackville?'

'Yes, it is.'

'Thank you Mr. Sackville,' said Kamani, 'for reiterating those points and your integrity to the court; your evidence has been most helpful. No further questions, sir.

33

NAIROBI

March

Day after day they returned to the courthouse, as the trial lingered on like an unwelcome guest.

Tessa was dreading her own call to the stand. She would be giving evidence against her husband and that was going to be anything but easy, even though in her heart she already believed he was guilty.

Finally, the call came for her.

'Good morning Mrs. Somerton,' Kamani greeted her with a reassuring smile. 'I'd like to begin with your account of what you knew about the attack on Nyara Camp, and where you were at the time?'

Tessa clutched the edge of the stand to steady herself. 'Ralph, my husband, woke me around six am on the morning of the sixth of June, last year, to tell me there had been a distress call from Nyara.'

'By *'Ralph my husband'* you mean, and are referring to, the defendant?'

'Yes.'

'And what was the call about?'

'He told me that Nyara Camp had been attacked in the early hours and that a woman, a client, was missing.'

'Mrs Somerton, can you please tell the court how you reacted when you heard the news of the attack and the woman's disappearance?'

'I was shocked of course. It was a dreadful thing to happen.'

'And your husband? What was his reaction?'

His reaction? 'He told me that he thought they must have appalling security and then he said, *'it'll take a lot for Nyara to recover from this once word gets out.'*

'How did you react to that?'

She shrugged. 'We knew nothing about their security and, as for making assumptions about their future, it seemed so unnecessary in light of the appalling situation.'

'Objection, this has no significance.'

'I agree,' said the magistrate. 'Objection sustained – can you please get to the point counsel?'

'Yes sir,' Kamani said. He turned back to Tessa. 'What did you do after you heard about the attack?'

'My husband and I agreed to call Nyara back and offer our help and Ralph wanted to participate in the search for the missing woman.' Sweat was trickling down her back and beading on her face from the stifling heat in the courthouse. There was supposed to be air-conditioning, but it never seemed to be working. She was feeling quite uncomfortable.

Kamani turned a page of his document. 'You say your husband offered to help in the search for the missing woman?'

'Yes, he seemed quite confident that he would find her. I said that she could have been taken anywhere – even across the border, but he seemed to think she was still in the Mara somewhere.'

'Did he say why?'

'No, but…'

Ajulu stood up. 'Objection, nobody could be certain of anything at that time surrounding the whereabouts of the victim. Not even the police knew.'

'Sustained. The defence is right.'

'I agree,' said Kamani, 'but the point is that the defendant seemed more sure than anyone else, at that point, that the victim was still in the Mara.'

'All right Counsel, continue.'

'Thank you, Mrs Somerton, you are doing very well,' Kamani assured her whilst he turned a few more pages of the thick pile of documents on the desk in front of him. 'You said in your testimony that you went to Nyara that very day.'

'Yes, both of us went, late morning, when our guests were out with their guides. We spoke to Alexia when we arrived and then Ralph spent an hour or so driving around looking for her. After he returned we drove back to Chui.'

'Did the defendant, your husband, go to Nyara to search for the woman again?'

'Yes. Ralph went up to Nairobi for a few days and on his return he went straight back out to look for her.'

'What did you think of this?'

'Well I thought it was vigilant of him, but also a bit strange.'

'Why so, Mrs. Somerton?'

'Nobody had heard from whoever had abducted her and there was no clue whatsoever as to where she might be. The

Mara is vast. It was like looking for a needle in a haystack.'

'Objection. There is nothing strange about someone wanting to search for a missing person.'

'Sustained.'

'I'd like to ask the witness something of her history with the defendant, with your agreement sir,' Kamani said to the magistrate.

'Allowed. Let me find this.' The magistrate leafed through his own set of documents, then waved Kamani permission to continue.

'How long have you been married to the accused, Mrs. Somerton?'

'Thirteen years,' she replied. God was it really that long? Where had the time gone?

'Where did you spend those thirteen years?'

'In Kenya,' she replied. 'In Chui Camp in the Masai Mara.'

'How much time would you say you generally spent at Chui camp?'

'Apart from the rainy season closures, just about all the time,' she replied.

'And you are both present, continually, during that time?'

Tessa shook her head. 'No. In recent times Ralph has spent a lot of time in Nairobi, perhaps a week every month and longer in more recent times.'

'And he left you to run the camp on your own?'

'Yes, with the help of our two head guides.'

'Were you aware of what your husband was doing, in Nairobi, when you were at the camp alone?'

'Only that he told me he was drumming up business for us.'

'Objection, Sir, I fail to see where this questioning is leading,' Ajulu protested to the magistrate.

'Counsel, is this a worthy path you are taking?' the magistrate questioned Kamani.

'Yes, sir, if I may continue.'

'All right, continue for the moment.'

Kamani turned again to Tessa. 'Did he tell you what he was doing in Nairobi?'

'My husband told me he was trying to save our camp, but I have it on good authority that although he made token efforts to speak to the tour operators he was rude and challenging to them. He spent more time bad-mouthing Nyara Camp than doing something about Chui…'

'Objection,' cried Ajulu, 'this is not evidence, this is slander!'

There was a titter from someone in the courtroom.

'Silence,' the magistrate commanded. 'Objection sustained; you are in danger, counsel, of going too far,' he warned Kamani.

Kamani paused and Tessa gathered he was trying to find a different way to word his questions about Ralph's feelings about Nyara Camp.

'In your opinion, did it in any way appear to you that your husband might have a grudge against Nyara Camp?'

'Yes.'

'Objection,' Ajulu shouted. 'Merely hearsay and when are we going to get to the end of this?

'Overruled.'

Tessa watched Ajulu sit back on his chair, tight-lipped.

'Can you give me any idea why?'

Tessa shrugged. 'Yes, he kept saying how he resented

Nyara Camp being there, how it had been stealing our clients. He was obsessed with it, in my opinion.'

'Objection,' said Ajulu. 'As the witness just said opinion, not fact.'

'Overruled,' the magistrate said. 'There is some interest here that I should like to hear a bit more about.'

Ajulu shook his head and sat down and Tessa guessed he felt the magistrate was being biased.

'Mrs Somerton, can you please tell the court why you have given evidence against your husband?'

'It is because I felt I had enough evidence to indicate that he had been involved in the plot against Nyara Camp.'

'Can you be more specific about the evidence?'

'I remember Ralph telling me that I shouldn't worry about Chui anymore. He said he had sorted it.'

'Sorted what?'

'That's what I asked my husband…the defendant.'

'Did he explain?'

'No, he just repeated that the problem with our camp was sorted.'

'Oh please, objection, this can hardly be construed as evidence,' Ajulu sighed.

'Mmm, I agree, objection sustained,' said the magistrate.

'Can you tell us more?' Kamani urged her. He didn't want to lose the attention he knew he had gained.

'My husband withheld the fact that he had met George Stephenson before the incident and, not once during our conversations about the attack and the victim and Mr. Stephenson, did he make any reference to it.'

'Objection, he may have forgotten,' Ajulu said gesturing with his hands.

'Sustained, Counsel. It is a possibility.'

'Could he have forgotten, Mrs. Somerton?' Kamani asked, using the objection.

Tessa knew beyond any doubt that he hadn't. 'The name appeared in the contacts folder on his telephone and several recent telephone calls, before anything had come to light about the missing victim. I thought that was suspicious.'

'Objection, this is all very loose circumstantial evidence that cannot be accepted as anything representing proof,' Ajulu pleaded with the magistrate.

The magistrate hesitated for a moment before replying. 'Sustained, counsel.' Then he turned to Kamani. 'Is there anything more that you know of, besides the name in the defendant's phone contact list to link him to Mr. Stephenson?'

Tessa knew that if George Stephenson was inside the courtroom he would be on his feet by now, shouting out that it was true.

Kamani turned to her. 'Is there, Mrs Somerton?'

'Not that I know of.' It would all come out with George anyway.

'Did your husband, the defendant, at any time during discussions you may have had together, say anything to link him to the attack at Nyara Camp.'

Tessa closed her eyes. She had to stretch her memory a long way back and sift through a lot of conversations, arguments, and angst.

'Take your time, Mrs. Somerton, I appreciate the enormity of the question I have asked you.'

Tessa's eyes flew open. 'Yes,' she said, and she heard the whole court draw in its breath, 'that is, I overheard my husband talking to somebody on the telephone about a package of his that had gone missing, and then he mentioned the fact that 'she' had better be found.'

'Did you think that the 'she' referred to was connected to the package?'

'Objection, counsel is deliberately leading the witness.'

The magistrate paused before saying, 'overruled. I'd like to hear the witnesses response.'

Ajulu sat down again with his lips drawn into an angry line.

'Yes, I did.'

'How did that make you feel?' Kamani ploughed on.

'My blood ran cold. I was sure, then, that my husband was involved. There were too many coincidences and it also explained his disappearances, his moods and his almost panic when I told him that the victim had been found dead. I had a feeling he was withholding something important from me.'

'Objection,' said Ajulu, 'this is just speculation, not real factual proof.'

'Objection sustained. I agree with the defence. It is all very well having feelings about such things, but feelings are not acceptable as direct evidence, although such things may sometimes be classed as circumstantial.'

'Yes sir,' Kamani acknowledged the reprimand. 'May I ask one more question of the witness?'

'Yes you may.'

'Mrs Somerton, was there any point at which you felt quite certain that the defendant was involved in the attack on Nyara Camp, and the abduction of Mary Stephenson?'

'Yes.'

'And what was this point in time?'

'When I overheard him refer to the package as a 'she'.'

'When you heard the package referred to as a 'she', Kamani repeated, and he waited a moment to let the words sink in before saying, 'thank you, Mrs. Somerton for your important testimony.'

The magistrate turned to Ajulu. 'You have your chance now counsel? I presume you will be cross-examining the witness?'

Ajulu approached the bench. 'Yes, thank you sir, indeed I will.'

Ajulu faced Tessa and she tried not to look concerned even though she was dreading the cross-examination. 'Mrs. Somerton, you have indicated to my learned counsel for the prosecution that things were not going so well at Chui?'

'It depends how you define well,' she replied.

'Well, let us say occupancy, repeat business etc.'

'My husband…' she began but he interrupted her.

'I'm not asking your husband, Mrs Somerton, I am asking you.'

Tessa shrugged. 'Occupancy was not as good as it should be. As for repeat business, I'm not sure camps have that much repeat business. For many clients a safari is a once in a lifetime trip.'

'But generally your occupancy rates were down?'

'Yes.'

'You were aware Mrs Somerton, that Chui Camp was losing money?'

'Yes, of course I was, which is why I was trying to do something about it.'

'And what do you think your husband was doing?'

Tessa glared at him. 'My husband was up in Nairobi spending our money on his leisure activities,' she snapped.

'A harsh reply Mrs Somerton, and I put it to you that, on the contrary, your husband was in Nairobi trying to keep your business going whilst you were doing your best to persuade him to pour money you did not have into it.'

Tessa gave a half laugh. 'He may have told you that, but the truth of it is this. If my husband had listened to the tour operators who were telling him he had to do something about it, way back, we wouldn't be in the mess we are now!' She was burning with indignation at the way in which Ajulu was trying to turn the tables on her.

'How much business do you think the camp was losing?' Ajulu asked.

Tessa pursed her lips, 'I don't know, perhaps up to two thirds during slacker times.'

'But you're not sure?'

'Well…'

'I put it to you Mrs Somerton,' Ajulu interrupted, 'that you have no idea about the camps financial position and difficulties because you did not bother to involve yourself in them.'

'That's simply not true,' she responded, indignant. 'I was running the camp single-handedly and keeping the books whilst my husband was up in Nairobi, allegedly meeting with people who were going to send us clients.'

'And I put it to you that your husband was up in Nairobi, trying to turn your fortunes around,' Ajulu countered.

'I wish that was true.'

'I put it to you, Mrs Somerton, that your husband had endured extreme stress and anxiety about his business failures and the thought that he might lose the camp, which was dear to his heart, owing to a long-standing family history. A prospect of which you seem less than sympathetic or understanding of.'

Tessa bristled. How dare he suggest it didn't mean anything to her after all the dedication and effort she had put into it. But she must not show her indignation at Ajulu's suggestions. 'It didn't appear that way to me,' she said evenly, 'and in fact I did understand, more than my husband appeared to accept. The difference was that I couldn't afford to dwell on it, because I was in the camp trying to salvage what I could of the mess we were in.' She was determined to press home that point.

'Have it your own way, Mrs. Somerton, but I wonder if you really knew what your husband was thinking or doing, at all.'

Twist it whatever way you like, Tessa thought, I'm not giving you an inch. 'I saw enough of him to know that he was determined to blame everyone except himself for OUR difficulties.'

'You seem to have very little sympathy with your husband and his situation, but dwell a lot on your own,' Ajulu challenged and before she could respond he had stepped in with: 'no further questions,' and the magistrate had called an afternoon recess.

'What an infuriating man,' she blurted out to Kamani, during the break.

Kamani smiled and shrugged, 'we are lawyers, what can I say. It is his job to be infuriating, butt is our job not to be ruffled by him.'

'Did I give the right answers?'

'You did very well,' Kamani assured her. 'You did not let him convince you that your husband was unstable which was where he was trying to lead you. He also neatly avoided cross-examining the last part of our discussion. He knew it could lead him into deep water. It is also why I chose not to re-examine you. Do you understand?'

'Yes I do. It was better to leave our part as it very much implicated Ralph, but his plan to show me up as a wife who did not understand or sympathise with her poor husband, who was supposedly fighting for his business and reputation, was very annoying.'

'I appreciate that, but you stood your ground well.'

'I hope I did enough to convince the assessors.'

'Time will tell.'

34

NAIROBI

March

Back in the courtroom half an hour later it was Esme's turn to be questioned. At least, now that she had given her evidence, Tessa could sit in on the rest of the trial. Tessa could see Esme's hands shaking as she took the oath. She tried to catch her eye to give her a positive smile, but Esme was too frightened to look anywhere but down at her hands.

'Can you tell the court how you know Mr. and Mrs. Somerton?' Kamani asked her.

'I was a maid at their house in Karen. I still work for Mrs Somerton.'

'Do you like them?'

'Yes, at least I like Mrs Somerton.'

'Not Mr. Somerton?'

'Not so much,' she mumbled.

'Please speak up Miss Adongo so that we can hear what you are saying,' the magistrate commanded.

'So you were not so fond of Mr. Somerton,' Kamani said, 'can you tell us why?'

'I never knew if he would be in a good mood or bad. He was often angry about something and then he would shout at me.'

Good for you, Tessa thought, you tell him girl.

'How often did you see him at the house?'

'He came to Nairobi a lot, more than Mrs. Somerton.'

'And Mrs. Somerton was away at the safari camp when he came back?'

'Objection, this is irrelevant information,' Ajulu interrupted.

'Sustained. I agree, can you move on please counsel.'

Kamani consulted his documents then he asked, 'where do you live Miss Adongo?'

'I live in Kibera.'

'Do you live alone?'

'No, I live with my brother, that is until he was arrested.'

'And what is your brother's name?'

'Yahzid Adongo.'

'Tell me a bit about him, for instance is he your older brother, or younger. What does he do…?'

'Yahzid is my older brother and my only sibling. He is a good boy but life has been hard for him.'

'In what way?'

'Our parents died, one after the other and then the Aunt who had taken us in. Yahzid wanted to look after me so he stopped going to school. He said I was smarter than he was and that I could go to university. He tried to get work but it was not possible so he searched the rubbish tips like some of the other boys, looking for things to sell. Then he met some bad people.'

'In Kibera?'

'Yes.'

'Why are they bad?'

'They drink the changa'a brew and then they don't know what they are doing.'

'Did your brother partake of this changaa?'

'Yes, he said it was to help him forget what a failure he was, but he is not a bad boy.'

'Were you aware that your brother and Mr. Somerton had become acquainted after Mr. Somerton paid him a visit in Kibera?'

'Yes. Yahzid told me Mr Somerton was trying to get him a job.'

'Did he tell you what kind of job it was?'

'Not really, but he said it was something that would pay enough money to help with my university dreams.'

'What did you think about that?'

'I didn't believe him. I thought it was the changa'a talking.'

'Do you think Mr Somerton bullied your brother …'

'Objection your honour,' Ajulu said.

'Sustained. Please do not put ideas into the witnesses head,' the Magistrate reprimanded.

'Very well,' said Kamani. He paused gathering his thoughts before he resumed the questioning of Esme. 'Miss Adongo, after Mr. Somerton was arrested you were found, were you not, in a lock up owned by Mr Somerton and located near Wilson Airport?'

'Yes.'

'Did you go voluntarily to this place?'

'No,' she replied in a strong voice. 'Mr Somerton came to the hut where I live in Kibera and told me to go with him because Yahzid had been involved in an accident and was in hospital. I was very frightened for my brother. On the way Mr. Somerton gave me a bottle of water to drink and after drinking some of it I don't remember anything else until I woke up in that lock-up at the airport. He lied to me about my brother just to get me to go with him.'

'Objection. That is supposition.'

'It is not supposition, sir,' Kamani addressed the magistrate, 'it is fact.'

'Overruled.'

'How long were you kept at the lock-up?'

'I am not sure, perhaps a few days?'

Kamani continued. 'Did Mr. Someton speak to you during that time?'

'Yes, he told me he was protecting me.'

'Did he tell you what he was protecting you from?'

'No.'

'And when he left you there alone, did he lock you in?'

'Yes.'

'So you could not leave of your own accord?'

'No I could not.'

'How did that make you feel, Miss Adongo?'

'Like a captive,' she replied.

'Thank you, Miss Adongo, I have no further questions for you.'

Esme was weary from the questioning and it was with a feeling of dread that she heard Ajulu say he wished to cross-examine her.

'Miss Adongo why did you not believe the defendant when he said he was protecting you?' Ajulu began.

'Because he had already lied to me about my brother to

lure me to that place.'

'If Mr. Somerton had asked you to go with him for your protection, would you have done so?'

'I don't know.'

'You don't know or you are not sure, so in fact you might have?'

'I suppose so.'

'Perhaps the defendant also knew that so he told you a lie for your protection. You knew that your brother kept the company of bad men so it could indeed have been the truth that he was protecting you.'

'I..I...'

'Could he have been telling the truth?' Ajulu persisted.

'I don't know.'

'That is right, you don't know so why do you insist that Mr. Somerton was holding you against your will?'

'Because he drugged me to keep me there.'

'What if it was an act of kindness?'

'I don't understand.'

'Perhaps he had to do something to stop you from leaving for your own good?'

'He drugged me,' she said with some conviction.

'So you keep saying, Miss Adongo but unfortunately there is no medical evidence to confirm this, so what you are suggesting is something that cannot be proved.'

'I spent most of the time that he held me, asleep. It was not because I was tired,' she replied in defiance.

In the courtroom auditorium, where Tessa had taken a seat since her own ordeal was over, she grimaced. She should have taken Esme straight to the police after all. It was her fault there were not any tests done which would have proved the drugging.

'All right Miss Adongo, let us turn to your brother Yahzid who is held in custody pending his sentencing for his part in the plot that ended with the death of a woman.' Ajulu paused before asking, 'can you tell us if your brother has ever been in trouble with the police before?'

It was a surprise question and Esme hesitated to answer.

Kamani knew it was designed to throw the strength of the truth of her testimony into dispute.

'Please answer the question. Yes or no.'

'Yes,' she said in a quiet voice.

'And what was his crime, and speak up so we can all hear you please?'

Esme lifted her head and looked out across the courtroom. 'Stealing, but he was just a young boy and we had lost our parents…'

'I didn't ask for a life history,' Ajulu interrupted. 'So your brother is known to the police as a criminal whereas my client, Mr. Somerton has no criminal record?'

'No,' she admonished, 'Yahzid was not a criminal he was just a hungry boy and looking out for me, his sister.'

'Well however you wish to entitle it, we have established that your brother has a previous record. The defendant does not. Can we assume that his testimony is reliable under those circumstances?"

'It was only one small crime which he committed because he was desperate, and my brother would not tell lies.'

'But he has admitted his guilt.'

'Yes, but that does not mean he is a li…'

'Thank you Miss Adongo, no further questions.' Ajulu's tactic had been to set about tarnishing the image of a prosecution witness. It was a cheap trick. Kamani had to try and salvage what he could.

'May I question the witness again,' he asked the magistrate who agreed.

'Miss Adongo, have you yourself ever been in trouble with the law?'

'No.'

'You are an honest young woman who suffered an abduction against your will?'

'Yes,' and her voice pleaded someone to believe her.

'Can you tell the court once more what happened on the day of your abduction?'

'Mr. Somerton came to my school and told me that Yahzid had been involved in an accident and was at the hospital. He said he was going to take me there to see him.'

'Had your brother been involved in an accident?'

'No.'

'Did Mr. Somerton take you to the hospital and discover it was a mistake?'

'No.'

'Do you believe that Mr. Somerton lied to you?'

'Yes.'

'Would you have gone with him if you had known he was lying?'

'No.'

'Thank you, Miss Adongo, no further questions.'

35

NAIROBI

March

In the days and weeks leading up to the trial George had been a lost soul. He wandered around the house, looking at pictures of Mary and the things that had belonged to her, and he wept when he thought about the terrible death she had suffered. It was almost more than a man could bear. He had thought about taking his own life but that was during the dark hours of night and, in the early morning light, he thought better of it. He needed to be alive to see justice done. He became a recluse, barely venturing out of the house or taking calls. Friends persevered for a while but then their attentions began to drop off. George listened to the messages people had left and although he appreciated their concern and support, he just couldn't bring himself to call them back. He had no energy for conversation and no desire to resume his life and enjoy himself and, more often than not, he was finding his way to the bottom of a bottle. It helped to obliterate the grief and guilt that he was feeling for Mary. George knew the anger and bitterness he felt towards

Ralph Somerton was combined with the guilt that lay at the bottom of his own heart, for putting Mary in such a vulnerable position.

How true it is, he mused, that you don't know what you have until its gone. Quiet and unassuming though she might have been, without her around he realized how daily he had come to heed her considered counsel over the issues in his life. What a rock she had been yet she had asked for so little in return. Her worries and concerns about the running of the orphanage she had hardly bothered him with. Not only had he lost a wonderful woman but so had the orphanage and the forgotten and abandoned children of Nairobi.

Now, in an uninspiring room at the courthouse, George waited for his turn to take the stand. It had seemed like an eternity until the start of the trial and he had suffered every day with depression and anxiety before, and since, its inauguration. He had long given up on all aspects of a social life and he spent most of his days alone in the house, from which his house staff had long since been dismissed, brooding on all that had happened. He refused all offers of help and comfort, preferring to deal with the tragedy in his own way. He had come to despise himself – the responsibility of Mary's death, he believed, lay not only at Somerton's door but also his own. He had neglected his wife and not realised the agonizing worry she had been going through, not only because of the collapse of their world in Nairobi, but also because of the cancer she had kept from him. The few weeks of euphoria just before the trip to Nyara, when it looked as though his business was at last going to get back on track, had vanished. He simply hadn't the heart for it. No Mary, no future. All George wanted now was justice for her and he would do everything in his power to bring down the man who had taken Mary's life and ruined his own. It was his mission to make sure that Mary received the justice she deserved.

He had heard that the defence counsel had referred to Ralph Somerton as: *a man of great integrity!* Is that what Ajulu thought of the man who had murdered his wife? It was shameful. George hoped with all his heart that Kamani had a good enough case to win – it simply must not be that Ralph Somerton could walk away, a free man. That could never, ever happen.

At last Kamani's clerk came for him and, with a deep breath and a hardened heart, he stepped up for questioning.

'Please tell me your relationship to the deceased, Mary Stephenson, and I apologise if this is painful for you,' Kamani began.

George cleared his throat, 'Mary Stephenson was my dear wife.'

'How long had you been married?'

'Almost thirty-five years.'

'So you knew your wife very well,' Kamani confirmed.

'Of course,' said George, 'as well as I know myself.'

'Can you tell the court in your own words what you and your wife were doing on the night in question at Nyara Camp in the Masai Mara.' Kamani went straight to the heart of the questioning.

'My wife and I had been at the camp for three days on a break. That night was the same as the other nights - we had pre-dinner drinks around the campfire and then dinner with the rest of the clients in the dining tent from about 8.00pm onwards. Mary went to bed a little earlier than I did, and I followed her sometime after that.'

'Approximately what time do you think that your wife went to bed?'

'About fifteen minutes past eleven.'

'And how long did you stay after your wife went to bed?'

'I would guess about an hour.'

'Did you speak to your wife when you returned?'

'No. She was asleep.'

'Was that the last time you saw your wife, Mr. Stephenson?'

George gulped, 'yes,' he said.

'Can you tell me what happened next, Mr Stephenson?'

'I don't know what time it was but something woke me up, but it was dark apart from the occasional flash of torchlight, outside.'

'What woke you up, do you think?'

George frowned. 'I thought I heard gunshot. Then I heard shouting and someone was crying. I thought it was Mary and I called out to her, but there was no answer.'

'You didn't see her or speak to her?'

'No. She wasn't there. I got out of bed with my torch and went into the bathroom tent to see if she was in there. It was then that I saw the canvas was slashed from top to bottom.' He paused to gather his emotions. It was difficult to speak about the events of that dreadful night.

'Take your time, Mr. Stephenson,' said Kamani, 'I appreciate how hard this must be for you.' He paused for a moment before continuing with his questions. 'So you had no idea where your wife was at that point in time?'

'No,' George said, shaking his head. 'I was very frightened, wondering what had happened to her and what was going on outside.'

'What happened next?'

'One of the members of staff, Silas, came to my tent and told me that the clients were gathering together in the lounge tent. I asked him what was going on and he told me that the camp appeared to be under attack. I was shocked and alarmed and I explained that my wife was missing.'

'He asked me to stay where I was and he went to fetch James Sackville.'

'What happened then?'

'He came back with James Sackville, and I showed them the slashed canvas in the bathroom area.'

'What was their reaction?'

'They conceded, at that point, that it was possible that Mary might have been taken. James Sackville said the police had been alerted, as well as the rangers and trackers. I wanted someone to go looking for Mary there and then, but I appreciate how difficult that would have been, in the dark.' George remembered his panic and how he had begged them to try and find her.

'Did you leave your tent, at that point, with Mr. Sackville?'

'Yes. He took me to the lounge tent to wait with the others. I was hoping that it was all a terrible mistake and that Mary would turn up.'

'I appreciate what a painful and anxious time it must have been for you Mr. Stephenson. Thank you for establishing what had happened on the night in question.' Kamani turned to the Magistrate. 'Sir, if it pleases you, I would now like to move the questioning from the night of the attack to the witnesses relationship with the accused.'

'Do you have further questions regarding the attack at the camp?' the Magistrate asked.

'Yes I do, but I would like to defer because of the relevance to my further questioning on this matter.'

The magistrate considered. 'Very well, continue your questioning.'

Kamani turned to George. 'I would like to take you back now to the first meeting you had with the defendant, Ralph Somerton. Can you tell the court when and where your first encounter took place?'

George cleared his throat. 'It was an evening last May, at the Norfolk hotel bar. We were both there alone and he offered to buy me a drink.' It was almost unbearable having to recall their meeting that night and, knowing what he knew now, George felt quite nauseous.

'Take your time, Mr. Stephenson, we all appreciate how difficult this is for you,' said Kamani.

'Thank you.'

'Was that the first time you had met the accused?'

'Yes.'

'What did you talk about?'

'The failure of our businesses - it seemed we were both there to drown our sorrows.'

'What were Mr. Somerton's sorrows at the time?'

'The failing of his camp business.'

'How did Mr. Somerton seem to you?'

'Well, apart from drunk, he seemed angry and bitter about it,' George recalled.

'Did it seem to you that Mr. Somerton, the defendant, had been drinking a lot?'

'Yes, he was slurring his words.'

'Objection,' said Ajulu. 'That is conjecture and irrelevant. It is not against the law to be a bit tipsy.' There was a trickle of laughter in the courtroom.

'Silence please. Objection is sustained.'

'Did Mr. Somerton tell you why he was angry?' Kamani continued.

'He told me his business had been ruined by another camp taking his clients.'

'Did he tell you to which camp he was referring?'

'Not at that time.'

'Did he say anything else about it?'

'Yes, he said he wouldn't mind finding a way: *'to get it discredited'*.'

'Objection!' Ajulu cried. 'This is just hearsay and cannot be proved.'

Kamani turned to the magistrate. 'On the contrary sir, this is evidence and it appears that counsel is calling my client a liar.'

The magistrate was cross and he demanded the presence of the two Counsels before his bench. 'I will not have verbal fisticuffs in my court,' he ordered. 'Temper your questions and interruptions accordingly.'

After apologising, Kamani went back to George. 'Did the defendant, at any time, in any of your meetings and conversations, refer to the camp he allegedly wished to be discredited, by name?'

'Yes, he told me it was called Nyara.'

Kamani leafed through his sheaf of papers, deliberately stalling to give his client some time to gather himself. He knew how hard it was for clients like Stephenson who had lost someone close to them. They often hadn't the heart to want to give evidence and were often still confused about the events, and however much you primed them for the trial they were still inclined to wander off the focus of the questioning. He wanted to make certain that he got the right responses from George.

'You said in your statement that you met with the defendant again?'

'Yes, but I hadn't planned to.'

'When was this?'

George thought for a moment. 'It was about a week later, on my way to the bank.

Somerton happened to be walking along the street at the same time.'

'And were you pleased to see him?'

'No, I tried to avoid him but he had already seen me.'

'What did he say to you?'

'He asked me where I was going, I told him and he said he had a good feeling about it.'

'What did you think of his remark?'

'I wasn't really paying attention. I wanted to get to the bank and back again as quickly as I could.'

'What happened after that?'

George gave a grim smile. 'It turned out he was right - when I got back to the government building they told me that I was going to be allowed to have some money released. It meant that I would be able to pay creditors as well as have some money to live on. I called Mary to tell her the good news but she wasn't home. On a whim I called Somerton. I don't know why, except that his premonition had been right and at the time I felt I owed it to him. He insisted we had a celebratory drink and I agreed.'

'Where did this next meeting take place?'

'At the Norfolk Hotel again.'

'What did you talk about on this occasion?' Kamani was not about to draw attention to George's lapse of reason.

'I told him how stressed my wife was about the bankruptcy, and how pleased I was to be able to tell her that we had a bit of money coming our way at last.'

'How did he react to that?'

'Somerton sympathised and said he felt the same way about his own wife.'

'What else did you discuss?'

'Out of the blue he suggested that I take Mary on a break, to Nyara Camp, when new season began in June. He said it was one of the best times to see the wildlife.'

'What did you think of the suggestion?'

'I was a bit surprised considering how down on the place he'd been when we last met, but he insisted that Mary deserved a break and a bit of luxury.'

'What was you response?'

'I said that if we were considering a safari break we would be more than happy to go to Chui camp.'

'Did the defendant comment on that?'

'Yes, he told me they were already full for the foreseeable future.'

'What did you do then?'

'I took his advice and went to see a tour operator who managed to make a reservation for us at Nyara.'

'So you are telling me it was Somerton's idea that you should go to Nyara camp?'

'Objection your honour,' Ajulu intervened. '

'What is your objection?' the Magistrate asked.

'The prosecution is putting ideas into the witnesses head.'

'I was merely confirming the witnesses own words your honour,' Kamani protested.

'Perhaps you could re-word the question so you are not telling him what to say?'

'Thank you sir, I will. Mr. Stephenson, what did the defendant say when you said you would be happy to go to Chui Camp?'

'The defendant said that his camp, Chui, was full.'

'And that was why he suggested, Nyara?'

'Yes. He told me that Nyara Camp was a great place to spoil someone.'

'And he was quite specific about it being at that time?'

'Yes, he was.'

'Did you question his reasons for making these suggestions of a break for you and your wife?'

'No. It seemed reasonable at the time. I just thought he had my best interests in mind.' George closed his eyes. How wrong he had been.

'Which, of course, he did not,' Kamani emphasised, in fact he had a very different interest in mind.'

'Objection!' Ajulu raised, 'counsel is making libellous assumptions.'

'Sustained, although I think you are over zealous in your comment.'

Kamani raised his hands. 'I am merely trying to make the point that it was the defendant's suggestion that my client and his wife should go to Nyara Camp.'

'Yes, yes, continue counsel,' the magistrate ordered.

'Mr. Stephenson, you said that the defendant remarked

that Chui camp was full?'

'Yes, he did.'

'In fact I have evidence to the contrary, your honour. Records show, and I have placed a document in your papers of an actual record of Chui Camp attendance, that Chui Camp was not full. It appears that the defendant was mistaken, or he was lying.'

The magistrate leafed through his papers and found the document. 'Yes, I see. Thank you counsel, we shall bear the evidence in mind.'

'Thank you Mr Stephenson, no further questions.'

'I presume you would like to cross-examine the witness?' the Magistrate said to Ajulu.

'Yes, sir, I would.'

Ajulu strolled across to the stand and stared at George for several seconds.

George held his stare even though inside he was dreading Ajulu's onslaught, as that was what he imagined his cross-examination would be.

'Good afternoon Mr Stephenson, I have just a few questions and I hope your answers will clear my mind of some discrepancies in your testimony.'

George frowned but he caught sight of Kamani shaking his head. Don't fall for it he was indicating.

'You said that you were both drinking when you met Ralph Somerton?'

'Yes.' George said – he couldn't deny it.

'Are you in the habit of drinking, for instance do you drink every day?'

George swallowed. 'Not every day, no.'

'Objection,' said the prosecution. 'I fail to see what this

has to do with the cross-examination.'

'I'm inclined to agree with you. What are you trying to establish?' the Magistrate demanded.

'What I am trying to establish, sir, is whether the witnesses account is reliable. If he was also under the influence of alcohol to the extent that it appears, then he may not be recalling the conversation with my client accurately.'

'Continue.'

'How much did you drink when you met with the defendant?' Ajulu asked again.

George 'I had two or three whiskies with him, on the first occasion, and a small beer on the second.'

'So when you had your conversations with the defendant it was under the influence of a considerable amount of alcohol?'

George half laughed. 'I don't think I was drinking excessively at all.'

'Not enough to make you relaxed and open to opportunities?'

'No, I don't know. I don't think so.'

'But you readily agreed to my client's suggestion that you take your wife on a holiday to a safari camp?'

'I agreed to his suggestion because I thought it was a good idea. I had no...'

'Thank you Mr. Stephenson,' Ajulu interrupted, 'you have answered my question. Here is the next one. I ask again, why did you agree to go to Nyara?'

'Because it simply seemed a good idea to give my dear wife a treat after all she had been through.' Why was Ajulu so fixated on the reason they had taken the break?

'So you agreed with Mr. Somerton's suggestion?'

'Yes.' George sighed.

Ajulu paused, thinking with great emphasis before he said, 'so let me get this right - you were in financial difficulties but you agreed to go to Nyara Camp, one of the most expensive camps – why, Mr. Stephenson?'

George turned up his hands in exasperation. 'I was desperate to do something positive for Mary, to make her feel a bit happier.' Instead he had led her to her death.

'Or perhaps you had other reasons for doing so?' Ajulu continued ignoring George's discomfort and his remark about Somerton.

George frowned, 'what other reasons?'

'Well, for instance,' Ajulu said throwing in a hand grenade of a suggestion, 'might you have been in collaboration with the defendant over your wife's kidnapping? Might there have been a plan to make some money together out of it?'

George's jaw dropped and he stared at Ajulu in horror. It was the police questioning all over again.

'Objection!' Kamani cried. 'The question is preposterous.'

'Overruled,' said the magistrate, and George realised he was intrigued.

'Dear God, I cannot believe you would ask me such a thing,' George said shaking his head in disbelief. 'I already told the police that I had absolutely nothing to do with it, apart from being unwittingly dragged in to Somerton's dreadful plan.'

'Well now I am asking you, and I would appreciate a yes or a no, were you or were you not, involved in your wife's kidnapping, however 'preposterous' it may seem?' Ajulu said, and he had to shout over the excited chatter in the courtroom.

'Order,' the Magistrate shouted. 'I insist on silence.' He banged his gavel and the chatter petered out.

'Objection, your honour,' Kamani said again, but the Magistrate overruled.

'Were you or were you not involved in the plan to kidnap your wife?' Ajulu repeated, and the whole room held their breath.

'No. Absolutely not,' George said firmly and with conviction. 'It is an abominable question to ask. I loved and cared for my wife and I would never,' he said, putting great emphasis on the word 'never', 'do anything to bring harm upon her.'

'Yet, based on your evidence and allegations, you went along with the whim of a man you hardly knew nor trusted and waltzed your wife into the heart of a trap?'

'Yes, but I didn't ...'

'Thank you, Mr. Stephenson; no further question.' Ajulu said and he sat down with a rueful smile.

'We'll take a recess,' the magistrate announced.

'With respect, your honour, I would like to re-examine my witness before we go to recess?' Kamani said.

George breathed a low sigh of relief. He knew that Kamani would be anxious that Ajulu's barbed examination should not be allowed to hang over them during a recess.

The magistrate considered. 'Will it take long?'

'No sir, not long at all.'

'Very well, go ahead, but if it appears to be protracted I will intervene.'

'Thank you sir, but that will not be necessary.' Kamani turned to George and said, 'I have just a couple of questions Mr Stephenson. You said that the break at Nyara camp was a treat for your wife?'

'Yes it was.'

'And why was it so important to treat her?'

'I wanted to try and make up for the mess I'd made of everything with my business, and see her smile again.'

'It meant a great deal to you, to see your wife happy?'

'Absolutely.'

'You had no ulterior motive?'

'None whatsoever,' George said shaking his head to reiterate his reply.

'So, when Ralph Somerton made the suggestion to you, about taking your wife to Nyara Camp, you were thinking only of her happiness?'

'Completely.'

'And you had no inkling or idea that that you were a pawn in his dreadful plot?'

George answered with passion. 'I had absolutely no idea. If I had done I would never have gone along with it. I stupidly fell for his trick and now I can never forgive myself for it.' His voice broke again.

'And how do you feel now, Mr. Stephenson?'

'I've lost my darling wife, the one thing that mattered in my life, because of that decision and quite frankly life does not seem worth living.'

Kamani nodded sympathetically. 'Thank you for your bravery on the stand, Mr Stephenson,' said Kamani, 'no further questions.'

Kamani hurried to speak to George as they emerged from the courtroom. 'I'm sorry you had to endure that cross-examination,' he said.

'How could the man suggest such a thing?' George said,

shattered by the questioning. He was slumped on a bench in a hallway jam packed with people who stared at him as they passed by.

'It's his job to question everything, but I'm surprised he went that far because of what it might have laid his own client bare to.' Kamani looked at the throng of people around them. 'Let's go somewhere quieter.' He stood up and steered George down the hallway and into a small windowless room. Kamani put on the light and shut the door. 'Sorry it's a bit stuffy.'

George shrugged. 'It's better than being on show like that.'

There was a knock at the door. Kamani wanted to ignore it but he called out 'who is it?' anyway, incase it was his clerk.

'Mr. Rama, with coffee.'

Kamani stood up and opened the door and George saw that it was indeed the courthouse cleaner, with two paper cups of coffee in his hand.

'Thank you, Mr. Rama,' Kamani said taking the cups the cleaner handed to him, 'that was thoughtful of you.'

'Very kind,' George added. It wasn't the first time the cleaner had showed him some kindness. Mr. Rama had found him a chair a few days ago and brought him some water. He had passed the time away with Mr. Rama, who had been understanding and sympathetic.

'Anything I can do for you sir, please you will ask me,' Mr Rama insisted. 'I have been here long enough and seen enough of the innocent and the guilty passing through to understand your need for justice for your poor wife.

Taking the coffee had helped to further show him as a friend to the poor man, someone George could rely on. It was not the last time they would speak with each other.

36

NAIROBI

September

Sophie poured two large glasses of wine, and she and Tessa took them out onto the balcony. A welcome breeze shook the tree canopy around them breaking through the thick humidity that clung to the city like a wet blanket. As night descended, lights peppered the city below.

Tessa leaned back in her chair with her eyes closed. 'So much artificial light,' she said, 'it's dazzling after the black of the bush.' How she longed to be there now, far away from Nairobi and its sticky air and harsh realities.

'So, it's Ralph on the stand tomorrow,' Sophie stated the obvious.

'Yes.' It was not a moment Tessa wanted to think about. His examination and responses would no doubt be peppered with lies and twisted truths. Part of her longed for him to be found guilty and sent to prison. He deserved to pay for the wrong he had done to others – to Mary Stephenson, George Stephenson, Esme and the Sackville's. Yet the other part of her could not imagine her husband serving out a sentence in a Nairobi prison. She knew she could never be completely free of him, no matter where she went. If she were in England she would think of him in prison; if she remained in Nairobi his proximity would stifle her, along with an obligation to visit. It was almost over but, yet, it would never be over. Her husband had committed a terrible crime and both of them were paying for it. And what of poor George Stephenson – he needed justice for his poor wife, but what justice could there be for a dead person.

'You're in a dilemma, aren't you?' Sophie said.

Tessa grimaced. 'Yes. I can escape the country but I can't escape my thoughts.'

'Poor you, but your plans to return to England make sense. Even I am brave enough to say that. In any case it will give me a reason to visit, but my God I'm going to miss you.'

'You'd better come and visit,' Tessa warned, 'Esme and I will welcome you with open arms.' She leaned back and looked up at the night sky, searching for stars, but the city lights obscured them. Another night, a million years ago, popped into her head when Ralph had showed her how to find Polaris, the North Star, using the Big Dipper. How she needed a north star now to show her the way. She brought her eyes back down onto the balcony again, choking back a sob. Why did he have to go and ruin everything?

The following morning they set out for the courthouse, where Ralph would be taking the stand. Tessa was subdued, thinking about what lay ahead.

'I know what you're thinking,' Sophie said, 'but you must be prepared for Ralph to behave like a complete moron.'

'Nicely put,' Tessa agreed with a wry laugh. 'If only he had pleaded guilty to the truth, rather than pleading not guilty – we wouldn't have had to go through a trial at all. I still don't understand why.' She looked out of the window as the car slowed to a crawl. The traffic was already heavy and they were jammed amongst the usual Nairobi traffic chaos, commuter cars, taxis, buses and trucks belching black smoke behind them; people on foot, women in their bright coloured batik wraps and headdresses with baskets on top, men in shorts, suits, traditional dress, children and animals all filled the highways and its surrounds. Everyone was hurrying to be somewhere in Nairobi on a thick grey humid morning.

Their driver pushed down on his car horn and soon they were surrounded by the sounds of a hundred horns.

'We'd be better off walking,' Tessa said. 'I'm feeling claustrophobic.'

'Take a deep breath and try to relax,' said Sophie. 'We'll soon be there.'

Tessa leaned back and closed her eyes. How could she relax? She was on her way to her husband's trial, but not a husband she knew anymore. She had spent hours trying to analyse what had made him change so much. Was it something she had done? Had he always been like it? Had he pretended to be different but then that pretence had run a gradual course and the real Ralph had begun to surface, the lone wolf, a single man in a marriage concerned only about himself?

She glanced across at Esme who was looking out at the myriad of people, her people, walking their daily journeys across open spaces and roadsides. Esme should be one of them this morning but, instead, she was on her way to the courthouse to face the man who had abducted her and

256

persuaded Esme's own brother to join in his crime. The man would now try and persuade the court that he was not guilty of the charges brought against him.

37

NAIROBI

March

He woke early in his grim surroundings, the morning of the day he was to stand trial. He washed in a bowl of cold water, was allowed to shave as best he could under supervision and then he dressed in the shirt, tie and suit that his wife had sent in for him. After a breakfast of mealie porridge and lukewarm coffee he was handcuffed, put into a van and driven off to the courthouse.

The media were awaiting his arrival. He was jostled and pushed by cameramen with flashing cameras and reporters trying to get a word from him and policemen had to rough handle them to get him through.

Ajulu was waiting for him. 'Do you still wish to testify?'

'Yes.'

'You know that after I have questioned you in the stand, the prosecution will cross-examine you?'

'Of course I do,' Ralph retorted.

'You have the right to remain silent and as your defence counsel I seriously recommend that you take this option.'

Ralph shook his head. 'No.' He wanted to show the

prosecution what he was made of.

Ajulu shrugged. 'So be it.'

Ralph guessed that his own counsel doubted his integrity but he also knew that he would do all he could in his summing up to prove his innocence. Ralph had paid him enough to do so.

They parted and went their separate ways into the courtroom. Ralph looked around, knowing that Tessa would be there, but it was a sweeping look. He didn't want to catch her eye.

The magistrate declared the session open and then Ajulu was there, in front of him, and the questioning began.

'Mr. Somerton, you are here today charged on three counts: count one of conspiracy to attack a camp, count two unlawfully taking from that place a person hereby named as Mary Stephenson, and holding them against their will and count three, the abduction of a person hereby named as Esme Adongo. You have pleaded not guilty to these charges, is this correct?'

'Yes sir.'

'You have pleaded not guilty because you are 'not guilty'?'

'Yes, sir.'

'I suggest to the court that the prosecution's evidence, from the myriad of witnesses he has gathered, has been flimsy to say the least. My client has been charged purely on the hearsay of one other, Mr. Yahzid Adongo, an unreliable changaa dependant witness with a criminal record, and that of several other witnesses who have, in my opinion, offered no hard evidence to link my client to the events in question.'

'Objection, the witness refers to Mr. Adongo who has pleaded guilty to his part in the criminal activities and has testified under oath to the defendant's guilt,' Kamani insisted. 'How much more evidence does the learned counsel require?'

The magistrate nodded. 'Sustained. Defense, please keep your questioning on the right path.'

Ajulu apologised and continued. He looked Ralph straight in the eye and asked, 'Mr. Somerton, you have pleaded not guilty to the charges made against you, is that correct?'

'Yes.'

'Why is that?'

'Because I cannot remember why I have been charged and I believe that I have been suffering from mental anxiety and exhaustion.'

'Objection. We have already been through this. The defendant cannot plead diminished responsibility.'

'Sustained, Mr. Kamani. I must agree with you. Counsel can you please get some control on your examination of your key witness.'

'I am merely trying to demonstrate that the defendant has suffered confusion and delusion.'

'This is a serious waste of our time,' the magistrate reprimanded.

'I agree,' said Ajulu, 'therefore I have no further questions.'

Ralph was taken aback. What was Ajulu playing at?

'Is that the extent of your questioning?' asked the magistrate, who was also a little surprised.

'Yes sir, it is,' Ajulu replied, 'my client has told the court that he is not guilty and so be it.'

'The defendant will remain where he is,' the magistrate

instructed and then he turned to Kamani. 'Will you cross-examine, counsel?'

'Most certainly thank you,' Kamani replied.

'Then please proceed.'

Ralph watched Kamani as he turned to face him and he knew he was going to have to fight for his life. Ajulu, it seemed, had abandoned him to his fate at the prosecutions hands.

'On the contrary Mr. Somerton you are guilty, are you not, of all the charges brought against you? Guilty of conspiracy, guilty of abduction and, because of your guilt, your actions led to the subsequent death of Mary Stephenson?'

'Objection,' said Ajulu, 'the victim's death was recorded by the coroner as *Death by Misadventure.'* My client cannot be implicated.'

'Sir, I am not accusing the defendant of the death of Mary Stephenson, merely the events leading up to it.'

'Overruled.'

The speed of the delivery of Kamani's accusation had taken everyone by surprise, including Ralph.

Over the gasps in the courtroom Ralph managed to reply, 'I cannot be guilty of something I cannot remember.'

Kamani smiled and pursed his lips. 'Clever, Mr. Somerton, but it won't wash with me. Tell me, would you lie to keep yourself out of trouble?'

'I'm not in the habit of lying,' Ralph replied.

'Are you not, Mr. Somerton? We shall see about that. In the meantime, can you tell me something about Chui Camp and what it meant to you before you were arrested? For instance, how long have you been the owner of the camp?'

'Chui Camp has been in my family for many generations

and I have owned and run it for the past thirteen years.'

'Is Chui camp popular with safari clients?'

'It was until the competition arrived.' He knew he shouldn't have mentioned it but he couldn't help himself.

'Can you be more specific about what 'competition' you are referring to please Mr. Somerton?' Kamani prompted.

'Oh there are all sorts of camps that are competition.'

'But you mentioned the competition arriving which I surmise means that it was a new rather than an already established camp. Is that true?'

'I suppose so.'

'Then can you please tell the court what particular camp you are referring to?'

Ralph was caught between a rock and a hard place.

'Perhaps I can enlighten you. Was the camp you are referring to, Nyara Camp?'

'It might have been,' he muttered in reply.

'The very camp that you are accused of instigating an attack upon?'

Ralph said nothing.

'No matter, Mr. Somerton, it was not a question and you do not have to reply to my comment. We'll get to the bottom of it some other way.'

Kamani opened another file and addressed the magistrate. 'If you please sir I would like to turn the questioning to the defendant's relationship with George Stephenson.'

The magistrate nodded and asked for a moment to retrieve the relevant documents.

'Mr. Somerton, can you tell me when you first encountered Mr. Stephenson?'

'I'm not sure.'

'Really Mr. Somerton, well let me jog your memory. You met him in the bar at the Norfolk hotel on two occasions in May of last year. Mr. Stephenson remembers the occasions in great detail and the barman has also testified to your presence on one of these occasions. Can you delve deeper into your memory?'

There was a moment whilst the court waited for Ralph's response.

'I do vaguely recall meeting a man I hadn't met before.'

'Dare I ask if you remember what you talked about?'

'No, I'm afraid I don't.'

'Well, according to Mr. Stephenson's statement you talked about your business failures,' Kamani prompted. 'How did you describe these?'

'I really don't recall,' Ralph said screwing up his face, 'but I might have been drunk at the time.'

Kamani ignored this reference. 'According to Mr. Stephenson you said you were losing your business to the opposition. You said, and I quote: *like to find a way to get that camp discredited*'.

Somerton shrugged. 'I don't remember saying that. As I said, I was probably drunk.'

'But you do remember meeting George Stephenson at the bar at the Norfolk Hotel?"

'I suppose so.' Ralph shrugged.

'But you don't remember saying and I quote again, that you would: *...like to find a way to get that camp discredited.*'

'As I said I'd been drinking and it was a long time ago.'

'I'll tell you what I think, Mr. Somerton. I think you are choosing not to remember,' Kamani pronounced.

'I have been through a great deal of stress and I believe it has affected my memory.'

Kamani pursed his lips. 'Mr. Stephenson has been under worse stress than you, and his memory is functioning perfectly well.'

'Objection, sir, that is an irrelevant jibe,' Ajulu protested.

'Sustained,' the magistrate agreed.

'What do you think, Mr. Somerton?' Kamani asked, somewhat provocatively.

'He has not been in prison for almost a year,' Ralph snapped, furious that Kamani should say such a thing and be allowed to get away with it.

It was just the sort of reaction Kamani wanted.

The courtroom gasped.

'Do not be rude to the court,' the magistrate warned Ralph, 'or I shall hold you in contempt.'

Ralph thought the reprimand was worth it.

'You discussed with Mr. Stephenson your camp failures?'

'I expect I told him something about my problems.'

'Let us assume you did. Why do you think there were such failures?'

'For several reasons...' Somerton began.

'Specifically?' Kamani interrupted.

'Well you could mention tour operators, the clients, the competition...'

Again Kamani interceded before Ralph had finished and he realised Kamani had drawn him in. 'Ah yes, the competition. There we have it. According to Mr. Stephenson you said to him, in the conversation which you conveniently seem to have forgotten: '...*I blame our damned new neighbours who were sponsored by a consortium to build a permanent camp, and apparently it's just what the punters want .... so this camp has been taking my clients and coining in the cash. I call that dishonest competition.'*

Ralph frowned. 'I was drunk at the time, so I could have said anything and that is a lot to remember.'

'Yes indeed you could and, allegedly, you did and when George Stephenson asked you what you could do about it you said, and again I quote: *'I could get them discredited.'* What exactly did you mean by that, Mr. Somerton?'

'I don't know what I meant.' Ralph was beginning to feel a little nervous and hot under the collar, but he knew he must not let Kamani get to him.

Kamani deliberately took some time again before he asked his next question. The courtroom rang with background noises: coughing, throat-clearing, people shuffling in their seats to relieve stiff backs and legs, as well as muted vocal reactions to questions and answers.

'Did you meet Mr. Stephenson again?'

'I'm not sure.'

Kamani rolled his eyes. 'Well let me remind you. According to Mr. Stephenson you bumped into him on the street in Nairobi and, later on when the bank had released some money to him, he called you and suggested that you both went to the Norfolk hotel bar to celebrate. Do you remember that?'

'It's possible – I spend quite a lot of time there.' 'Indeed, Mr. Somerton, and the police file contains positive evidence from witnesses amongst the staff who recall that you were there on that occasion, with the plaintiff.'

'Then I probably was.'

'It is alleged, during that second meeting with Mr.

Stephenson, that you should suggested he should use some of his newly released funds to take he and his wife off to Nyara Camp during the new season in June of last year. Do you recall suggesting this?'

'I really don't remember.'

'Goodness me you have a TERRIBLE memory, Mr. Somerton,' Kamani said, 'or is it that you just won't admit the truth?'

'I agree,' intervened an equally exasperated Magistrate. 'If you don't start co-operating Mr. Somerton I shall adjourn all the proceedings, hold you in contempt of court and you will return to Kamiti prison until I see fit to resume this trial whether in a week a month or a year or several years!'

'I'm sorry, I am doing the best that I can,' Ralph apologised.

'No, Mr. Somerton, you are not,' was the Magistrate's sharp response. 'You must do better.'

'Did you or did you not suggest that George Stephenson take he and his wife on a safari to Nyara Camp?'

'It's possible.'

Kamani nodded. 'Let us agree that you did.' He paused to consider his next question. 'Can you explain to me why you might have suggested Nyara camp to Mr. Stephenson, the camp that you regard as your rival, instead of your own?'

Ralph shrugged. 'I presume Chui Camp was full.'

'That's indeed what you are alleged to have told Mr. Stephenson, but I have here records to prove that it was not true at all. Why would you suggest that he should go elsewhere when you have been telling us that you needed all the clients you could get?' Ralph did not reply and Kamani launched an attack. 'I put it to you Mr. Somerton that you made that particular choice because you had already decided that the Stephenson's were going to be your stooges in a plan, in which Mary Stephenson would be taken from Nyara Camp and held against her will, just long enough for Nyara Camp to be ruined.'

'That's ridiculous.'

'Is it, Mr. Somerton?'

'Yes, I mean why would I suggest such a thing and as for saying there was a plan…' His voice ran out and Ralph clutched at the edge of the stand so hard his knucklebones stood out, gleaming like ivory.

'Yes, Mr. Somerton, you were saying about the plan?'

'I don't recall a plan.'

'Well, Mr. Somerton, I suggest that you are lying when you say you don't recall a plan, or remember a time, or a conversation or remarks about Nyara Camp. I suggest that you are guilty, of the charges made against you, of the conspiracy to attack Nyara Camp and to abduct and confine Mrs. Stephenson, the deceased. What do you say?'

'I don't know, because I don't remember.'

Kamani calmly turned his attention back to his papers before looking up and addressing the magistrate. 'I would like to refer my questioning to the relationship between the accused, Mr. Yahzid Adongo, and the accused Mr Somerton.'

Then the magistrate intervened. 'May I suggest that this is an appropriate time to adjourn. It has been a long session and I would like to refer this new line of questioning to a new day. We will reconvene tomorrow morning at 9.30am.'

Ralph gave an inward sigh of relief. He could do with a rest from Kamani's relentless questions and even relished returning to his cell rather than standing in the dock for a moment longer. He noted with some satisfaction that Kamani was unhappy about the interruption.

38

NAIROBI

March

'Mr. Yahzid Adongo has confessed and pleaded guilty to his part in the conspiracy and abduction in which he implicates the defendant, identified as Ralph Somerton, as the chief conspirator. Mr. Adongo has sworn under oath that the defendant approached him in the month of May last year, in Kibera, and asked him to help in a plan in exchange for a considerable amount of money.'

Kamani opened the cross-examination the next morning. 'Did you, or did you not approach Mr. Adongo about the alleged conspiracy and abduction and offer a large sum of money in return for his co-operation in this plan, Mr. Somerton?'

'I may have spoken with Mr. Adongo but I don't recall what it was about.'

'You did, in fact, speak to Mr. Adongo on several occasions, but I am referring specifically to the first time you approached Mr. Adongo about the conspiracy.'

'I don't remember.'

'Well, I am telling you Mr. Somerton that, when you spoke to Mr. Adongo during that visit it was about the alleged conspiracy and abduction of Mary Stephenson, and you did ask him to play a part in it.'

'I...' began Ralph but Kamani cut him off.

'It was not a question and I require no answer.'

Ralph waited whilst Kamani leafed through his notes, wondering what was coming next and why Ajulu had not yet raised any objections to the line of questioning.

Kamani looked up suddenly and said, 'did you ask Mr. Adongo to arrange for two men, who are since deceased, to abduct Mrs. Stephenson from Nyara Camp during their visit in June?'

'I don't remember.'

'Do you not? Do you not remember visiting Mr. Adongo in Kibera, in May last year, to ask that very question? Are you certain, Mr. Somerton?'

'I am not certain, but I don't remember.'

Kamani shook his head. 'You are making my cross-examination very difficult, Mr. Somerton, with your dreadful lapses of memory.'

'I apologise, but I have been very confused and...'

'Yes, yes, you have already explained this to the court. Take your time now, Mr. Somerton. The answer to my question is very important.'

Ralph swallowed hard. He was finding it difficult not to give a proper answer, but he could not.

'You can be charged with perjury,' Kamani warned.

'No, I cannot,' Ralph said boldly. By not remembering and thus not answering the questions he considered that at least he was not lying. That would have been perjury.

Kamani shook his head.

Ralph could see the frustration he was trying to hide, on his face. Good, let him sweat a bit.

'Let us leave this line of cross-examination for a moment. I would like to question you about events after the attack on Nyara Camp.' He turned to the magistrate, 'you should have these documents, sir.'

The magistrate looked through the papers in front of him. 'Yes I have them, please proceed.'

'You were at Chui Camp when you heard the news about the attack on Nyara Camp and the victim, Mary Stephenson, going missing?' Kamani began.

'Yes.'

'And you offered to help in the search for her?'

'Yes.'

'Well at least your memory is improving, Mr. Somerton,' Kamani said with a cynical smile. 'Why did you offer to help search for her?'

'It was the least I could do,' Ralph said. 'Us camps have to stick together in a time of crisis.' Now he felt on safer ground.

There was an audible titter of disbelief from the courtroom.

'Silence,' the magistrate warned.

'Or,' said Kamani turning provocatively to the court as though he were addressing everyone, 'was it because you knew where to find her?'

'That's ridiculous,' Ralph muttered.

'Is it? I put it to you, Mr. Somerton, that you offered to help in the search because you knew precisely where to find Mary Stephenson, because you had planned and instigated her abduction and agreed with the abductors as to where she would be held?'

'No.'

'Yes, Mr. Somerton.'

'No.'

'On the contrary, I suggest that your plan was to bring her back and claim the glory for it.'

'That's not true,' Ralph said. He looked at Ajulu. Object he willed him.

'What is not true, Mr. Somerton?'

'I, I, don't remember.'

Kamani laughed. 'Just because you don't remember something it doesn't mean it didn't happen,' said Kamani. 'After the attack, did you go to Nairobi?'

'It's possible.'

'You did, Mr. Somerton and when you were there you contacted Mr. Adongo. Dare I ask why you contacted him?'

'I don't remember contacting him.'

Kamani held up a sheaf of papers. 'I have here Mr. Adongo's phone history and I can assure you that you called Mr Adongo just after midday on the day you returned to Nairobi, and you also contacted him the day after the death of Mary Stephenson. Why did you feel the need to contact him at that time?'

'I don't remember why or even having done so.'

'Well we have it on record that you did so I think we will accept that as the correct version of the truth. Please tell the court why you found the need to contact him, not once, not twice but on at least three occasions?

'I don't know, it was probably about some work. My wife had asked me to help him.'

'But I think you do know exactly what it was about, Mr. Somerton. Your terrible memory will not wash with me. I have got all the time in the world to get you to admit your guilt. Now, according to Mr Adongo, you made the call to express your concern about the death of Mary Stephenson. He alleges that you were angry with him because she had managed to escape her captivity. What is your response to that?'

Ralph did not reply. His mouth felt dry and he desperately wanted a drink of water. This was not going quite as he had planned it would. He gave Ajulu a pleading look again.

'Mr. Somerton?' the Magistrate prompted.

'May I have some water, please?' It would give him a few minutes of stalling.

The Magistrate relented and waved his hand at a clerk who went off for the requested water.

Whilst Ralph drank, the courtroom fidgeted along with Kamani, he noted with satisfaction. He drew it out as long as he could.

'Continue now please,' the magistrate ordered.

'Referring to my last point, you made the call to express your concern about the death of Mary Stephenson, according to Mr. Adongo. Why would you have discussed such a thing with him?'

'It was on the news?'

'So you did speak to him?'

'Well, it is possible, but perhaps it was about the work I was hoping to get him.'

'We are all getting tired of your stalling, Mr. Somerton. I put it to you that you called Mr. Adongo because your plan had gone wrong and you wanted to discuss it with him.

Now you had a dead woman on your hands. Mr. Adongo said that in that phone call you both discussed payment to the two men for the kidnapping, and you said you would not pay them because they had not fulfilled their role and safely returned Mary Stephenson. Is that right, Mr. Somerton?'

'I...'

'Don't remember, Mr. Somerton?'

Ralph noted the edge of sarcasm. What should he say?

'On the contrary I insist that you do remember but you refuse to accept it. Did you not also end up agreeing to pay those two men half the agreed sum?'

'I don't remember.'

'And a plan was made for you to take the money to the bus station?'

'No, I...'

Kamani ploughed on without mercy. 'I put it to you Mr. Somerton, that you are lying when you say you don't remember. The evidence points clearly to your guilt. You remember all of it because it is true but you refuse to admit your culpability.'

Best thing was to say nothing, but the Magistrate addressed him. 'You should answer something Mr. Somerton. I could have you charged with obstructing the court's proceedings.'

Ralph sighed. 'I apologise but I was in a very anxious mental state at that time and events are blurred. I'm not sure what is the truth and what is not.'

'Oh come now, Mr. Somerton, you cannot expect the court to fall for that,' Kamani guffawed.

'Objection,' cried Ajulu, at last. 'Counsel is taking his brief a step too far.'

'Overruled,' the magistrate dismissed. 'On the contrary he is dealing with a difficult situation.'

Kamani continued, relentless now. 'Did you or did you not have a conversation with Mr. Adongo on the day you returned to Nairobi, the day that you learned of Mary Stephenson's death?'

'If the records say I did, then I suppose I must have done.'

'Well, that's a little better than not remembering. Why did you call him?' Kamani asked again.

'I told you, I had been trying to help him find a job so it might have been about that.'

'Yes you told me Mr. Somerton, and I put it to you that you had already found him a job which was the hiring of the men who abducted Mary Stephenson. Mr. Adongo has testified under oath that this was the job in question.'

'No.'

'Yes, Mr. Somerton,' Kamani insisted, 'it was that very job and you are the only person who denies it. Why, I have testimonies from a number of people who confirm it.'

'Why do you believe Mr Adongo over me? Ralph protested.

'Because Mr. Adongo's memory appears to be a lot better than your own.' He turned a few pages. 'Do you recall a trip to the bus station in Kibera, the bus station where you were supposed to meet someone who would collect a bag from you?'

'When was this supposed to have taken place?'

'You tell me Mr. Somerton.'

'A year is a long time to remember days and dates.'

Kamani produced a long-suffering smile. 'Let me

enlighten you Mr. Somerton, again. It was just a few days before your arrest and I'm sure you haven't forgotten about that. Perhaps you can tell me who you were meeting there?'

'No.'

'Now I happen to know that your answer of 'no' is the truth and probably the first truthful reply because Mr. Adongo has alleged that only he knew. I can enlighten you now. It was supposed to be Esme Adongo, but she was unable to attend. Do you know why?'

Ralph was taken aback. He had no idea that it was Esme he would have been meeting and now he knew why nobody had turned up. What to say? What about the truth again? 'Yes.'

'Then please explain,' Kamani said opening an arm in a gesture to the courtroom.

'I had taken her to my airport lock-up for her own safety.'

Kamani raised his eyebrows 'for her own safety? From what evil did you feel the need to protect her?'

'I was worried about the company her brother was keeping. He was drinking changa'aa with other men and it does terrible things to the mind. I thought it was best to take her to a place of safety.'

'An admirable reason, Mr. Somerton, but why not take her to your own house, where she was employed?'

'I thought those men might know about our house. The lockup near Wilson seemed a better option.'

'Why did you feel the need to drug her?'

'You must answer the question,' the magistrate ordered.

Ralph bit his lip. 'I knew she would not come with me, nor stay there of her own accord. I was just trying to protect her. '

Kamani gave him a long look. 'So you admit that you held Miss Adongo against her will, in a drugged state, at the lock-up near Wilson Airport?'

Ralph was feeling confused and tired. He didn't know what answer to give any more.

'Yes or no, Mr. Somerton?'

'I'm sorry, I am feeling confused. I suppose the answer is yes, but I did not hold her there as a kidnap victim. I wanted to protect her,' he insisted. Why couldn't they understand that?

The prosecution shook his head in disbelief. 'No, Mr. Somerton, you are not confused you just don't want to answer a question that might implicate you and you refuse to admit to the plain fact which is that you are guilty. Guilty, guilty, guilty and yet you continue to deny it.'

'Objection, your honour,' Ajulu intervened at last. 'The prosecution is attacking my client with his accusations.'

'I am merely trying to get the witness to accept his accountability,' Kamani insisted, 'yet not only does he refuse to admit it, he refuses to remember. Surely he is holding this court in contempt?'

'Objection overruled, but try to be a little less cavalier in your approach,' the magistrate suggested.

'I repeat Mr. Somerton,' and Kamani turned to face him again, 'you are guilty of all the charges made against you and you were in your right mind when you committed them. You conspired in a pre-meditated plan to abduct the deceased during her visit to Nyara Camp, and to hold her against her will until you conveniently found her, returned her and claimed the glory.'

'I did not abduct Mrs. Stephenson.'

'No, not physically, but you were culpable in that abduction,' Kamani said then he turned to the Magistrate, 'your honour, may I draw your attention to the Laws of Kenya, the penal code, Chapter XXV – Offences against liberty, the section which refers to definitions of Abduction : items 259 and 261. Item 259 states: *Any person who kidnaps or abducts any person with intent to cause that person to be confined is guilty of a felony and is liable to imprisonment for seven years. Item 261 states: any person who knowing that any person has been kidnapped or has been abducted and confines such person is guilty of a felony and shall be punished in the same manner as if he abducted such person with the same intention or knowledge, or for the same purpose, as it conceals or detains such person in confinement.*'

'Thank you, Mr. Kamani, I have made a note of your reference, you may continue,' the magistrate acknowledged.

Kamani turned to Ralph Somerton. 'Do you understand what that means? Do you understand that regardless of whether you personally abducted Mary Stephenson, but paid others to abduct her on your behalf, it will not exonerate you from your culpability?'

'Yes,' Ralph replied.

'And do you still maintain that your smokescreen of lies and denial absolves you from the crimes you committed?'

'Objection,' cried Ajulu, 'the prosecution is sabotaging my client.'

'Overruled.'

Kamani pulled out his best card, the one he had been waiting for. 'Sir,' he said addressing the magistrate, 'may I now be allowed to show the photographic exhibits?'

'Come to the bench please,' said the magistrate,

summoning both Kamani and Adongo.

Ralph's head was pounding from the pace of the cross-examination and his efforts to stall Kamani's efforts. Now there were going to be photographic exhibits? Please God let the magistrate adjourn the proceedings so he could prepare for it.

The magistrate banged his gavel to call the court to attention. 'The prosecution has requested the display of some photographs taken at the scene of the crime. However, I am not sure they should be shown to all and sundry and, I would like the court to adjourn until we have established the legalities of what can or cannot be bandied about. We will recess for thirty minutes whilst we discuss this matter.'

Ralph breathed a sigh of relief for the short reprieve during which he hoped to gather himself enough to get him through the next session.

The court session resumed two hours later. Press and official photographers were unable to enter until the photographs had been used as evidence and then removed to a place to be kept under lock and key from prying eyes. The magistrate ordered that anyone entering the courtroom must surrender their mobile phones so that the cameras on those phones could not be used to wrongfully photograph or video the material.

'Are we ready for the photographic exhibits?' the Magistrate asked.

'Yes your honour,' both counsels agreed.

'These are being exhibited for you to see as well as those remaining in this courtroom, Mr. Somerton. I would like to ensure that you will do so.'

'I will,' said Ralph. George Stephenson, he noticed, had not returned to the courtroom. He reckoned it was going to bad but that he could deal with it and he faced the screen with resolution. Even he was not prepared for the pictures that appeared. There were gasps and cries of horror from those who had been allowed to remain in the courtroom, revealing their own shock and distress at what they were seeing. It was not for the faint-hearted and even the toughened rangers had been distressed by what they had found. Nobody could have identified the remains as belonging to any particular individual. They were too mangled and some body parts were scattered across the scene. It was that, and the wedding ring they had found on a severed hand, that had persuaded the police to formally accept the remains as those of Mary Stephenson. Ralph put a hand to his mouth. Visible horror showed then on his face and he even let out a sob. George must have been devastated when he had seen them.

'What we have seen Mr. Somerton,' said Kamani, when the images had disappeared, 'is the result of your evil conspiracy. Those terrible images show the remains of an innocent woman whom you used in your reckless, spiteful and evil plan to discredit another camp. You may not have killed her but you are, are you not, culpable in the responsibility for her ultimate death?'

Ralph heard the gasps and the snarls that erupted from the people in the courtroom, from their revulsion and horror at what they had witnessed. He couldn't speak; all of a sudden the absolute madness of what he had done and the terrible consequences of it hit him like a runaway train. It was over; he could not go any further. He felt smothered by a heavy blanket that was suffocating him.

'We are waiting for your response, Mr. Somerton,' Kamani reprimanded.

'I never meant for her to die,' he whispered.

Kamani heard him and he held up his hand for silence. 'Can you please repeat what you just said, so that the whole court can hear you? The counsel wanted it rammed home to everyone in the courtroom.

Ralph looked up at the people in the courtroom. 'Yes,' he said. 'I am guilty, but I swear on my life that I was supposed to find her alive and return her unharmed. She was never meant to die. For that I am truly sorry.' He put his head in his hands.

The court began to erupt again with the sounds of people reacting to what had just been said by the defendant.

'Silence!' shouted the magistrate and banged his gavel several times.

When it was quiet again, Kamani spoke. 'The prank that went horribly wrong?' he asked, pushing and turning the knife.

'Yes,' Ralph whispered.

'Objection,' called Ajulu, 'my client has been forced into a submission. The trial should be adjourned.'

'This court IS adjourned,' said the magistrate, 'until further notice. I have noted the defendant's admission. I would like to see both counsel's in my chambers.' Then he stood and swept out of the courtroom, with Ajulu and Kamani hurrying after him.

Before he was taken away Ralph sought out Tessa in the courtroom. He saw her white face, the look of horror and disbelief written there. How could he blame her? How could he ever explain that he had been driven by a demon

- a plot hatched in despair and mental instability. Now he could see what he had done, and he could not hide from the consequences of it.

He had no answers. What was done, was done and he could not talk back the clock. Could not blame anyone but himself. He knew that now but it was too late. He had lost the two most important things in his life, his wife and, more importantly, he had lost Chui. His inheritance, his pride and joy. In the end it had all been for nothing.

39

NAIROBI

March

'It's over,' said Sophie as they watched Ralph being taken away. 'He's confessed.'

Tessa nodded, unable to find words to reply. It had been such a traumatic experience, and the photographic evidence had shocked her beyond belief. Ralph's confession had been almost an anti-climax.

'I need to get out, now,' she said, scrambling to her feet, a hand at her mouth from sudden nausea.

'Out of the way please,' Sophie shouted to those who were ambling towards the exit and she elbowed her way through them, holding on to Tessa's arm. It was hot and humid in the courtroom, enough to make anyone feel ill without the added factor of the events that had taken place. They pushed through the throng to the exit and out into a courtyard. The oppressive air wasn't much of a relief, but at least they were free of the claustrophobic environment of the courthouse and its myriad of people.

Tessa leaned her hand against a tree, bent over, overcome with despair and emotion. She heard Sophie called to a vendor, and then she was by her side with water. A few sips of it helped to steady her.

'Are you okay?' Sophie asked, with a comforting hand on her back.

Tessa wanted to reply but the words would not come out. What words were there to say or to describe how she felt anyway?

The van carrying Ralph back to prison passed by right in front of them.

'Jesus,' Tessa exclaimed, and she began to shake.

Sophie hugged her. 'Its okay Tessa, you've been so strong but I'm not surprised today has cracked you.'

Tessa shook her head convulsed now with tears. 'I feel so guilty,' she wailed.

'Why? It's not your fault.'

'I should have seen what he was capable of, what he was being driven towards. That poor woman,' her hand went again to her mouth.

'No, you could never have known he could be capable of something like that. You said yourself he was acting like a man you didn't know,' Sophie said. 'This is not about you, its about Ralph and his actions. I won't have you trying to blame yourself and taking on his responsibility.'

Tessa gulped back her tears and wiped her face on a tissue Sophie proferred, 'thank God I've got you around to keep things in perspective for me.'

Sophie gave her a half-smile. 'God knows it was enough to finish anyone off today, but it's almost over now.'

'Is it? What happens now he has admitted his guilt? Will the trial be null and void? Will they just jump straight to sentencing? What will they do?' Tessa shook her head in despair.

'I don't know, but at least you won't have to sit through anything like that again.'

Tessa grimaced, 'I couldn't bear it.'

Her friend hugged her again. 'Poor Tessa, you've been so brave and strong, but it's taken its toll of you.' She pushed her back a little, looking her up and down. 'Goodness me you feel like skin and bone.'

'I haven't had much of an appetite,' she confessed. 'How am I going to get over this?'

'You will get over it, in time, sweetheart.'

'I suppose I might learn to live with it, but I don't think I'll ever get over it.' She turned to Esme who was standing beside them, listening to their conversation, with distress and anxiety in her troubled expression. 'Oh Esme, I'm so sorry you had to go through all this too, what with your brother in prison, and then standing as a witness and the things Ajulu said to you.'

'Yahzid must face up to what he did and bear his punishment,' Esme said with a solemn voice, 'and I hope he will learn from this. As for the rest of it, it is in God's hands.'

Tessa was not sure if God should take all the responsibility, but she appreciated Esme's feelings. 'Will you come to hear what the court has to say about Ralph?'

Esme shook her head. 'No. I have missed too much of school and I must go back to Kibera. I do not want to miss my exams – they are my only chance at finding a place in a university.'

'I understand. We'll get the driver to take you there,' Tessa said. The girl had been struggling since her turn on the stand and the days at court were draining her. The guilt

285

of her brother was a great weight on her shoulders and Tessa wanted to take it from her.

'Thank you but I just want to go to the bus station. You have both done so much and I am very grateful but I will take a matatu to Kibera. Don't worry, I will be fine, I am used to it, after all.'

Tessa hugged her when they dropped her off. 'Promise me you will let me know how you are and we will let you know what happens. Good luck with your studies.' Then Esme was gone, vanishing into the cram of people getting on and off the buses.

'Poor Esme,' Tessa said to Sophie as she got back into the car, 'she has been through so much.'

'She'll be fine. She's tougher than you think and she'll soon be out of it and on a plane to England with you and her future. Now, what we need is a drink.'

Tessa couldn't help but laugh – it was Sophie's answer to everything. 'You make us sound like alcoholics.'

'No darling, it's just that there's nothing like a good glass of cold white or mellow red to cheer the spirit.'

40

NAIROBI

March

Ajulu arrived in Ralph's cell, grim-faced and furious. 'You could have saved a whole lot of time if you'd pleaded guilty in the first place. The only saving grace is that your plea of guilty gets me out of the onerous task of trying to prove otherwise.' He opened his briefcase and pulled out some papers.

Ralph stared at him. 'I apologise, but I realise now that I was wrong. Something, perhaps confusion or some kind of madness, blinded me into thinking otherwise,' he paused before saying, 'it was only after seeing the photographic evidence that the full realisation of what had happened, hit home.'

Ajulu shrugged. 'What's done is done. Now I need your confirmation that you have changed your plea to guilty, so that I can take that information back to the magistrate.'

'What will happen then?'

'That's up to the magistrate to decide but, one of two things could happen. One, the charge will be put again and you can change your plea to guilty or two, the trial will continue. Counsels will sum up, the lay assessors will give their verdict and depending on that it will go to a judge who will decide what he or she thinks. That verdict will be standing. If it is 'not guilty' then you will be free to go, If, on the other hand you are found guilty as confessed, you will return to prison to await sentencing.'

'Right,' said Ralph. 'I'm presuming the outcome will be guilty.'

Ajulu shrugged, 'as I said that is up to others to decide. As for me, I just want the money you owe to me for representing you.'

Ralph was left in no doubt about Ajulu's feelings on the matter.

He lay down on his bunk and thought about the trial. The prank that went horribly wrong. Is that how Kamani had styled it. Yes, he supposed it had been a prank. After all he really had meant no harm to come to the woman. She should have been held in a secure place until he had 'found her' and returned her to safety. That was all. God, if only she hadn't taken it upon herself to escape. If only the stupid men, Yahzid had found to do the job, hadn't left her on her own. How could he have imagined that such a plot could ever have been the right thing to do, for the sake of Chui? The photographic evidence had brought that home to him and now he was realising the full impact of the consequences.

A month later the magistrate took the number one path. The charges were put again under Ralph's plea of guilty, and all that remained was for Ralph to be sentenced. Whatever that sentence might prove to be there was one thing Ralph knew for sure, and that was that his life was over. He'd lost it all.

He'd failed his ancestors, given in to his own selfishness, created the awful circumstances, surrounding a woman's death, for his own selfish fulfilment? Yes, he was guilty of all of the above. He had baled out of the responsibility of his inheritance, left Tessa to put up with his absences and punished her for her ability to manage without him. How long had he been in that downward spiral, blaming everyone else for his own failures? He had wanted to punish someone or something and had focused on Nyara, but instead he had ended up punishing the one person who might have helped him get through it. Tessa. Now he saw the madness of it – the wrong path he'd taken and where it had led him. He longed to tell Tessa he was sorry but he doubted he would ever see her again and who could blame her. Ralph would have given the world to have Tessa on his side again. He had lost everything, but more than that, he had lost the one person who had mattered to him.

Unbeknown to him, somebody else was feeling exactly the same.

41

NAIROBI

August

A harsh light of a Nairobi morning woke Tessa. She got up and went out onto Sophie's balcony, hugging a fleece around her, looking out across the cityscape of apartment blocks, office buildings and hotels, spectres in the omnipresent humid haze that suffocated the city. The never-ending traffic inched along the roads below. A smell of coffee rose up on the damp air, along with the sound of a loudspeaker broadcasting a call to prayer, the booming bass from car radios and the daily hum of the city. Far away, beyond the buildings, she imagined she could see the edge of the Nairobi National Park whose boundary came so close to the city. There the necks of giraffes would replace the sea of building cranes, and animals roamed and filled the landscape instead of cars and people.

How she longed to be back in the bush with all the dreadful events of the last year behind her, but it held no place for her any more. She was leaving her precious Africa for the second time in her life and this time there was no guarantee that she would be back. Yet how could she not? Nobody who had Africa in their soul like she did could stay away for too long, even if they wanted to. It drew you back like gravity, like the waxing and waning of the moon, and the ebb and flow of the tides. Africa, she thought, is a place that makes you aware of how alive you are. Yet it also slams home to you how narrow and fragile the gulf between life and death can be, how success and failure are intertwined.

That fragility could catch you up and take you out like a sniper's bullet, sudden and unexpected, just as had happened to Mary Stephenson. I didn't see it coming, she thought, even though I knew things were going wrong. I didn't face the problem head on and deal with it. I moaned about it and I chastised Ralph and wallowed in my own self-pity but I didn't face our crisis it until it was too late. I suppose I didn't want to admit that things had gone wrong.

Today she would face the momentous outcome of that fragility - the day of the final verdict by a Judge. The day when she would find out if the man who was her husband, who had brought so many to ruin, whose actions had led to the death of an innocent woman would be found guilty and, if so, what sentence he would receive.

She shivered as a breeze danced across the balcony. I have been sentenced too. Sentenced to exile and whatever that future may bring. But at least I will be free.

42

NAIROBI

August

The once pristine tiled hallway of the courthouse had been scratched and dulled from the relentless trudge of footsteps of the guilty, the not guilty, the prosecutors and the defenders, the judges and magistrates, assessors and watchers. In the far corner stood Mr. Rama, who cleaned the floor every day, leaning on a mop that stood in a filthy bucket of water. He was watching those people go by with a keen eye for whom was what and what would be.

As soon as he arrived, George headed for the washroom. Mr Rama had just finished cleaning it and was removing the 'wet floor' notice as George approached.

'Is it okay to go in?

Mr Rama looked at him and smiled. 'Yes all done.' As George stepped inside he called after him. 'The one on the left is the better of the two.'

'Thank you,' George said with a quick smile.

As he left the washrooms he thanked Mr Rama again- a stranger who had shown him some kindness. The cleaner nodded and carried on mopping the hall floor.

A flurry of activity alerted George to the fact that Somerton must have arrived. He thought of him in handcuffs, flanked by policeman pushing their way through the sea of photographers and press, all clambering for a word from the accused – the guilty.

Then the Judge entered and the whole court rose. 'I declare this session open and I shall now give my verdict in the case of the Republic versus Ralph William Somerton, defendant.

I will now convey to you my own consideration and judgement of these charges. *'Ralph William Somerton you stand here today in the matter of your plea of guilty to the following charges. I have considered all the evidence put before me and find the following: In the matter of the first charge for your culpability in conspiring to attack a camp referred to as Nyara Camp in the Masai Mara - I hereby find you guilty as charged.'* A huge cheer erupted from the onlookers. 'Silence please until I have finished,' the Judge ordered, banging his gavel onto the desk. *'In the matter of the second charge of 'culpability in the abduction of Mary Stephenson' I find you guilty as charged.'* Again the judge could not stop the sound of approval in the courtroom and he waited a few moments for the sounds to subside. *'On the charge of 'actual abduction of Miss Esme Adongo', I find there was insufficient evidence to find you guilty and therefore declare you not guilty of this charge.'* Now there were mutters of disapproval and he had to bang his gavel a few times for silence. It was not a verdict most people desired, including George. He wanted Somerton to be found guilty of everything, including murder, but that was not to be. He wondered how the girl, Esme was feeling about it.

'Silence please' came the cry from the courtroom clerk. 'The judge will speak again '

Silence fell for they knew that the important part of the proceedings, the sentencing was about to begin.

'I hereby wish, which I do, taking into account the charges that you subsequently confessed – to impose a sentence with a strong message to others who try to fool the law. Therefore, my sentencing is as follows:

'Ralph William Somerton, in sentencing you I have taken into consideration your guilty plea. Therefore, I sentence you in total to seven years but, taking into account the year you have already served in prison, your sentence from this day forward will be six years. That is my final decision. Now you will be taken from here to your place of confinement.' The Magistrate banged his gavel and stood up to leave. *'Court dismissed,'* called the clerk, but those last two words could hardly be heard. The whole courtroom had erupted, once again, with the cacophony of people reacting to the judge's words. Reporters were clamouring for statements and there was an explosion of blinding flashes, as photographers took their pictures.

George barely listened to the sentencing. He looked at Somerton and felt despair and anger at the sentence the judge had meted out to the man. He felt cheated for Mary. This was not justice it was an insult to her name. Why had the judge not seen it? The man should have gone to prison for the rest of his life: a life for a life.

What had to be done must be done. In the midst of the chaos around him George reached his hand inside his jacket and pulled out the small handgun that Mr. Rama had concealed for him, in the men's washroom. A gun obtained at a considerable price. He turned now without hesitation and fired it directly at Tessa Somerton who was standing nearby.

The sound of the gunshot froze the chaos in the court. For a split second there was a stunned silence then the noise resumed, but now it was full of fear, of screams and crying and the thunder of people trying to get to the exit.

Tessa had slumped to the floor and several people had gathered around her.

'Now we're even!' George screamed at Ralph who was being dragged from the dock, **'murderer,'** he yelled, but his voice was lost in the noise and frenzy of the crazed throng around him. He watched as Ralph twisted and pulled, like a tethered animal, trying to tear himself away from the two policemen either side battling to hold him in his handcuffs. 'It's my wife,' Ralph shouted, 'let me go to her.' Instead they began to propel him towards the door to get him out of the courtroom. He was straining and bellowing like a tethered buffalo, trying to launch himself up into the air to see over the heads of the crowd of people who had gathered around the spot where Tessa had fallen. George stared at her, lying on the floor in a spreading pool of blood. Kneeling by her side was Alexia Sackville.

He heard Ralph let out a long wail of denial and turn his bewildered eyes to the man who had shot her. But there would be no explanation. In the seconds before he was over-powered, George Stephenson had turned the gun on himself.

EPILOGUE

In front of her stretched a sea of black robes and hats, line after line of them down towards the stage, each person waiting for their own chance to shake the hand of the Dean and receive their degree. Her heart pounded as she waited for one person in the crowd to take her turn. It was an amazing achievement, the culmination of all the hard work of a girl who, against all odds, had chased and captured her dreams. Dream, believe, achieve – that was the mantra she had drummed into her through the toughest of times.

At last she was there, centre stage.

'Esme Adongo, Post-graduate Certificate of Education, specialising in primary education.'

Tessa thought her heart would burst. She heard Esme's university friends clapping and whistling as Esme took her certificate, thanked the Dean, shook his hand and walked off the stage. It was all over in a matter of seconds but those few moments would be forever remembered and treasured. As Esme returned to her seat she blew a kiss into the audience. Tessa knew it was for her.

Later on, when it was all over and everyone was filing out, she waited for Esme to come and find her.

'My darling girl, I'm so proud of you,' she said through tears of pride and joy when at last Esme was standing in front of her. Over the past years she had come to love the girl as her own. They had been through so much together and had been each *other's support and lifeline.*

Her phone pinged and a text from Sophie appeared on the screen.

'Hey girls, where are the photos?'

'I'll reply,' Esme said and took the phone from Tessa, then she bent down and took a selfie of them together which she sent with a short message back to Sophie.

'Oh you two look fabulous, I can't wait to see you,' came the quick response, 'love and congratulations.'

Tessa stared down at the photograph on the screen as Esme pushed her wheelchair to the lift, back down to the ground floor reception area that was mobbed with graduates and their families. How different she and Esme looked now to the time of their arrival in England. Tessa had spent three months in hospital before they had even been able to leave Nairobi. Her injuries had been severe, and she was left partially paralysed. She had undergone physiotherapy to try and gain some mobility but the intensity of it had taken a toll on her. In England she had spent almost a year in rehabilitation and, through sheer perseverance and determination, had ended up with limited movement in her lower body. It meant that although she still had the need to use a wheelchair to get out and about, she was able to move around at home with the aid of a walker. Tessa had also received counselling for the trauma of having been shot by George Stephenson and the fact that he had turned the gun on himself. In many ways Tessa was thankful for that and for the fact that she wouldn't have to face yet another trial, but her guilt over the hurt and suffering he had endured had taken a long time to come to terms with.

The stress of the trial and her brother's imprisonment had also affected Esme and she too had undergone counselling. It had taken some time to see her to smile again – a smile that now lit up her face and turned her into a beautiful young lady. The photo proved that lives could change for the better. Tessa leaned down and kissed the picture on the screen.

'Hey Mrs. Sentimentality,' Esme teased.

'I know, I know, but you've got to cut me some slack for feeling this way.'

'I will always allow you whatever it is you wish,' Esme replied in earnest. 'I owe you so much.'

'Rubbish,' Tessa dismissed, 'now you must go and find your friends if you want to. Don't feel you have to stay with me. I've got the hang of moving this thing you know.'

Esme laughed, 'I know you have and that's why I will not leave you alone with it. You are a crazy driver! I have spent the past four years with my friends and now they are here with their families just like me, and it is those people that we want to spend our day with - the people who helped to make all this possible.'

'It's your achievement, not mine,' Tessa said, thrilled to hear Esme refer to them as family.

'But it would not be mine if it were not for you,' Esme insisted, and then they both laughed.

'Yahzid will be very proud of his sister,' Tessa told her.

'I am so looking forward to seeing him and I am also proud of him now he has his new job as the car mechanic in the aid organisation.'

'Yes, his time in prison was well spent learning a trade,' Tessa agreed. 'Yahzid has proved that he can be a better man and Sophie says he has avoided the old influences.'

Esme nodded solemnly, 'I am grateful to your friend for finding the place for him. Now he is helping other young prisoners to help themselves when they are released. What can be better than to do such a thing?'

'You'll soon be reunited in Kibera,' said Tessa, 'and the school in Mashimoni will be lucky to have you as a teacher.' Tessa felt a lump in her throat at the thought of not having Esme around anymore but she would have to live with it. The girl had her own life to lead and an important job to fulfil. She knew their bond would never break and, although Tessa would not live in Kenya anymore, it did not mean that she would never visit. She had toyed with returning to Kenya to live there again but she knew in her heart that it wouldn't work – going back was never the same and it certainly wouldn't be in her position. But they were going together, for Christmas and New Year, to Nyara Camp at the kind invitation of the Sackville's. After that Tessa would return to London alone.

During her years at university, Esme had come back to Tessa's flat in Chelsea as often as possible. Sometimes she brought friends with her and Tessa had cherished the sound of young chatter and laughter within the walls. They had taken her out to restaurants, pushed her along by the river, taken her on a riverboat, even on the London Eye, cooked for her and generally spoiled her. It was Esme and her friends who had helped Tessa to get through the dark days, when she had resigned herself to a new but restricted life in England, confined mostly to a wheelchair. Looking forward to Esme's visits had kept her going and the girl had encouraged Tessa to start making that new life work for her too. In turn, Esme had encouraged Tessa to embrace her own dream of writing a novel and they had found her a writing group for support. She'd made some good friends in that group and now the novel was almost ready for submission to an agent. It was that exciting next step that kept Tessa going. She thought briefly of Ralph, confined in a different way. She had been told how he had raged and demanded to see her after she had been shot but all his raging had fallen on deaf ears. 'Let's go and sit outside,' she said feeling the need for fresh air to blow away her melancholy thoughts.

'Are you looking forward to our trip?' Esme asked, and Tessa heard the anxiety in her voice. 'I don't want you to come just because of me.'

'Of course I am, you silly girl. Christmas and New Year at Nyara Camp with you and Sophie – in the lap of luxury? I can't think of anywhere else I'd rather be.' It was partly the truth, but still she wasn't sure how she would feel, returning to the place where the nightmare had begun.

'I just wondered because…'

'Because that's where it all started?' Tessa finished for her.

'Yes, and because you will be back in the same country as your husband and all the memories…'

'I mean to not think of him at all,' Tessa interrupted. 'I don't want thoughts of him interfering with my precious moments back in Kenya. We will make the most of those last days together and then I shall come back to England and be a famous novelist, and you will start a brand new phase in your life.'

She marvelled at the way in which the shy young girl had blossomed into a confident young woman. She was sure Esme would do well for herself, and she was proud to have been a part of that development.

Esme gave her an uncertain smile. 'I am excited about it, but I shall miss London and I shall miss you.'

'You can come back here whenever you like,' Tessa said. 'I might keep your room for you,' but there was a twinkle in her eye. 'Perhaps you'll come back one day for my book launch.'

'I will not miss that for the world,' Esme promised, 'and maybe I will bring Yahzid with me.'

In the middle of December they boarded a Kenya Airways flight from Heathrow and, as they descended towards Nairobi's Jomo Kenyatta airport through the familiar thick and towering grey clouds, Tessa's heart bounded with excitement. It had been so long to be away from the land she loved. It was an absence that often pained her. Now she couldn't wait to see it again.

Sophie was waiting in the arrivals hall and could hardly contain herself when they emerged. She enveloped them both in a huge hug. 'Oh girls I've missed you so much! She looked down at Tessa and said in a waering voice, 'as for you, I don't think I can bear to let you go away again.' Then she got behind the wheelchair and Esme took the trolley from the luggage porter. They headed out of the airport with Sophie talking nineteen to the dozen about everything that had happened or changed since they had been away. Tessa let it all wash over her. She breathed in the thick Nairobi air with its familiar sweet and sour smells, and revelled in the landmarks and surroundings she knew so well.

In Sophie's untidy and chaotic apartment she noticed, with a grateful smile, how her friend had tidied and rearranged things to make it all more accessible for her. Chairs and tables moved, rugs lifted, books and magazines usually scattered on the floor were piled in a corner and doorways cleared. Sophie helped her out of the wheelchair and into a chair. Esme got down on her knees and began to rub some life back into the weak circulation in Tessa's legs. 'That was a long time sitting.'

'You were very brave to make the journey,' Sophie said, and put a cup of tea on the table beside her, 'but I'm so glad you did.'

'Me too.' It was so good to see Sophie again. They skyped on a weekly basis but there was nothing like seeing such a dear friend in the flesh.

'Would you like to sleep now?' Sophie asked.

'Oh no, I'm raring to go,' Tessa said. She looked down at Esme. 'Thank you sweetheart that feels a lot better.' Some faint feeling was returning in her legs, enough to allow her to stand up and lean on the walker. 'I need some walking exercise.'

'I've hired a van and driver for the whole time you are here, so we can get to lots of places without worrying about parking,' Sophie told her. 'Have you thought about what you'd like to do?'

Tessa looked at Esme. 'We will visit Yahzid in Kibera, of course, and then I'd like us to be tourists.' She wanted to take Esme to places that she had never been to before.

'Going where?' Sophie asked.

'Giraffe Manor, the Elephant Sanctuary, Karen Blixen's museum… a picnic in the Ngong's for starters?' Tessa said. 'What do you think Esme?'

The girl looked uncertain. 'I would love to but I think I will feel like a fish out of water even though it is my own country.'

Tessa sought to reassure her. 'Nonsense. Even though you have grown up and become independent and confident, you are still the same person inside no matter what happens.' She thought of a well-known saying and adapted it: you can take the girl out of Africa, but you can't take Africa out of the girl. Well that was true for both of them.

Sophie put up her hand, 'all agreed but today, and I insist, we will go no further than lunch.'

The following day, Tessa and Esme went to Kibera together, first to see Yahzid. It was a tearful reunion for brother and sister and Yahzid introduced her with great pride to the people who *were part of his new life. Both of them would be working in their own community, in jobs that assisted in bettering the lives of Kibera's younger generations.*

They moved on to Mashimoni, where Esme would soon be back in the heart of her community, helping Kibera's children to achieve an education to enable them to go on to university or to apprenticeships in skilled professions.

For the rest of their time in Nairobi they explored the city like tourists, eating in the popular restaurants, visiting museums, galleries and having that perfect picnic in the Ngong Hills. Every day Tessa's anxious feelings about being back in the city were being replaced by a sense of peace and reconciliation. Friends clamoured to visit and entertain her. Their care and concern warmed her heart. The past was forgotten, or at least not talked about, and for that she was grateful.

Soon would come the next part of the rehabilitation – Christmas at Nyara.

Tessa looked out of the small bush plane window and traced the familiar land of the Masai Mara below her: the curve of the river, the hippo hollow, the acacia trees on the rolling landscape and the place where Chui Camp had once stood. She fought back a rush of emotion and tears; this was not supposed to be a melancholy occasion it was a time of reconciliation – time to put the sadness and regrets behind her. She was glad to be back and her heart sang for it, but still it wasn't easy.

The bush plane touched down at the airstrip and Esme and Sophie helped Tessa from the plane into the folding wheelchair the stewardess handed down from the back of the plane. Esme pushed her across the runway towards a waiting truck. Tessa tilted her head back to feel the Mara sun on her face. It warmed her soul.

As they drew nearer to the truck a Masai strode with purpose towards them, his red and purple checked robe wrapped around him and a huge smile on his face. Tessa gasped. It was Jackson.

'Good morning,' he said.

'Good morning Jackson, it is very good to see you,' she replied with respectful restraint, even though she wished she could leap up and hug him in her joy.

'I have work at Nyara Camp,' he said.

She was delighted that her recommendation to Alexia had paid off. 'I am so pleased to hear that.'

His eyes twinkled. 'I think you will find everything at Nyara camp will be to your liking.'

Then, to her surprise, he bent down and scooped her out of the wheelchair and planted her into the seat beside him.

'Very special place for you.' He fetched their bags from the plane and loaded them onto the back seat with the folded wheel chair, and Esme and Sophie climbed aboard. They sat in silence for a moment, before he turned on the engine, listening to the breeze brushing through the grass, the gentle lowing of wildebeest, the distant hum of the departing plane. Tessa saw impala on the edge of the runway, the tall necks of giraffe moving through the bush, the gentle rolling hills beyond, and her heart felt as though it would burst with so much joy and emotion.

'What do you think of this, Esme?' she asked. It was a new experience for the girl who had never been into the bush before – had never seen such a vast wild empty wilderness, nor listened to such an impossible silence.

'It's just beautiful,' she breathed, 'I cannot say how beautiful – it is as though God wanted to show us a piece of heaven, here on earth.'

'Stretched out in front of us like a painters dream,' said Sophie.

Jackson nodded. 'God was wise to choose Africa for this purpose.'

ACKNOWLEDGEMENTS

I would like to thank all those who kept me going with this book. It has taken a long time to reach publication passing through many, many drafts and, without the restraint of friends the drafting might never have come to an end.

Thank you Rhian Kirk for your first reading, way back when it was in its early stage; your feedback and encouragement made me think it was worth persevering with.

Thank you to Eve Seymour at Writers Workshop, for your editing feedback of an early draft, for putting the whole book into perspective for me and showing me where moments and people needed to be extracted, despite the pain I suffered from doing so! I hope it has become a better book for that.

And, to my lovely husband, who has to put up with me and my blank face when I'm away with the book writing fairies; for the hours he doesn't see me when I'm hiding out with my computer, thank you for putting up with me and making it possible.

val harris

Val lives near Farnham in Surrey.
She has previously published four novels: Whisky and Ginger (2007),
The Siren (2008), Sea Creatures (2009) and its sequel,
The Song the Waves Sing (2013). Hunting Ground is her fifth novel.
(All books are available as Amazon kindle editions.)

Val has lived and worked in the Middle East, in Abu Dhabi and Saudi Arabia.
She was involved in cross-cultural training programme for Africa at Farnham
Castle, at Chatham House in London, and later taught English as a
foreign language.

To find out more about what Val is up to you can visit her website:
www.valharris.co.uk